THE LUCIFER MESSIAH

FRANK CAVALLO

Gold Imprint
Medallion Press, Inc.
Printed in USA

Published 2006 by Medallion Press, Inc.

The MEDALLION PRESS LOGO
is a registered tradmark of Medallion Press, Inc.

Copyright © 2006 by Frank Cavallo
Cover Illustration by Adam Mock

Printed in the United States of America

10 9 8 7 6 5 4 3 2 1
First Edition

ACKNOWLEDGEMENTS:

Thanks first to my parents, for everything. And to the rest of my family, who supplied me with many of the anecdotes herein, as well as lots of little details about old New York that aren't in any book. Thanks to the folks at Medallion, who gave my weird little idea a home; to my agent Rebecca, who took me on blind; and to Haewon Yom, who spent many hours of her time with my imaginary friends.

Finally, a nod each to the gang from Marguerite Street, the boys in the Corporation, and to all the former residents of Snaithville, about whom I need say nothing more.

BOOK I
"Old Friends"

ONE

NEW YORK CITY
NOVEMBER 19, 1946

SEAN STAGGERED.

A stench crawled into his nostrils. Garbage. Rotten food. Shit. Even the shadows stank.

They were still out there. Somewhere. Stalking him.

He forced himself to move, creeping through the filth and the darkness. His gut ached. He felt the blood drooling out of him. It trickled into his pants, ran down his leg. It was sticky and wet.

He had to keep going.

He recognized the street ahead. Ninth Avenue and the corner of West Thirty-Sixth Street. The edge of Hell's Kitchen.

Street lamps buzzed overhead; an electric swarm of pale, flickering light. Across the way, the minute hand of an old gothic clock moved one click. That made it 1:13 AM.

Sean didn't care.

Steam exhaled from a sewer vent. Sulfurous ghosts

washed over him. For a moment he welcomed the warmth. But he couldn't linger. He only bathed in the hot odor for a moment.

He fell, toppling a half-filled trashcan. Noise was the last thing he needed. He didn't get up, not right away. First he grabbed his dented felt hat from a puddle. His overcoat was already ruined, but that hat meant a lot to him—sweat stains and mildew notwithstanding.

A sedan turned from around the far corner. Headlights skimmed the street. Tires squeaked on blacktop.

Sean scrambled to his feet. He stumbled backward, hoping to reach the safety of the reeking dark.

His chin dripping sweat, he watched as the car drove by. It was motoring slowly, agonizingly so as it rolled past his little alley-hovel, then beyond him, and finally around the next block.

He counted in his head.

One, one thousand. Two, one thousand. Three . . .

After what he figured was enough of a pause, he chanced an appearance. Hobbling out into the dangerous light, he gasped for air and hurried across the street.

He only made it halfway.

A pair of shots ricocheted. The sedan screeched from around the corner. It roared like a mechanical predator. Lead and fire and noise spewed from two *Thompson* submachine guns.

Sean faltered. He dragged his feet with an urgency that was nothing short of panic, across the bullet-marked street and into a second alcove.

The grinding steel-on-steel whine raced behind. He made it into the narrow passage between a bakery and a shoe store. His feet crushed broken glass. He slipped as he ran. Before he could gain much distance, with the sedan plowing toward him through the debris, he came face to face with frustration.

A ten-foot iron fence blocked his way, mocking his flight in rusted silence. Razor wire ringed the top, though the barbs were barely visible through the shadows and the steam. The headlights were on him.

Gunfire clanged at his feet.

He winced. The bullets were close, but there was something else. He shivered, though not from the cold, closed his eyes tight and fell backward.

The gloom swallowed him.

A moment later, the sedan skidded to a halt inches from the fence. Rocco Gallucci heaved the passenger-side door open. He bounded out with a Tommy gun braced in his arms. The barrel was dripping smoke.

"We know you're out there Mulcahy. The boss wants a word with you. He ain't gonna shed no tears if we bring you back in pieces," the fat man shouted.

Two others joined him from within the massive automobile.

"He ain't back here," one whispered.

"He's here. He ain't got no way outta here," Rocco said.

A rustle stirred behind a dumpster. Jolted, the third gunman squeezed his trigger, firing off a pair of rounds. His comrade was quick to grab him. Rocco rebuked him just as fast.

"It's just rats Gino!"

The smoke from the shots took a moment to clear. When it did, they saw a brood of rodents, nine or ten strong, squealing and crawling over one another. The pests scurried in a half-dozen directions, a mess of whiskers and scaly tails burrowing through a pile of old clothes—a dented felt hat and a once-fancy overcoat among them.

"Looks like they ate some bum," Gino said.

The men continued their search. They rifled through every inch of the trash in the alley, but of the fugitive they had cornered, there was nothing. Just some blood smeared on the lower links of the fence.

"He's gone. There ain't no two ways around it," Gino said.

"That's impossible," Rocco answered.

"Unless he climbed the fence."

"Climbed the fuckin' fence, my ass. You wanna be the one to tell Mr. Calabrese that we lost 'em? After what that son of a bitch did to the new guy?"

"We gotta tell him something. And I don't see nobody back here," Gino said.

Rocco spit. He cursed again, this time in his native Sicilian dialect. Within a few moments, they were back in the sedan, and gone from the alley.

A short while later, after the block had settled back into the slumber from which it had been so rudely awakened, Sean Mulcahy limped out of the alley. He was still dressed in the tattered overcoat and the beat-up felt hat.

A rat scampered across his shoe. It climbed up and disappeared under the leg of his pants.

He was finally home.

TWO

THOUGH LATE INTO THE NIGHT, THE DOORS WERE STILL open at the *Catanzaro Sunset Cafe and Social Club*. None of the patrons, all regulars who were mostly arguing and conversing along the bar, ever called it that. Most of the locals on Mulberry Street knew it simply as *The Sunset*. And most knew that despite its congenial name, it was not an establishment that welcomed outsiders.

When Rocco and his men came in through the entrance on Hester, all the talking stopped. It didn't take long for the guys at the bar, or the ones seated at the back table to recognize them. Their chatter soon picked up unabated.

Rocco clapped his hands in the direction of the barkeeper, who looked much older than the place's aging turn-of-the-century décor.

"Hey, Mikey, is he in?" he asked.

The bartender nodded. A second later he shifted from his nearly incomprehensible *Campania* dialect into only barely comprehensible English.

"He's upstairs, been askin' about you all night," the olive-skinned *Napolitano* answered.

Rocco had only one word, which everyone in the joint understood.

"Shit."

✢ ✢ ✢

Salvatore "Sam" Calabrese's lips curled in a grin that stretched between bloated cheeks. His fingers twisted over the naked breasts of a dancer. His breaths came in short, excited huffs. Though he did not at first notice it, the door to his office slowly opened. Rocco Gallucci entered quietly, his cronies in tow.

"Jeez, boss, I'm sorry. The guys outside, they didn't tell me nothin'," he said.

Calabrese shook his head.

"Relax Rocco. If I didn't want to be disturbed I'd have left word," he answered.

He extended one of his plump hands, and the three men stepped into the room. They closed the door behind them.

Calabrese's private hold, a converted loft above the Sunset Club, was an oasis of luxury amid dingy surroundings. Once merely an office, a recent swing of his fickle mood had spurred a remodeling of the entire place.

Seven hundred dollars and three missing workmen later, it resembled something of a harem. Plush-cushioned furniture lined every wall. Oriental rugs lay spread across the floor and silk tapestries dangled dangerously close to rows of black candles. Aside from the occasional intrusion of headlights through the windows, the golden whispering tapers provided the only light in the room.

Like some regent on a barbarian throne, Lower Manhattan's most despised loan shark reclined in a silk robe, his girth spilling out everywhere. The three men approached with caution. They did not have good news.

"Well gentlemen? Shall I assume from your less-than-joyous demeanor that you have returned from the night's errand with my wishes unfulfilled?" he asked.

His words were spoken with uncommonly perfect enunciation, distinctly more refined than any other local hood, or even his own usual diction. The three of them, two the illiterate sons of Italian immigrants, and the third a native of Palermo, stared back at him in silence. It was a reaction that Calabrese had produced often among his associates, as of late.

"C'mon, spit it out, Rocco, before I have ta smack ya. Is he alive? Is he dead? What?" the sprawling man demanded, his grammar shifting completely in an instant.

The three ignored the sudden change in syntax. Rocco responded accordingly.

"He got away. We hit 'em, I think. There was blood on the fence. I don't think he coulda got too far."

Calabrese sighed, wiping tiny beads of sweat from his forehead. With a delicate manner, he let his other hand slip from the dancer's shoulder. A vaguely effeminate wave informed her that she was dismissed. Then, his eyes bulging, he turned to the other men. He spoke as if reading off a roster.

"Rocco. Gino. Vig. Where is the other I sent with

you, Michael?"

There was a long, desperate pause before the large man called *the Vig* mustered the courage to speak.

"Mulcahy. He got loose. The new guy, he tried to stop 'em. The mick bastard killed him."

Calabrese nodded.

"Would the two of you give us a few moments, please?" he asked, his tone clearly directed at the two men beside Rocco.

Rocco, as though he knew what such a suggestion meant, wasted no time in pleading.

Calabrese ignored him. His voice fell into a whisper, an almost reptilian hiss. Every sibilant syllable prickled Rocco's ears.

"We need a few moments alone Rocco," he said.

The door closed with a thud.

Outside the office, Gino and the Vig shuffled toward the stairwell. But the hall was blocked. A tall man stood in their way. A stone-faced giant with reddish-brown skin and sharp features. They recognized him. Indian Joe was his name. He was the only Indian either man had ever seen, aside from the matinee. But his sight would have been striking to any men, if not for his height and his broad frame then for his hair alone. Black as pitch and board straight, it hung long to his waist, a natural contrast to his double-breasted silk suit.

That peculiarity might otherwise have made for an amusing novelty, if not for the man's entirely morbid reputation.

"Mr. Joseph. We was just leavin'," the Vig said, careful not to actually call him Indian Joe.

The Native-American nodded, though he remained silent as the two men cowered beneath him. The stories about Indian Joe well preceded him, both among those who worked for Salvatore Calabrese and among the rest of the local underworld denizens.

He had appeared at the big man's side three months back, without the benefit of anything resembling an explanation. Since that time, he was said to have cut the scalps from seven debtors of his employer, all left alive save for the last, whose heart the longhaired man was reputed to have eaten.

Gino and the Vig had no more than a moment to consider those gruesome rumors.

A scream peeled from behind the office door. Shrieking in deep, foul tones followed. Both men shuddered. Neither could manage a word from their lips. They stood paralyzed for several long minutes. They heard horrible sounds.

Howls. Cries. Pleas.

When it was done, and the screams had faded into whimpers and the whimpers into silence, Indian Joe motioned toward the stairs. All through the terrible moments, he had remained stoic, as though the savage sounds were of no concern. The two thugs quickly hustled away.

The Native-American entered the office without knocking. Calabrese greeted him warmly.

"Lycaon. Come in, I've been waiting for you."

"Rocco?" the Indian asked.

The gangster shook his head, nothing more than the hint of smirk to suggest anything out of the ordinary. There was no sign of a struggle, or of a body. Indian Joe didn't seem to mind.

THREE

VINCE SICARIO DID NOT HEAR THE STATIC CRACKLING from his radio. He was asleep, after a fashion. An empty whiskey bottle rested on his slowly heaving chest. Spread out across his dirty couch, in his dirty apartment, he only moved occasionally. Usually to settle his head or to scratch himself, which he did with his good arm, his right one, stained inky blue-black across the bicep. It was all that remained now of what had been, in his younger days, a tattoo of a woman poised over an anchor.

A crumpled mess of yesterday's *New York Herald-Tribune* lay scattered on his floor. He didn't even budge when a shrill ring echoed through the apartment.

A second ring followed. It lasted only half as long as the first. Eventually, the noise roused him, but only a little. He moved his head forward, just enough for his greasy bangs to slide down over his eyes.

Some minutes passed before the sounds of scratching and a knock emanated from the door. While the sound was louder, it had no more effect than the doorbell.

Then, the ringing began once more. Vince wriggled

on his couch to ignore it. This time it did not cease so quickly. The noise continued, on and on, as though the bell had been stuck in place.

Finally, with a groan that was not unlike a sickly wheeze, he shook from sleep. His thick arms stretched upward and then outward as he got up from the sofa, tenuously at first. Barely balanced, one hand waving in front of him, he dragged himself across the room.

"Jesus!" he muttered, unfastening the chain lock. "I'm comin', I'm comin'. What do you think . . . ?"

His words ended as abruptly as the buzzing when he opened the door. Sean collapsed into his arms then and there, dropping his dented fedora and smearing warm blood across his chest.

❖   ❖   ❖

Sean was bandaged and wrapped in a blanket, but his face was pale as he lay on Vince's couch. The apartment was dark now, shades drawn closed and only one lamp lit in the whole of the place. A glass of water in his hand, Vince knelt down beside his guest. As he did, the youth stirred. He winced and opened his eyes.

"Didn't expect you to wake up so fast. Have a sip," Vince said, offering the glass.

Hands trembling slightly, Sean took a long drink. He finished and exhaled a deep, but clearly painful sigh. Still he said nothing.

"What? Do I gotta say something now? How's about

a 'thanks,' huh?" Vince said with a sneer as he got up from his knee.

Sean smiled.

"Thanks."

Vince paced, his hands clasped behind his back. Though the whiskey still stung his temples, concern tensed his face. When he spoke, his words were direct, and as clear as if he were sober.

"That's it? No *Hey Vince, thanks for fixin' me up* or *Hey, Vince ol' buddy, sorry for bargin' in on you and spillin' my guts all over the place?*"

Sean did not seem the least bit moved by his host's ire. Again, he replied simply.

"I said thanks."

Vince made his way over to the front of the couch. A chuckle grew up in his belly. His look of sarcasm melted into a grin. He pulled a chair to the side of the couch, spun it around backward and sat himself down bow-legged.

"I gotta hand it to you. You're a piece of work. Man, is that really you? I still can't square myself with it. Sean Mulcahy, on my goddamn couch. Bleeding like a stuck pig, no less."

"Sorry about that, old buddy."

"I'll bet. I'd ask you where the hell you've been, but you don't look like you're in any shape to tell me a story."

"I know, long time, huh? I meant to write," Sean managed, still wincing and still obviously in pain.

"Yeah, sure."

Mulcahy laughed and guzzled the last of the water.

Vince ran his hands through his tangled black hair, that suspicious smile still spread across his face. Then, the young man breathed heavily, and passed out again.

Vince grabbed a pack of Lucky Strikes from the floor, snapped a match and lit his last cigarette. He tossed the empty pack away blindly and reached for the phone on his bureau.

He paused before picking up the receiver. Partly because he wasn't sure if he remembered the number, and partly because he wasn't sure he could make the call even if the digits came to him.

The phone rang three times on the other end before a lady's voice answered through a yawn. Vince's eyes shut for a long moment. He swallowed hard before speaking.

"Maggie? It's Vince. Get outta bed, I got someone here who needs to see you . . . don't ask, you wouldn't believe me if I told you."

FOUR

MIST CLOUDED THE EARLY MORNING, AND THERE WERE few people about on the streets of Lower Manhattan. A hard autumn frost had swept in over the night. Not many souls had chosen to brave the cold in the opening hours of a November day.

Argus and Arachne moved through the dew-spotted fog slowly. They owned the empty sidewalk, a small frame beside a large one, a tiny hand held in the grasp of one much bigger.

From the opposite direction, Irene Cahill, a woman of fifty-three years, approached the silent pair. A baker's wife, she'd risen hours before the sun. For her, as it had been almost every day since her marriage, first light signaled her first break from the ovens.

Kerchief tied hastily around her hair, and a wool shawl held about her arms, she breathed in the chill and strolled at a leisurely pace. It was quiet, as though the fog had smothered the normal rustles and shuffles of a New York morning.

The mismatched pair was not at first visible, cloaked

by the whitish haze. But soon enough they emerged, and she was able to discern their features.

Arachne was the taller, still a girl really, with long blond hair that rested over her shoulders. From her unblemished face, silky white with lips of pink, Irene guessed her to be no more than eighteen. Her dress was mostly hidden by a long, black raincoat. To Irene's eye she was likely married, judging by her companion.

The boy Argus who bounded along beside her brought an immediate smile to Irene's face. He was tiny, no more than four or five, a toddler really. But he was dressed in the smartest little suit, a shiny black tie set against an equally small white button-down shirt, all tucked behind an embroidered maroon vest. On his little torso and legs, he wore the most elegant matching pinstriped jacket and slacks. There was a white carnation that looked uncommonly huge pinned to his lapel.

Just about the cutest thing Irene had ever seen, and she didn't mind saying so, either.

"What an adorable little one you have Miss!" she gushed as soon as she was within a few feet of them. "Why, he's just like a teensy little doll, he's so precious."

The young girl simply sighed. She did not respond, except to shrug as the baker's wife knelt down before the youngster.

"Well! Aren't you just the cutest thing? What's your name?" Irene asked in her best baby-talk voice.

Argus, his chubby cheeks red from the cold, did not reply at once. As Irene busied herself fussing gently over his lapels, he trained his eyes directly at hers. Something about them, the uncommon hint of crimson in the pupils, maybe, was distinctly un-childlike.

"I'll thank you to refrain from fiddling with my jacket," he said, in a voice colored by a weird, indeterminate accent.

Irene's hands dropped from the lapels. Her mouth and eyes widened.

"As for my name, I doubt whether you'd seriously be interested in learning it were I not presented to you in such an unfortunately juvenile form."

Irene stammered. She glanced up at Arachne. A scowl greeted her.

"Now, if you are quite finished admiring my tailor's handiwork, expensive though it is, I'll thank you to step aside, for we really must be on our way," the strange child said.

Irene, dumbfounded, did just as the boy requested. Without even a second glance, both he and Arachne continued walking.

The mist soon reclaimed them from her sight.

"Was that necessary? You could have humored her. She'd have been none the wiser," the blonde asked her tiny companion.

"My patience wears thin Arachne, and we've no time for distractions this morning. In any case, I'll be free of this puerile coil soon enough," the boy answered.

"Not a moment too soon, I'd imagine," she replied. "But it will be remembered, certainly. And I can always say that I tended to the wizened Argus when he was just a little child."

They both laughed, though he couldn't help but frown as he did.

✤   ✤   ✤

The pair did not wander much longer through the hazy morning. As the early rush of traffic clogged the avenues with fumes and noise, they found their way to a quiet corner of the Lower East Side. On a dead-end street, set off from any main arteries, they came before a church. It was fairly nondescript, perhaps once notable for the four spires that bore a passing resemblance to the Cathedral of St. Patrick, much farther uptown.

Not a person was about as they neared. Like familiar patrons, however, they unlatched the rusted iron-gate along the sidewalk, and ascended the front steps. The hinges very nearly screamed when they turned, as though the metal joints hadn't been disturbed in years. Though the stained-glass windows of the gray façade were largely intact, it was clear from the boards nailed carelessly over the doors that the house of worship was no longer in regular use.

The rest of the street seemed oddly removed from the neighborhood that encircled it. There were no residences, no offices, just a scattering of empty lots and some abandoned tenements. On the whole, as quiet and eerily serene as it was, it almost seemed as though the rest of the city had forgotten about it.

Arachne did not withhold her impression. "What a gloomy place."

"Yes. Just as I remember it. Perfect I think, for our purposes," the child Argus answered.

"Charybdis should be inside already," Arachne continued. "She said she had news."

Argus nodded. With a last glance at the boarded-up entrance, he motioned for his companion to follow him toward the cemetery set against the south wall. There was a cellar door beneath the distorted trunk of a maple tree that had grown too close to the building. He opened it with his tiny fingers and the two of them disappeared into the bowels beneath the church.

Inside it was musty. The air hung heavy with stirred-up dust. They took a winding staircase up from the basement in total darkness, but found some light there to greet them in the expansive main hall.

A woman called Charybdis stood waiting for them, at the center of the aisle between the pews, above a metal grate in the floor. She was black, with stern, West African features that looked to be aged about forty years. Standing almost at attention, her figure was obscured by a man's flannel suit. Her hair was cropped down to the scalp.

She did not greet the pair, and instead opened in a deadpan voice. "Lucifer has been found. He is here, in New York."

Arachne paused when she heard it. She turned to look at her companion. He too stopped in his tracks. While she seemed suddenly out of breath, he looked almost relieved.

"So the rumors are true?" Argus replied. "Are you certain of it, Charybdis?"

"There can be no doubt," the African woman answered. "Last night, the Keeper located and apprehended him. He fell into the Morrigan's hands well after midnight, on the West Side, Eleventh Avenue and West Thirty-Eighth Street."

The words, though deeply spoken, seemed distant, dwarfed somehow by the vast emptiness that cradled them. The three figures came closer together beneath the ruined cathedral rafters. Finely crafted columns stood silent guard over them, charred black by a long-dead fire. A circle of candles provided both the only light and the only heat in the cavernous hold. Their breath condensed when they exhaled.

"The neighborhood the locals call Hell's Kitchen," Arachne said. "If the Morrigan has him, he's probably already dead."

"I would imagine," Argus replied.

"No. The Keeper did not succeed. I am told that Lucifer was held in check by only one of our kind. The rest of the agents were not of our ilk, conscripted by the Morrigan from the ranks of her unwitting *indigenous* associates.

"Before he could be brought to face the queen, Lucifer killed his captor and escaped. He may have been wounded, but as far as I have been able to learn, the Keeper does not have him, and his whereabouts are now unknown," Charybdis finished.

"Who was the one of our own that he killed?" Arachne asked.

"Caeneus."

"Caeneus? Wasn't she killed in Spain, during the civil war?" Arachne asked.

"The elder Caeneus, yes. The one who died last night was new to our fold, only brought into the circle three seasons past. He had just taken the name. Now it will sit vacant on the rolls once more," Charybdis answered.

As his associates continued the exchange, Argus wandered over to the back of the platform upon which they stood. A half-burned crucifix rested there, fallen from the place on the wall where it had once presided. He paced across the altar area, scanning the toppled offertory and the scorched Lenten vestments that lay beside it upon a carpet of soot.

The others became quiet as the child paced.

A fire just before Easter 1941 had ruined the once opulent cathedral. Tight budgets during the War had prevented the diocese from restoring it, and in the intervening years its parishioners had slowly filtered away to other neighborhoods. Thus did it remain abandoned, forgotten by all but a few parish bookkeepers and the locals who generally avoided its dark and unsafe confine.

Argus knew all of that. He also knew that hardly anyone else shared the information.

"This place will do just fine, I think," he said, talking to the walls.

"Fine for what?" Arachne asked.

"We may have been given a rare opportunity, my friends. One that I had thought lost to us long ago. Lucifer must be found, but not by the Morrigan," Argus replied.

"Are you suggesting what I think?" Charybdis asked. "We haven't spoken of that in ages."

"There will never be a chance such as this again. If we do not act now, we might have to wait for another hundred years, or longer," Argus said.

"But can it be done? If he is found, I mean?" Charybdis asked.

"The hours are running short. We will make him understand this time. There is no other way," Argus said.

"Have we any idea where he might have gone?" Arachne asked.

"We have some notions, but nothing concrete," Charybdis answered. "The Morrigan brought us all to New York because of Lucifer, because of the rumors that his first life was spent here. It is likely that he will seek out family or friends now that he has returned, but we've little more to go on than that."

FIVE

PAT FLANAGAN SNARLED. HIS EYES NARROWED. HE raised up his left hand in a fist.

"That's as far as you go, grease-ball. Didn't you see the sign? NO DAGOS ALLOWED."

Vince snarled too. He lifted his chin in the direction of the Irishman's knuckles.

"Well, they let you in. So I figured the place was open to all sorts of lowlifes," he answered.

The red-haired man laughed, swelling and deflating his prodigious belly. His fist melted into an open hand, and he laid a rough pat on Vince's shoulder.

"How's my favorite ex-partner? Haven't seen you in a while," he began.

"Gettin' along. Yourself?"

Flanagan shrugged. He arched his back for a moment, rubbed his bulging gut through his ill-fitted shirt and burped. Then he answered.

"Can't complain. I mean I could, but who the hell'd listen? Not my wife, I'll tell you that much."

Vince smiled. It was good to be in his old station house

again. The faces had almost all changed in the seven years since he'd left the NYPD, but the place still had the same feel. Same ugly mold-green tile along the floors and the lower half of the walls; same dull black paint still peeling from the iron railings. It smelled the same, too. Badly.

"Yeah, how is Mary?" he replied, halfheartedly.

"She'll be the death of me, that's how she is. Many's the day I wished I was rid of her."

Vince sighed. He inhaled and craned his neck. Right away, the other man knew what that meant.

"Oh, hey ol' buddy. I'm sorry, I didn't mean nothin'. How is Maggie, you two talked lately?" Flanagan said, realizing that he'd touched on a sore spot.

"A little. That's why I'm here, to be honest."

"Anything I can do, you know that," Flanagan said, gulping the last drop of his third cup of coffee.

"What do you know about a shooting? Happened near here last night. Late, after midnight," Vince asked.

"Yeah, woke you up did it?"

"You could say that."

"Turf war. At least that what's we think."

"Whose turf?"

Flanagan yanked his spotted tie a little looser, tugging on the sleeves of his rumpled coat. He walked toward the front of the precinct house, and the door.

"Well, this is kind of on the hush-hush, if you know what I mean. The papers have an idea somethin's happenin', but we're trying to keep a lid on it, at least until *we* know what's goin' on."

"Which is?" Vince asked as they stepped out of the station.

Flanagan lit up a cigarette. He offered one to his old partner. Vince took a second to look at the brand. It was a Parliament. He politely declined.

"Some kind of trouble inside Sam Calabrese's crew. I wasn't on last night, but I heard some talk this morning that they think the thing last night had somethin' to do with his guys. Let me tell you, it's gettin' nasty out there Vince. Ain't like when you and me walked the beat."

Flanagan sucked down a long, satisfying drag. He let the smoke slide slowly out of his lungs.

"We picked up one stiff from last night's fun and games. Guy had his face mutilated. We're talking serious bodily damage. Eyes punched in, brains scrambled up like grade-A farm-fresh eggs and yanked out through his fuckin' nose. I didn't see the photos yet, but I heard it was so bad it even made some of the crime-scene guys puke."

Vince knew that his old partner was given slightly to the dramatic, so he quietly filed away what he imagined was probably an exaggerated description.

"Who was it?" he asked.

"We don't know. New guy, nobody'd ever seen him before. That's why we're thinkin' some new blood's been movin' in on Sammy's action, and last night he sent a message."

Flanagan flicked the ash from the end of his cigarette with a shrug. Then he finished his thought.

"All's I can say is, I hope whoever was supposed to get it, got it. Cause this kinda shit gives me chest pains, you know?"

✤   ✤   ✤

The morning came and went, without Sean Mulcahy taking note of it at all. When he did stir, shortly before half
past twelve, he found himself still laid out on the couch
where Vince had set him down. Though his sight was
clouded with the haze of slumber, he quickly saw that the
debris and trash that had littered the floor the previous
night were gone.

Obviously, someone other than Vince had been there.

An aroma next caught his attention, familiar, though
long forgotten, and he wasn't quite sure why he hadn't
sensed it immediately upon waking. It was the smell of
soup. Chicken soup, he thought. For an instant, either
from delirium or pure exhaustion, he let his nerves ease.

The eye of his mind drifted over a forty-year-old memory.

It was his mother's kitchen. It was winter. And she
was cooking. Irish mothers were hardly renowned as the
best of cooks, but in that moment Sean thought fondly on
the deep smell of boiling broth, and how the heat from the
oven used to warm the whole of their tiny cold-water flat.
But the soft moment was not long to last.

His attention turned back suddenly, violently, to the
present.

There *still was* someone else in the apartment.

He could hear breathing, and the click of shoes against
the hardwood floor. From the sound of it, he knew it wasn't
Vince, too delicate, too measured in stride. Definitely

human, though, or at least pretending to be. Though he couldn't see from behind the couch, he could tell that the stranger was approaching. Under the quilt that covered him, he slowly raised his right hand. Though the pain in his side made it difficult, he concentrated. He felt his fingernails begin to grow, and to harden.

As the unknown figure neared, footsteps softened by the living-room carpet, he gently twiddled his fingers. The tips of them were now solid, bony, and sharp like claws. When he moved them they tore at the fabric of the quilt, ripping four tiny holes where his hand had been.

Once behind the couch, near enough for him to hear every rustle of whatever it wore, the stranger turned. Whoever it was, it was going to come at him from the front. He shifted, gripped the quilt to fling it off, and readied to strike. Just in case.

The other stepped around. Sean turned, first glimpsing shoes, then a belt as his clawed hand swept out from under the covers. The blow was already in motion when he caught sight of a face. A female face. A familiar face.

Then, as abruptly as he had begun, his reflexes froze. His unnatural hand remained hidden.

"Well. We're up, are we?" It was a voice he hadn't heard in decades, and a face he had missed for as long. "I didn't mean to startle you."

"Maggie?"

"Haven't forgotten us, I see. I suppose that's something, after all this time," she answered, with a tone that somehow managed to convey both humor and sadness at once.

She smiled, and put a ceramic bowl on the table beside the couch. Entirely oblivious to the danger that lurked only inches from her throat, she took a chair and set it down, taking a seat beside Sean, whose hand tingled as it slowly regained its human shape.

Margaret Reilly, *Maggie* to her old friends from the neighborhood, retained a youthful smile, though the years had etched fine lines into the corners of her face. Her eyes were the same as always, though, sparkling and blue and exactly the way Sean remembered them.

They greeted him with a gaze that put his tensions at ease.

"Vince called you?" he asked, his eyes wandering unconsciously over her figure.

She wore a checkered apron tied over a dark wool suit. The folds of a white blouse peaked out from under her belted jacket. Uncrossing her legs, her stockings shimmering gently in the half-light, she reached out to lift the bowl from the table. Sean was less interested in the steaming soup than he was in the sight of her.

Her auburn hair was bound up, not like the pigtails she'd worn it in the last time he'd been so close to her. As she lifted the spoon to his lips, he thought he noticed a streak of gray running through it.

When he opened his mouth, it wasn't to sip, but she stopped him in mid-breath, before he could say a single word.

"You need to eat. Then we'll talk," she said. For an instant he felt as though he'd been scolded by a schoolteacher, rather than the first girl he'd ever kissed.

Whatever the case, he simply nodded, content to enjoy the long-lost taste of oily chicken broth, and to watch her smile as she spooned it up and fed it to him.

His nerves soothed, Sean lasted only long enough to sip half the broth. Then his head spun and he faded from consciousness once more.

✤   ✤   ✤

"Shhh. He just passed out again," Margaret whispered when Vince barged in through the door a few moments later.

"He was up? Did you get a chance to talk to him?"

"Vince, he's not in any condition to talk. Look at him. He's been shot for Christ's sake," she answered, making no attempt to mask her hostility.

"Yeah. I know, Maggie," Vince said as he knelt down and adjusted Sean's blanket, pausing for a moment to turn the sleeping man's face toward them, and to look carefully at it. "I'll tell you, he aged pretty good, you know? Look at him; guy looks exactly the same as he did thirty years ago. Now how the hell did he pull that off? That's what I want to know."

"If we don't take him to a hospital soon, you'll probably never find out," she snapped.

Vince shook his head.

"We went over this last night, we can't do that. I just got a hold of an old partner of mine, you know him, Paddie Flanagan. Anyway, he's still on the job, and I got from him that they're lookin' at this for a mob hit last night. Big

Sammy Calabrese's guys.

"Whatever the hell Sean's gotten himself into, he's in deep right now. We can't move him, at least not until I look under a few more rocks, and see what else turns up."

SIX

LA PIAZZA SAN MARCO WAS QUIET. A RARE THING FOR that most bustling of Venice's many ancient squares. The hour was late, and growing later with every wave that washed against the bulwarks of the Doge's palace.

Sean was there. And he was smiling.

He sat beneath the magnificent stone arcade, along the south side of the plaza, at a wrought iron table with a glass top, in a chair of similar fashion. Across from him, gleaming, sparkling as she smiled with him, was Orlanda.

Orlanda Santina.

Her skin was dark, all the more in the dappled light of moon-glows and candle-flames. Her hair was shoulder-length, dark and curled at the ends. But her eyes . . .

Her eyes reflected the warm evening glare, but not all of it. As Sean watched them, followed them when she shrugged or laughed, he knew that they held back some of the light they seized. Held it back deep within that dusky gaze. It made him think of Homer, and the "wine-dark sea," and it made him happy.

She wore little in the way of cosmetics, a touch of rouge

on the apple of her cheeks, a hint of gloss over her pink lips. A simple girl, her beauty was natural, the kind of face that make-up only muddies.

He thought he could watch her forever, and thought maybe he was going to, when the *cameriere* finally brought them a pair of espressos and their bill on a handwritten slip of paper.

Sean didn't remember paying, or drinking the coffee, for that matter. But if he had stopped to consider it, he'd have been sure of doing both. As it was, the very next instant they were walking together on the other side of the square, under Byzantine towers that loomed high over the bay with their truculent spires.

"*Resti con me, insieme, per sempre,*" she whispered.

His command of the lyrical romance language was not perfect, but he had spent enough time in Italy to understand her. Sometimes even without words.

Often, in fact.

"*Sì.* I will stay with you forever."

He couldn't help but respond in English, even though she didn't understand a word of it, if only to help him gather his thoughts for the translation. "*Ti voglio bene, per sempre.*"

The words were not exact, but the sentiment was all the same.

"*Promesso?*" she asked.

"I promise. *Sì.*"

So they kissed. And they walked. And they kissed.

They strolled along the waterfront, by where the ferries and the gondolas were tied, rocking along in the wind-tossed sea.

They passed across a footbridge, over a canal between two very old buildings. They wandered through winding, shadowy, dusty streets that were more like corridors of plaster and stone than actual roads.

Hours stretched meaninglessly, the waltz of the moon across the cloudy eve like the silent melody to their endless dance.

Venice was tranquil, stirred not at all but for their footsteps and their laughter. It was not a city of wild nightclubs and all-hours parties. It wasn't like Paris, or Munich, or his own, long-lost New York. It was serene, and it was theirs. All theirs.

Until there came another.

It was just shuffling at first. A rustle in the darkness. But then it was more. The sound of feet. Whispers.

Orlanda noticed it. She broke from their embrace.

Few were out and about, to be sure, but the city was never completely deserted. At least that was what Sean assured her. They were safe. Nothing would bother them.

He promised.

Again they stopped, and they kissed. Lost in the contemplation of each other, neither of them saw the dark figures as they emerged into the light.

They surged forth from the dim, born whole from the shadows, expelled from the belly of the night. Everything about them was as drab as the dark from which they sprang, long coats, flat-brimmed hats, trousers, and shineless boots. All was black, except their scythe-like blades.

Those shone silver. Menacingly. Evil in their sharpened elegance.

The three moved as one. They swept upon the lovers like a plague.

Orlanda screamed when she saw them. It was already too late.

The moments seemed to accelerate, as though the violence had disturbed the orderly flow of time itself. Sean reeled. He thrust Orlanda behind him. The assailants were on three sides. The canal was at his back, several feet down.

A swipe cut at him from the left. Another slashed from the right. Blood spilled from his arm.

Orlanda screamed again. He parried. His swing missed, opening up his middle for an instant. The third man stabbed at him from in front. The strike cut his shirt. Razor-edged steel tore across his chest.

He felt the blood, but his return blow was already in motion. This time his punch landed. Sean's roundhouse connected with a crack. The force of it knocked the mystery man's hat from his crown.

Sean gasped between breaths.

The corrupted face of a middle-aged man stared back. But what startled Sean was his fractured jaw. His fist had ripped the man's lower mandible from his face. Teeth were scattering like raindrops mixed with blood. A piece of the bone dangled from a tether of raw skin.

Sean recognized the sign immediately. He was facing his own kind. The Morrigan had found him again.

He had no time to ponder it.

Another blow came, from the side. Another angry slice opened his veins. Orlanda, behind him, had quieted her screams. She was reciting *Ave Marias* one after another like a drone.

"We don't want to hurt you Mulcahy. Come with us. Join the fold. Don't make us kill you," the one on his left said.

The man spoke in an eerie whisper, a tone that was far too intimate for the circumstances.

"The girl must be killed, unfortunately. But you need not die as well. Save yourself. Join with us," said the other.

The third breathed heavily from the gaping red wound where his mouth had been.

Sean did not bother to respond. He could dispatch them all in an instant, but not with Orlanda there. She couldn't see. She couldn't know.

Why couldn't they just let him live?

Why couldn't they just leave him alone?

An instant later the decision was made for him.

A final blow caught him across the throat. It knocked him from his precarious foothold at the canal's edge. He tumbled in a bloody mess, down past the stone blocks and into the cold, cloudy brine.

Then the three closed in on Orlanda, crimson dripping from their blades. She tried to scream again, but found that her voice would not oblige her.

Time had grown short. Though the streets were still deserted, her cries would soon bring others, and the killing this night was to be kept to a minimum. The one with half a face held her, wrapped her in his thick arms. Her throat bared, he forced her down to the cobblestones like a hunted beast. The other two raised their daggers.

An instant of peculiar calm fell over the grisly scene. One of the men raised his knife.

The blade fell, but it did not pierce flesh. It clanged and broke against the street when its wielder was suddenly, violently hauled down from behind. The man's face smashed against the ancient stones. He never saw the thing that had torn him away from the deed, for even as the tentacle that had coiled about his ankles loosened, his mangled head tore free from his shoulders.

The others, and Orlanda with them, did see the slayer, however. They saw it in all its savage, demonic fury as it closed in on them.

It was a beast for certain, but nothing that could have been spawned from nature's noble pantheon. What skulked up from the murk in those agonizing moments was horrid. Green, or maybe black of skin, if it even had skin. The moonlight reflected off it in a myriad of foul shades. A dozen or more writhing tentacles lurched at its base, the bony spikes on their ends chipping the old Venetian stones.

It stank of the oily, briny bilge from which it crawled.

The torso was insect-like. The seven arms that sprang from either side of the exoskeleton bore claws that resembled swords, black, serrated blades as wide and fearsome as Scottish claymores. Sticky red ooze drooled from the one that had ripped the first assailant in half.

Most ghastly of all was that the creature, despite its

hybrid, unnatural madness, bore the face of a man. An all-too-human head and neck grew from the nape of the beast. As it glowered upon the three, it appeared for all the world like some poor, damned soul had been swallowed by the hideous abomination.

That poor soul was Sean himself. It was his face that bore down upon the cowering trio.

This time, Orlanda's voice did not fail. Her scream was the equal of a banshee.

The two who had only moments before tried to kill her, now feebly attempted to use her for a shield. It was to no avail. Two of the claws melted from their armored state, shifting in an instant into a pair of very long, but very human-looking hands.

They took hold of Orlanda, gently, and wrested her from the grasp of the two remaining assassins. They set her aside, screaming all the while as she stared in horror at the defiled face of the man she had asked never to leave her side.

The two did not even bother to mount a defense. They knew that their moment had come. They were not given much time to ruminate on the fact.

The living blades cut them to shreds. In a whirl of organic steel, their clothes, their limbs and their very skulls were sliced and chopped so many times that there remained at the end nothing more than chum to be shoveled into the canal; fish food and scraps of cotton in a broth of almost-human blood.

When it was done, he turned to Orlanda.

Then she saw something only possible in nightmares, something no one should ever have to see, and few humans before her had. She stood dumbfounded, beyond words or cries, as the beast contorted, compressed, and turned in upon itself. She watched in disbelief, still, despite all that she had seen, as the skin of the creature shifted like muddy water. Stinking yellow pus oozed from the joints where arms or limbs were receding into the core of the thing.

It didn't take long, though, but then why should it? Something so terrible and unreal?

In a few moments, Sean was standing there before her again. He was naked, dripping in slime and blood. But it was clearly him, and she'd seen every second of his horrid metamorphosis.

"I should have told you. I wanted to. But how could I?" he said, taking a moment to find the words in her language, and then repeating the phrase so she could understand.

She simply stared back at him. She wasn't hurt. She wasn't in pain. But her face had changed. Those eyes that had once been so warm, so dark and so sweet were now cold. Their stare was empty, like a corpse.

He reached out a hand to her, and took a step. A siren blared, and police arrived just around the corner.

"Please. I only want to be with you. I'm sorry," he said.

But she just ran away.

He wanted to run too, to follow her, but he couldn't. He knew he couldn't.

Instead he fell to his knees. Tears blended with the muck on his cheeks, and he screamed out her name.

"Orlanda! Orlanda! Orlanda!"

✛   ✛   ✛

Then he woke up.

Maggie was there by his side. She had a wet towel pressed against his forehead.

"It's only a dream. You're okay. It's just a nightmare, Sean," she assured him.

He opened his eyes. He saw her through the tears.

"What is Orlanda?" she asked, wiping the sweat from his brow.

"Who," he answered. "Who."

SEVEN

VINCE WAS NO STRANGER TO THE SUNSET CLUB, OR to the connected guys who patronized it. His years on the force had been marked by their constant association, payoffs, kickbacks from numbers games, and during Prohibition, the occasional raid. It was unavoidable, a simple fact of life, and not at all as glamorous or exciting as the movie houses made it out to be.

The reality of it was that the rackets were a closed shop, from the beat cops and the back-room bookmakers all the way up to the detectives and the street bosses. The thing they never got right, those Hollywood types with their natty cardboard-cutout lawmen and sneering George Raft bad guys, was that the whole lot crawled out of the same pool. It was a dirty, polluted cesspool of petty fraud and wink-and-a-nod sanctioning, kept alive by enough hard cash to go around, and jolted every now and again by murder when there wasn't.

But it was still just one pool.

Vince had grown up with most of those guys, with their brothers and cousins, mentored by their fathers and uncles. He knew better than most that among the dingy pubs and taverns of the West Side, the Bowery, and the Lower East Side that cops and hoods alike spent as much time rehashing twenty-year-old stickball games and sordid tales of the girls back in the day as they did discussing their actual business.

Which wasn't to say that nothing ever got done. When the busts were made, they were made. When there was a score to settle, it got settled. Bad blood fueled more posturing and backstabbing than just about any other motive, except perhaps the old reliable green.

But two sides? Cops against robbers, white hats against black?

It had never been, nor would it ever be that simple.

Nevertheless, Vince found himself taking a few deep breaths as he crossed Mulberry Street at the corner of Hester. The steamed-up kitchen windows were open at Gennaro's across the street, slathering the cold breeze with welcome drafts of breaded veal cutlets frying in olive oil. He politely sidestepped a pair of hunched little widows in black shawls chattering to each other in Sicilian, and pushed open the creaky old side door to the Sunset.

It was suitably dim and quiet inside. The thick shades were drawn over the windows, as always. The house lights were set on low.

Vince scanned the room. The un-lacquered tabletops were bare. Some of the chairs were still upside-down on top of them. The black-and-white tile floor was wet in places from a recent mopping. But near the back, a few seats were occupied. One in particular caught his attention, beneath a cheap painting of Garibaldi holding a tri-color emblem.

"Hey, Paulie Tonsils," the ex-cop said, recognizing an old pal with a cigar and a bad comb-over sitting under the hero's portrait.

Paulo Giannini had gotten his nickname when he was seventeen, almost half a decade after he began working for Sam Calabrese. Most kids had their tonsils out in grade school, or a little later. Paulie, however, had been laid up for weeks when his throat glands finally got bad enough to require extraction—about a month before high-school graduation.

The boys had kidded him about it for so long, getting a child's operation when he was almost eighteen that the name had stuck. Now pushing forty, his hair was thinning, and a lifetime of pasta and *vino* was beginning to put a belly on him. But the name lingered.

"*Paesan! Che si dice?* You lookin' for some action?" he answered, watching Vince approach from the other side of his own exhaled smoke. "Rangers look pretty good this year."

"I don't bet hockey," Vince replied as he sat down.

An Enrico Caruso recording was playing low from a phonograph in the back. It was scratchy from over-use. It skipped a little disconcertingly while Vince settled into the chair.

"Right, smart move," Paulie answered. "I think we got some college basketball going on, if you want to put somethin' down on that."

"Yeah, I might lay down a few bucks. St. John's is

playing at the Garden, right?" Vince said.

"Yeah. I'll put you down for your usual. Good spread on this one, just between you and me. I think you'll make out on it."

"Thanks, Paulie." Vince turned then, out of habit when he heard the door open behind him.

He watched discreetly as a pair of men he had never seen before entered the place from the same unmarked side door he had come through, the door only regulars and good customers ever used. Strangely, though, no one paid them any mind. Not old-time Freddie who sipped his espresso in the corner. Not Mikey, the ancient-looking man behind the bar who never seemed to leave, and not any of the four runners playing cards at a table near the back.

That alone was odd. What was odder still was how the two looked. A bald man so short he was probably a midget, and a guy who Vince imagined would make a good Tonto from the Lone Ranger radio show. Vince wasn't quite sure what to say.

"Who the hell was that?" he managed, once they had passed.

The balding wiseguy smiled half a smile. He looked like he wanted to say a lot, but he responded briefly.

"Coupla new guys."

The answer did not satisfy the ex-cop.

"I heard you had some new faces around here. But what gives? Frankie don't trust nobody that didn't grow up within spittin' distance of the neighborhood. And I can tell you right now those freaks ain't from the neighborhood."

Paulie took a long draw from his Macanudo. The full, sweet smoke seemed in no hurry to ease its way out of his mouth. He rather carefully checked to his left and to his right before he spoke again, trying hard not to look like he was trying hard.

His voice fell into a self-conscious whisper.

"He didn't. I don't neither. Ain't you heard, though? Frankie ain't around no more. Hasn't been for about three months."

"No. I didn't hear anything. If somebody took out Little Frankie, I think I'd have heard something."

Paulie shook his head. His eyes strayed away from Vince's sight. For the moment, the plain surface of the table was all that he wanted to see.

"We don't know that somebody took him out, not yet, anyway. Believe me, I don't mind tellin' you Vince, cop or nothin', if I knew anything, I'd take care of it myself. All we know is that he left one day and nobody's seen him since."

"And Sam? What's he say?"

Paulie looked up, just so Vince could tell that he wanted to conversation to end.

"Tell you the God's honest truth, he don't seem to care one bit. But the boss ain't really been himself lately. Gettin' a little nuts in his old age, if you know what I mean."

"So I heard. Listen, I'll be back tomorrow to pick up my cash. Good spread, right?" Vince said, getting up to leave.

"You know it."

With one more look to the rear, where the newcomers had settled in the shadows, Vincent buttoned his coat, paid his respects to old Freddie, and left.

"Who was that, Paulie?" Indian Joe asked, not a moment later. Paulie had not heard him approach.

"Oh, him? Vinny Sicario. Used to be a cop around here, grew up over on the West Side, Hell's Kitchen, you know? Good guy, good customer. He drops a couple hundred in here every summer."

"Every summer?"

"Yeah, you know, baseball season. Big Yankee fan, old Vince. You gotta get with the program here Joey, what the hell do you do all day upstairs?" Paulie tried to use humor to mask his unease at dealing with the giant Native American. It usually didn't work.

"What did he want?"

"Nothin'. Just talkin', you know."

Joseph nodded, and walked away.

❖ ❖ ❖

The little bodega store was out of Lucky Strike cigarettes. That meant Vince was going to have to settle for Marlboro, or maybe Pall Mall. It also meant he was going to be in a bad mood for the rest of the day.

Having met with failure seeking the first item on his informal list, he ran quickly through the other things he needed. Juice. Canned soup. As usual, he couldn't remember too many. Maggie was going to be mad at him.

The place didn't sell bandages, but they had dishrags and twine, good enough to dress a wound temporarily.

There wasn't any hydrogen peroxide either, which meant he'd have to make due with another disinfectant. He looked at rubbing alcohol, a large bottle. At least then he wouldn't have to waste any more whiskey.

Vince had been a cop for almost twenty years, from the time he got back from the Navy in the spring of '22 until he drank himself off the force in late '41. Those years walking the streets had done several things for him. They'd left him with a slight limp and a near-suicidal drinking habit. But the time spent wandering the streets had also honed his instincts. Even years removed from his days in blue, his senses were keen. He knew when things weren't quite right. And that was the feeling that came over him as he compared the sizes of rubbing alcohol bottles in the back aisle of the store.

Someone was watching him.

He could feel the gaze. It was heavy, the way a cat watches a mouse before pouncing. The stillness was what gave it away. The lack of ordinary movement. When a guy follows you, Vince knew from experience, he tends to focus on you to the exclusion of everything else, including his own demeanor. It was a pitfall that he himself had always sought to avoid, but had fallen into often, nevertheless.

That was what he sensed now, even before he turned around. The area behind him was too quiet, too still.

Cognizant of the presence, he did nothing. It was exactly what he was supposed to do. He continued browsing, picked the bottle of alcohol with the cheapest price and made his way toward the register at the front. As he walked, he pretended to scan the aisle to his left. It was a magazine rack, filled with pulp rags and tabloids, but it was what lurked behind the rack that piqued his interest.

It was a man, Spanish from the look of his skin, olive like an Italian, but with eyes that were too narrow to be a paisan. The fellow was short, and somewhat disheveled, with matted black hair that hung over his eyes. Vince was certain he was the one.

He didn't keep an eye on the man. He just kept walking. At the front register he greeted the elderly woman behind the counter, made idle chit-chat and paid for his stuff. When he left he caught a glimpse of the other man pausing, and then following.

Brown paper bag braced in his arms, Vince walked in the exact opposite direction of his apartment.

The other man kept a good distance, and Vince was sure that his pursuer was unaware that he was on to him. He crossed at Forty-Second and Eighth, over to the east-side of the street. There he set his bag on the ground and knelt down. He untied and then retied his shoe, and got his best look yet at the Spanish man, who waited in an unassuming manner on the other end of the busy intersection.

Even from a distance, the man's bizarre features were obvious, such that Vince marveled that they hadn't garnered his attention before. His face was narrow, but long with a chin that sported bristle-like whiskers. His nose was also long and thin. It came to a near point at the end, extending over a floppy black mustache that hid the man's lips. In all, he looked more like a sewer rat than anything else.

Vince waited until the light changed to tie his other shoe. Sure enough, the rat-man blended into the crowd and crossed in his direction. He had now gone several blocks in the wrong direction, and the chase had grown tiresome. He was going to have to lose him.

Around the corner he went down into the subway. He darted into a newsstand, and then right back out the other end. Down the stairs into the subway entrance he walked for a few feet until he was shielded by a crowd. Then he doubled back.

As he crossed back over to the entrance, he saw the rat-faced man pass by, still looking ahead, unaware that Vince had eluded him. If it had been another time, Vince thought, he might have turned the tables and followed the follower, but Sean still languished in his apartment, and he needed the supplies.

He bounded up the stairs, in an effort to make up for lost time. As he did, he caught a glimpse of something out of the corner of his eye.

A girl.

She was perched like a pigeon, on the top of a ledge at the exit doorway. Not so far off the ground, but high enough that few people would ever sit there. That wasn't really what drew his eye though. It was the way she sat there.

Lots of bums and vagrants found their way into odd places, but she was none of those. Her blond hair was unbound, and it flowed long and free over her bare shoulders, despite the chill. Her pale face and icy green eyes seemed to peer down, directly at him, as he left the terminal. It was as if no one else saw her. Vince paid her an eye for only a moment, though, strange though her sight was.

Arachne just smiled as he turned his back and walked away.

EIGHT

WARD'S ISLAND WAS A PECULIAR RUNT OF A PIECE OF land. A misplaced, weed-ridden lump in the East River, awkwardly wedged between Manhattan, the Bronx, and Queens.

A black Cadillac sedan drove along its desolate vista past the whitewashed, ghostly edifice of Manhattan State Hospital. The sight spurred a cackle or two from somewhere within its labyrinthine halls, muffled by the filter of iron gratings that guarded the upper windows. Trailed by a cloud of gravel and dust, the car turned around the empty park and into the unpaved lot just beneath the Hell Gate Bridge. Noon was creeping up on the city, but the river overlook was deserted.

A last desperate call echoed from the confines of the lunatic ward as the sedan vanished under the behemoth structure. The wind was tormenting the Hell Gate currents with gusts that were every bit as violent as the cries escaping the nineteenth-century asylum.

It smelled like dead fish at low tide.

Another car was already waiting when it pulled up into

the noisy shadows of the stone pylons. A train was clattering over the rails above, screeching eerily as it slowed. The monstrous white columns that formed the base of the bridge's stone arch seemed to be the only thing the railcars didn't rattle as they rumbled along far overhead.

Indian Joe slipped out of the first sedan, his black pinstriped suit pressed and creased in all the right places. Taking the man's appearance as a kind of cue, a grungy Chinese youth in a black leather coat exited the other vehicle, his hair jutting out from under an old hat and his beard half grown in. They greeted each other casually, but kept at arm's-length.

The Asian opened the door to his car, allowing Victor Huang to step out. He was a slight fellow, a fifty-ish gentleman also of Chinese birth, though much better dressed than his young associate in a sepia-brown suit with a starched yellow shirt, a striped tie and a matching handkerchief tucked into his coat pocket.

"How are you this morning Mr. Huang?" Indian Joe asked, bowing in an awkward, almost insulting fashion.

The Chinese man merely shook his bald head. He brushed a quick hand over his pointed gray mustache. That sort of ignorance no longer bothered him. He had been around too long.

"Is all this really necessary?" he began, his English devoid of any foreign accent. "Our places of business are not a mile apart. Why all this secrecy?"

"You'll have to excuse our methods," Joseph answered. "But you must understand that under some circumstances these types of precautions become necessary."

The answer did not satisfy, but Huang left it alone.

"Is my money here?" he replied, his manner already betraying some of his ire.

Joseph simply shook his head.

"I am merely the driver, Mr. Huang. Mr. Calabrese waits for you as we speak. I'm sure he can answer all your questions."

Joseph pointed the other man in the direction of the ornate sedan from which he himself had exited. The back door opened from the inside.

Huang, with a look back to his guard, entered.

Inside, protected from the noontime sun by purple velvet curtains drawn across the windows, Sam Calabrese sat patiently in an absurdly cartoonish white suit. He was polishing a gaudy gold bracelet encrusted with diamonds in a spiral pattern. Even in the daylight shadows, his belly and chin and legs seemed to sprawl out across the seat cushions. He didn't even look up when the other man entered, and closed the door behind him.

"Mr. Huang, I see you've spoken to Joseph. As I'm sure he's told you, these added security measures must be taken from time to time. I trust it will not affect our little arrangement."

Huang made no attempt to conceal his unease.

"Mr. Calabrese, I don't know what kind of quantities you usually deal in, but I'd hardly call our arrangement little."

"A euphemism, my friend. I merely wish to put you at ease. Assuming all goes well, you'll have nothing to fear from me, despite what I'm sure you've heard. Trust me when I tell you, the old Salvatore Calabrese is no more, appearances to the contrary aside, of course."

The other man did not appreciate his reference. Calabrese chose to move on with his business.

"I know that I have asked you for a great deal, and that the amounts we've discussed are significantly larger than your usual transactions. That is why I have taken such steps to give you extra time to accommodate me."

"I understand that, but . . ."

Calabrese interrupted.

"Because no one wants this arrangement to end with violence. Not your Tong, and certainly not me," Sam said. Finally, he looked up from his gold bracelet. He stared directly into Huang's eyes.

It took a lot to intimidate a man like Victor Huang. More than a few men would have died for his word, and he hadn't made his living for thirty-five years with his sense of congeniality. But when Sam Calabrese looked right at him, through him really, the Chinese man couldn't help but shudder.

It was the coldest stare he had ever seen. Vacant. Soulless. It was almost inhuman.

"I have done my best to fill your needs. And I continue to work on it. My people are dealing with this day and night. I don't know what you're planning here, but I'm not certain I'm equipped to handle this kind of order," he finally said.

"Nonsense," Calabrese answered. "Your operation

has done excellent work thus far. The supplies of hashish and heroin have been superb, top quality in fact. And to be honest, I really never expected you to be able to locate any absinthe. I wouldn't worry about that. So in actual fact, our matter is very nearly closed. All that remains is the shipment of opium, along with the pipes and other incidentals."

Huang gathered his resolve to answer.

"Well, that has proven difficult. You must have some very old-fashioned friends, Mr. Calabrese. There isn't a large market for straight opium anymore. I have had great difficulty amassing a supply large enough to meet your demands."

Calabrese smiled. The grin did not put his associate at ease. In fact it made him more uncomfortable.

"Perhaps this will aid you," Sam said, lifting a leather satchel and handing it to Huang.

He opened it, and quickly realized that it contained much more than the fifty thousand dollars they had negotiated.

"I trust that will go part of the way to smoothing over any problems you might encounter. I'll need my full amount satisfied in three nights' time."

Again, Huang seemed uneasy. He was about to reply when Sam preempted him.

"Three nights. That is not negotiable."

Just then, the door opened from outside. The expression on Indian Joe's face told Huang that the conversation was over.

NINE

SEAN WAS SITTING UPRIGHT, IN AN ANTIQUE ROCKING chair that looked almost as out of place amid the disarray of Vince's apartment as Maggie did. While his torso remained bandaged, his arm had been placed in a makeshift sling crafted from a sweat-stained T-shirt. It was dark outside, and getting late. His head was spinning, and he felt deathly cold, but he was awake.

That was a start.

"Time to change those sheets, they're starting to stink up the place. And that's hard to do in this sty," Maggie said, rustling up the dirty linen on the couch beside him.

He couldn't really help, with his arm immobile and the pain that still lanced his side with every breath, but watching her there, he wished he could. Maybe that was why he felt the need to break the uncomfortable silence that followed as she folded up the old cloth and spread out the new.

Maybe it was that. Or maybe something else. Maybe he just wanted to talk to her, *with her*, again.

"If I haven't said so yet, thanks. I appreciate what

you two are doing for me. Especially with the way we left things," he stammered, through a cough that brought the warm taste of bile into the back of his throat.

"I haven't forgotten about that."

"But you haven't mentioned it, either."

"You haven't exactly been in any shape to be talking about ancient history lately," she replied. "Considering that we had bigger problems to deal with, I figured it could wait until you were better."

"I'm better now. A little, anyway," he said without a hint of irony while a heavier cough plagued him with every breath.

"You're not better, not by a mile. Do you really want to broach this subject?"

"I don't want to wait another thirty years. That's for sure. Go ahead," he answered.

Maggie was reluctant. His skin was so pale. He was sweating even though his forehead was cold to the touch. This wasn't the time to dredge up dirty laundry. Nevertheless, she began anyway.

"Well, I was mad at you, for a long time. I still am. A little, I think," she said.

"Mad at me? How's that?"

"For leaving the way you did. Maybe just for leaving. For all the times that I needed you here."

There was a lot she wanted to say, but her thoughts only came out in fragments.

Sean's reply seemed like more of a sneer than anything else. "You had Vince."

"That's not fair, and you know it. What happened, happened. I made a choice, and I've had to live with that ever since," she answered.

"I could say the same for myself."

"Yeah. I suppose you could. But at least I had the courtesy to tell you about mine. Do you think that was easy? It tore me apart, but I did it. I did it because you were my friend and I cared about you. When you ran away you didn't even say goodbye," she said, finding it easier to let her feelings out the longer the conversation went on.

Sean, on the other hand, answered flatly. His tone was so vacant that the words seemed totally absent of emotion. "I hate goodbyes. I've made too many of them in my life. Always saying goodbye to someone, or someplace."

Maggie shook her head. He could still disappoint her, even half a lifetime later.

Leaving him on the chair, she turned her back, and walked to the other side of the room. Sean almost settled his head back down, expecting her to have lost patience. She hadn't, though, and she proved it by opening Vince's old phonograph.

There were a few records piled next to it. One was already on the turntable. She placed the needle down gently, and the single spun. At first there was just the familiar crackle and static, then a hint of a tune that almost felt distant, until the horns blared.

"Do you remember this?" she asked, her back still turned.

Sean perked up his ears. The music was soft, but

it had a strong tempo. He couldn't quite place it. He knew it, but it had been so long. As soon as he heard John McCormack's tenor voice, though, he remembered. He remembered everything.

Up to mighty London came an Irish lad one day
All the streets were paved with gold
So everyone was gay!

The first line brought it all back.

"It's a Long Way to Tipperary," he said, a certain satisfaction clear in his voice. "I haven't heard this in years."

Neither one spoke for a moment. They just listened to the old tune, to a song that seemed to have been everywhere during the War.

Singing songs of Piccadilly, Strand and
Leicester Square
Till Paddie got excited and he shouted to
Them there

"I played it earlier, but you were passed out. I used to cry every time I heard this. Especially after you were gone," she said, turning back to face him from across the room.

It's a long way to Tipper-ary
It's a long way to go
It's a long way to Tipper-ary
To the sweetest girl I know!

"I'm sorry."

It was all he could think to say.

"Sorry?" she shot back.

"For that. For this. I was angry in those days. You were my world, you and Vince. When you told me you were gonna marry him, it was . . . I don't know, it wasn't like anything, really. It was the worst thing I could imagine, the worst thing in the whole world, so I thought."

His bout of coughing grew worse then, and he had to clear his throat of what he guessed was blood, from the sickening flavor of it. Finally, he was able to finish his thought.

"If I had to do it again, I would have made different choices. If I'd known then what I know now."

His fit did not end with the close of his words. Maggie rushed from the phonograph back over to the chair, holding his head as he choked on the blood and phlegm. In only a moment he was passed out. She found herself pondering his words alone, with only the scratchy old recording to keep her company again.

"Yeah. I might have too, if I'd known then."

TEN

THE CHILD-WHO-WAS-NOT-A-CHILD, WHO HIS ASSO-ciates called Argus, sipped his tea with the hand of a connoisseur. In his elegant, but uncommonly tiny suit, he sat quietly, feet dangling from the edge of his chair. There were only a few others in the diner to notice him. A cabbie with a day-old beard growth sat nibbling on dry toast at the end of the counter. *A lady of the evening*, still done up for a night on the town, waited for her late-night snack as she counted her trick money before calling it quits.

It was quiet, almost surreal for Manhattan, a town that was buzzing seemingly at all hours. Outside the slightly steamed restaurant windows a few trucks made their way through mostly empty streets, accompanied only by the rush of the sewer vents and the occasional homeless strag-gler. It was Argus's favorite time of the day.

During the dawn hour, when the moments seemed to stretch longer than at any other point of the day, he often found himself drawn back over the many years of his long, long life. The older he grew, in fact, the more he enjoyed casting his thoughts backward, rather than forward.

The child-who-was-not-a-child had seen that sun rise more than five hundred thousand times. And with each one there was a memory.

Prague, December 1923 was the one that drew his attention this morning.

He could still hear the icy water rushing over the rapids of the *Vltava*, just beyond the Charles Bridge. He could almost see the battlements of the castle *Pražský Hrad*, bastion of ancient Czech kings, rising defiantly through the early day's haze. And he could still smell the pungent odor of a man who had not bathed; a stink that he well recalled had carried downwind from where the disheveled figure sat along the riverbank.

He had been huddled, wrapped in a urine-stained cloak beneath a barren tree. A steaming mess of yellowish puke had oozed over the near cobblestones, an empty bottle of vodka at its center.

Argus had approached him carefully, for he had walked with a cane in 1923, a thing he distinctly remembered, perhaps better than any of the other details of that day. His thin, withered legs had not been able to carry him swiftly in those days, and he had several times brushed long, white hair from his eyes as he neared. Charybdis had been at his side then, and he well recalled how his loyal aide had looked in those days as well.

1923 had been a good year for Charybdis. *He* was strong then, tall and broad-shouldered, with the Nordic features of a Dane or a Swede. An aristocratic beard on his chin lent him the bearing of a noble in exile. A perfect watchman for the *little old lady* named Argus, as *she* neared the drunk at the edge of Prague's central river.

"Are you certain of it?" Argus questioned, his voice the shrill whine of a hag.

"As sure as I can be without seeing him myself. The owner of the bar described the scene to me personally. If his memory was even close, then we may be in luck," Charybdis answered.

"What did he say again, exactly?"

"That a woman wandered into his beer hall three nights ago, tall, beautiful, and speaking English with an American accent. Every man in the place bought her a drink, and by midnight she was utterly drunk. One of the bolder of the patrons retired with her to the rear of the hall, to a private room."

"Not much to speak of so far, Charybdis," Argus interrupted as they neared to within several yards of the tree where the lone beggar sat.

"It will be. Only the girl and the man, a regular at the tavern, entered the private room, and the owner assures me that no one else was back there. Then, about five minutes later, after some loud and unusual sounds echoed from that area, a single *male* stumbled out of the room, half dressed in the clothes of the man who had entered. The second man, who no one had seen before, ordered a drink and secluded himself in the shadow of a corner booth. A few minutes later, someone checked the room and found—are you ready?

"The man who had entered with the girl, knocked

unconscious and naked. No girl anywhere in sight—just her clothes scattered on the floor."

"Interesting."

"So the owner checked the booth where the male no one recognized had sat down a few minutes earlier, and what did he find? The blond girl, alone and dressed in the guy's clothes, finishing the drink that the unknown man had ordered."

"What did he do?"

"The owner grabbed her by the arm, and picked her up to demand an explanation. A second later, he dropped her."

"Why?"

"Because when he looked at it in the light, the arm was a snake."

"He was drunk as well?" Argus chided.

"Maybe, but there's more. After he dropped the snake the girl slumped back into the booth, again, all in shadow. When she got up a few seconds later, it wasn't her, it was the strange guy again, and *he* walked out of the bar, stumbling, drunk, and laughing."

"Sounds like one of us," Argus said.

"Based on his description, I'd say that huddled scavenger over there is our man," Charybdis replied.

The pair walked slowly, like hunters stalking prey. Slumped and quivering, the quarry did not appear dangerous to all outward appearances. If he were indeed the man they suspected him of being, however, then they knew that he was likely the single most dangerous man in Prague, if not in all of Europe besides.

They neared with great caution.

Argus placed a shriveled hand on the beggar's shoulder, fighting back his instinct to choke on the brew of stale alcohol and human waste that hung about him. Charybdis waited beside him, prepared for trouble if it should arise.

"My son. Let us help you," Argus said, gently lifting the head of the unfortunate wretch.

Immediately he realized that his search had ended. The face was that of Sean Mulcahy, just as he remembered it from the first and only time he'd seen it, in St. Petersburg, Russia, in 1918.

Argus recalled taking hold of the young drunk, and carrying him to a waiting carriage. From there they had taken him to a small two-story home in Zizkov, a sheltered neighborhood outside the bustle of the city center. They'd used the side entrance to avoid dragging the dirty young American through their spotless foyer.

He had awakened after a bath and a drink of black coffee. Argus laughed as he thought on it, for the young man's voice and manner had been, in those days, almost as foul as his odor.

They wasted little time. Once Sean regained his consciousness, they settled in the central room of their suite. Still somewhat woozy, Sean nestled into the folds of a soft ermine couch next to a crackling fireplace. The little old lady in the black dress and stringy white hair left briefly, leaving him alone with the tall Viking.

"Where am I?" Sean asked.

"The Haven of the Three Shields," Charybdis answered

from beside him.

A moment later the tiny woman returned. Hobbling on her gnarled cane, she clutched something large close to her breast. It was a book, which she presented to Sean when she sat down beside him on the couch, the Nordic man still standing.

"Our home, here in Prague. Your home as well, if you wish it to be," Argus added.

"I ain't got no home," Sean said.

"Very well, many of us are wanderers. For whatever you choose to do, know that you may stay here as long as you like. You are safe here, my son."

"Safe? From what?"

"From the outside; from those who do not understand us and who fear what they do not understand."

"Us?" Sean questioned, sitting up fully as Argus opened the ancient book across his lap. "What is this?" the American asked.

"Take it, my son. It may answer some of your questions," Argus replied, settling the leather-bound volume to rest comfortably in his lap. The hide cover was beaten and timeworn. The pages cracked when he opened it. Argus pointed a knobby finger to a gold leaf that jutted out from the middle of it. "Here, the page where I've marked it. Begin there. I've brought the English translation."

Sean cast an incredulous eye at the old woman and her tall aide, but he did as the lady asked.

"The words of Nestor, second Keeper of the Lore, as spoken to his scribe, the honored Galatea."

It did not take long for him to offer his own commentary, however.

"What the hell is this shit?"

"Read," was all the old lady Argus replied.

"In the early day, as the green glen cradled the mist, and the sparrows announced the coming of the sun, he came to me as if spoken from a dream. First merely words, then words made flesh and earth and stone, brought to life in the haze that spread in every direction."

Sean cringed, but he kept reading.

"When mortal men walk among the clouds, like the gods their fathers banished, he will come. Unlike any born of the human line before, a trickster who will shed all bonds. Seek him when the master grows weary, sated from fifty feasts, the Keeper will fall to the bringer of the light, the one who was, and who will come again.

"Then shall there be a new dawn. The star of morning will lead the flock back to their peace long lost. From across the veil of night, far in the cold north by way of the western sea. Lucifer of old will be reborn."

The end of the page brought yet more comments from the young New Yorker.

"There. I read it. Happy, lady? I didn't follow a damn word."

"No? You should, Lucifer," Argus said, moving closer to him and pointing at the words on the yellowed page.

"What? You really are a crazy old coot aren't you?"

"You've no idea how right you are," Argus answered, getting up from the couch to stand before Sean.

"See, at least we got somethin' between us. Now, if we're all done with the mumbo-jumbo, it's been nice talkin' with you guys, but I've got some Czech beer with my name written all over it."

"About my age, that is. I am one very old creature indeed. In fact, you're far more right than you could possibly know."

Sean merely sighed, but he delayed his exit long enough for Argus to finish her words.

"I was born in the year you know as A.D. 395, *anno Domini* in the language I was taught to speak as a boy."

"As a boy? Right." Sean almost smiled, now he knew the old hag was nuts. "I'll give you credit, you look good for your age. I stand corrected. Nice talking with you."

"Wait. I am telling the truth. I was born in Milan during the first year of the reign of Flavius Honorius, son of Theodosius the First. As a child I saw the Visigoths ride south toward Rome in 402. Later, I was a consort to one of Charlemagne's knights. Even later I stood beside Duke Godfrey, and saw Jerusalem burn in 1099. But you have no reason to believe any of that."

"You're right there."

"But you will believe this," she said, her voice falling into a whisper. *"I know what you are."*

Sean felt a sudden, uncomfortable chill. He knew exactly what the old woman meant, even though he wished with all his heart that he didn't.

"Yeah, what am I? I ain't crazy, I'll tell you that," he finally answered, mustering all of his street-kid false bravado.

"No, but you are quite a rare breed, only one or two like you in a century."

Sean's expression went cold.

"Don't worry. You're among friends here, I assure you. Others of your kind. Well, maybe not exactly your kind, but very much like you, in any case. Including me, by the way."

"And you are?"

"They call me Argus. And I would very much like to be your friend."

✣   ✣   ✣

A soft touch on his shoulder broke him from his spell, and Argus found himself back in the diner, back in New York and 1946. It was Arachne. There was a dire look played out across her delicate features.

"You must come quickly. Charybdis has sent me to find you," she said in a hushed tone.

Her cheeks were red and there was a hint of sweat in her blond hair. She paused after she spoke, to regain her breath before finishing.

"Something has happened at the church!"

ELEVEN

THEY HAD HUSTLED AS FAST AS POSSIBLE THE SEVEN north-south blocks and four long east-west blocks back to the burned-out cathedral, Arachne resorting to carrying her boyish master the last three. Charybdis was waiting for them when they arrived.

A shriek echoed from inside as they stopped.

"It's begun," the dark-cloaked African said as they hurried into the shelter of the cathedral.

Inside was a scene of the macabre.

Nearly a dozen people were gathered on the broken-down altar at the rear of the place, each holding a candle that made for the only light in the musty hall. They were encircled, and chanting in an ancient, labyrinthine dialect. The long shadows from their tapers danced upon the walls in a slow, hypnotic rhythm.

In the middle of their ritual circle something writhed on the sooty ground.

And it screamed.

Argus and his aides rushed to the altar. The inhuman howling reaching a fever pitch as they neared.

"When did it start?" he asked.

"Not more than three hours ago. I had the local hospitals under our watch, as per your orders. An ambulance brought this one in from off the street. No one knew what to do with her. Our people spirited her out and brought her here," Charybdis answered.

"Do we know who it is?" Arachne asked.

"Not yet. She was already in the midst of it when we rescued her. She has not come out yet," the dark-skinned woman replied.

"Is this the first?" Arachne asked.

"That we know of, at least. It's still early, but it means the time is rapidly approaching. Within days the condition will afflict all of us," Charybdis answered.

Argus, though the smallest of the gathered folk, moved through the circle with a wave of his palm. Then he saw firsthand the source of the awful screams.

It was spread out on the floor, covered in a bluish slime and flapping a series of appendages against each other like a deformed seal. The bulk of it, approximately six feet in length, was vaguely serpentine, but with limbs, or the remains of limbs, jutting out from every side. There was no head, but something that resembled a human chin and mouth struggled in pain at one end. It was there that Argus knelt, his tiny hand on the slippery skin of the thing.

"It hurts. I know. But you are safe now. Do not fight it. Just let it happen, my child. Let the change overcome you," he assured it.

✛ ✛ ✛

"The end stage," Charybdis said, from her vantage a few paces back.

Arachne was beside her. The blonde tugged at the sleeve of the African's silk suit, a strange look clear on her face.

Charybdis knew what it meant.

"You have seen her? My lost beloved?" the black lady questioned.

"I am fairly certain. The Keeper has had a young Latino thug following a man named Sicario for the last day. My contacts indicate it is your once-betrothed, Scylla."

Charybdis breathed heavily. Arachne noticed a slight quiver in her long torso. She almost looked frightened.

"It's been so long. I was beginning to think I'd never see Scylla again. This complicates matters."

"What will you do?" Arachne whispered back. "If the Morrigan learns that you two have broken her command, she'll see you both dead."

"I have only one choice then, haven't I?" Charybdis answered.

✛ ✛ ✛

The chanting continuing at his back, Argus stroked the fishlike exterior. He watched with an expression that was something like pride as the chin and mouth pushed forth from the snakelike body. With them came the beginnings of a face, a young man's face, and then a head as well.

"There, the pain is going away, isn't it? You're almost through it," Argus continued as a neck followed the head. Then two human arms broke free from the fluttering quasi-limbs.

In a few more minutes the chanting ceased, and the gathered circle lowered to their knees. Their candles they held forward, to shed light on the naked form of a young man who sat, quivering, next to Argus. A steaming, slimy husk of *something* lay discarded beneath him.

"Welcome back to the fold, Galanthis. It has been a while, hasn't it?" the boy-master said.

"Argus?" the young man replied as a blanket was wrapped about him.

The child-who-wasn't nodded.

"It has been a while. You're looking very young these days, aren't you?"

TWELVE

SOMETIMES A LITTLE FRESH AIR DID A MAN GOOD. Unfortunately, there wasn't much of that in Manhattan, so Sam Calabrese had to make due with the occasional breeze off the river. Every so often, if he walked around long enough, the wind would clear out the stench of garbage, bus fumes, and human waste.

But not nearly as much as he liked.

Still, it was better than the staid confines of his abode, where Indian Joe kept the strictest of security in place at all hours. He was doing exactly what he was supposed to do, of course, ever the vigilant protector, but even the master needed a break from time to time.

So he walked. As always of late, he walked under guard. The man called simply the Vig was on his left, a crew-cut giant who had earned his name for a savant-like ability to calculate interest. On his other flank was Gino Tonetti, the pug-faced former associate of Rocco Gallucci, who had reportedly left the neighborhood for a long vacation. A permanent vacation, some whispered.

Calabrese ordered his men to stop when he caught

sight of a Spanish youth nearing from the opposite side of the street. They were in front of a newsstand. Sam directed his men to dismiss the elderly proprietor. Then he took up residence inside the booth. When the Spanish man arrived, he was welcomed inside as well.

"What do you have for me, loyal Scylla?" he said, without looking at the rat-faced man.

"Very little, I'm afraid," the other answered, reluctantly, it seemed.

"We haven't much time. You know that. Tell me what you have learned."

The Spanish man yet seemed hesitant, and he paused. He took a quick look at the Vig and Gino, guarding them outside the booth. He recognized them. They were not like him. They were human.

"Would it not be better to converse alone, master?" he said, motioning toward the two loyal enforcers.

Calabrese shook his head.

"*Alors, en français?*" he questioned, quietly, but with a flawless Parisian accent.

"Fear not. Those men owe their loyalty to me alone. You may speak in their presence without fear," Calabrese answered.

"Very well, master. At Lycaon's request, I have spent the past day's time on the trail of a man named Vincent Sicario. He was asking questions at the club early yesterday morning, only a few hours after the incident."

"And?"

"As of yet, nothing. He's a hard man to follow. When I

have been able to check on him, I've watched him visit a police station, a drug store and several bars, but I haven't seen him do anything that would lead us to the one we seek."

"Very well, check with Lycaon, but that route may have proven a dead end. If so, we'll have need of your skills elsewhere."

"It may not be that simple."

"Why is that?"

"There are others following him as well."

"Others? Of our kind?"

"I do not yet know. It is possible. Since the War ended our folk have been scattered. The Havens in Leningrad, Paris, Hong Kong, and Prague were all destroyed. If it is one of us, it could be someone from there."

"Prague. Argus's followers. They are gathering here, that I do know. Your beloved *is* among them, if you were wondering," Calabrese replied.

It was almost a taunt.

"Of that I was unaware, master. By your command, as always."

"She has been by the ancient one's side since he came to this place, and remains there as we speak."

The rat-faced man stayed silent. His beady eyes grew even more sullen, and his mustache hid a sharp frown.

"I know I need not remind you of my decree, Scylla," Calabrese pointed his fat finger directly into the Spanish's man's face, his voice nearly fallen to a whisper. "I have permitted you to join us here to share in the festival season, and to allow you one final chance to atone for your past failure. Until that is done, you are to have no contact whatsoever with Charybdis."

"I am thankful for the opportunity," he answered.

"Do not defy me," Calabrese answered, with a tone that was all too clearly menacing.

The rat-looking man called Scylla nodded, almost bowed.

"Very well. You will use your skills to keep watch on both Mr. Sicario and these others who are seeing after him. If they are indeed followers of Argus, I must know immediately," Calabrese said.

"Do you suspect the ancient one of treachery?" Scylla asked.

"I suspect everyone," Calabrese replied. "But I fear him the most. If Lucifer were to fall under Argus's influence, then I have no doubt that he would move against me."

✠ ✠ ✠

The Vig was a whiz with numbers, but in every other respect, he was a certifiable imbecile. Nobody was better at breaking legs, or arms, or anything else that needed breaking, though, which was why he was one of the most trusted men in what had been Little Frankie Pentone's side of the Calabrese operation. Trusted, but not well regarded for his brains.

When he came into the Sunset with a worried look on his face, Paulie Tonsils perked up immediately. The Vig was too stupid to be worried.

"What's up Vig?" he asked, from his usual seat along the far wall, espresso in hand.

"I just heard something you might be interested in, boss."

"Ok, quiet down kid. Why don't you have a seat? Talk about it."

The Vig did as he was told, and Paulie smiled when he sat down. The big man never really looked comfortable doing anything but hurting people.

"You know that Rat guy, right?" he asked, in the manner that a child might ask his father if he knows the President.

"The new guy, yeah, the Spanish kid."

"Well, I was walkin' with Mr. Calabrese this morning, and the two of them met up and talked."

Paulie laughed. Not too much, though. He knew the kid meant well.

"So?"

"They talked about Vinny Sicario. That Rat guy's been tailin' him since yesterday."

Now Paulie was interested.

"Sicario, huh? Did they say why?"

"I couldn't follow, but I think it has to do with the guy that got killed the other night."

"Damn."

"What's up boss? I don't get it," the Vig said. His face was the picture of bewilderment.

"That night, who was you lookin' for?" Paulie asked.

The Vig paused and considered for a moment. Most Irish names sounded more or less the same to him. *O-this,*

Mc-that. But this one wasn't any of those. It was different.

"Some mick. I think his name was Moe? Or maybe longer, like Moe-kay-he or somethin'."

"Mulcahy?" Paulie asked.

"Yeah, that's it. Rocco and Gino were with me. We lost the guy. Why, you know him?"

"No, but I know Sicario. Guy grew up in the middle of the biggest Irish slum in the city. Get a hold of Gino, I think we need to pay our old buddy Vince a visit."

THIRTEEN

THE RAT-FACED MAN WAS ON HIS TAIL AGAIN. VINCE caught sight of him just after he picked up his morning paper. He got his coffee as though nothing were out of the ordinary. This time, he decided, it was his turn.

The little dance routine of theirs had gone on long enough.

He had left Sean and Maggie at his apartment, against his better judgment. She had told him that their long-lost friend had awakened the previous night, for a short time, but he had not stirred much since. Maggie had stayed the night, resting in a chair beside the couch. Vince, for his part, had gotten very little sleep.

He needed to figure out what Sean was into. Whatever it was, he was sure it wasn't good. When he found the rat-man watching him surreptitiously from across the street for the second day in a row, the deal was sealed. Sean was in big trouble, and he knew that he might be too, pretty soon.

He played it calm. This was his backyard, his neighborhood. He knew Hell's Kitchen backward and forward.

Some stranger wasn't about to outwit him on his own turf.

First he had to lull the pursuer, draw him in closer, make him think he had nothing to worry about. Then he would turn the tables. The rat-man was about to get a free tour of the West Side.

It lasted for hours, well past noon. Vince moved deliberately, never looking like he was meandering, even though that was all he was doing. The whole time, he made sure to keep his pursuer in the corner of his eye. He hit four pubs, three stores, a pair of churches and a diner. He even paid a visit to Sacred Heart, where he'd gone to school as a kid, and hardly ever since then. Old Father Gallagher was still there, still doing the rosary, and still as big as a house.

Then it was time for the move.

Vince knew a place, on the corner of West Thirty-Eighth and Ninth. It was a deli, next to a bar, but it hadn't always been two places. When he had been on the job, the bar had been twice as big. The owner, Jimmy O'Connor, had fallen on hard times during the War, some investments hadn't panned out, and he'd been in the lurch for some cash. A buddy of his, Dirty Mike Sullivan, had stepped in and bought out half of the place. Without a liquor license, he'd converted his side into a sandwich shop.

But the division was largely cosmetic, and Sullivan had paid off a few inspectors to skirt the building code violations his arrangement had created. One of them, in particular, was that the two places shared one cellar.

Vince knew both men. He ducked into Dirty Sully's Deli, happy to see that the owner was behind the counter.

It was no problem for him to slip downstairs, and over to the other side of the twin establishment.

The rat-man waited outside for well over fifteen minutes, Vince could see him from the window of the bar next door. He could tell the odd-looking figure was getting frustrated. The Spanish guy finally ventured into the deli, but he exited only a moment later, clearly agitated. He walked south.

Now it was Vince's turn.

He waited until the rat-man was distant, but not too far away. Then he left the bar, and blended into the crowd, a hat borrowed from Dirty Mike low over his forehead. He followed the man over to Times Square, then into a subway, and onto a downtown car. That was the hardest part. Trying not to be noticed on the train. Luckily it was more crowded than usual.

The rat-man got off in the Village, at West Fourth Street. Vince hated that part of town, hated the whole area around NYU, but he got out anyway. He needed to see where the guy was going.

It didn't take long. Just out of the subway, the Spanish-looking stranger took a left, then a right, and then another left. The path led to a small side street just outside of Washington Square Park.

The rest of the neighborhood was trendy, which was why Vince hated it. Most of the kids who circulated around there, the artists, the musicians and the students, they weren't *real* New Yorkers. Not the way Vince thought of them, anyway. Some were from the city, sure, but most were imports, and even those who were locals didn't know his city, his life.

This one block, however, looked like the *avant-garde* attitude had skipped it entirely. There were no coffee shops full of pretentious Bohemians, no tiny storefronts selling fake antiques. Just a row of dingy, poorly maintained buildings, and a lot of trash that hadn't been picked up in a while.

The rat-man moved quickly to a nondescript two-story building, with a plain stone-gray façade. There were no windows, but a small hand-painted sign above the door said **BLEECKER STREET HAVEN** in black letters. *That's weird*, Vince thought, *since I'm not on Bleecker Street.* But that wasn't the only thing that bothered him.

He knew the place. He just couldn't remember how, or why.

❖ ❖ ❖

The law offices of Preston, Howe & Stephens occupied the entire twenty-third floor of a fairly new office building in the mid-fifties on Madison Avenue. It was a part of town that a man like Salvatore Calabrese rarely got to in his line of work. He had dressed in his finest Italian suit for the occasion.

J. Rutherford Preston, Esquire always wore expensive suits, with monogrammed cuffs and a diamond-accented gold tie tack. Behind his mahogany desk, with the obligatory green-shaded lamp and a scattering of papers, three framed degrees decorated the wall. At the center, raised a notch above the rest, was his license as counselor and attorney at law of the State of New York, flanked by twin certificates from Yale, one a bachelor's degree in economics, and the other his *juris doctor.*

He got up from his red-velvet chair when his secretary buzzed. It was just past one o'clock, and he had been dreading this client all day long. He fidgeted as the door opened, trying hard to keep from shaking visibly when the corpulent man with the grim reputation stepped into his office.

Indian Joe was beside him, dressed just as sharply, but with hair longer than Preston had ever seen on anyone, male or female. He caught himself lingering just a moment. He prayed that neither man had noticed.

"Good day, sirs," Preston said, knocking his wastepaper bin with his knee as he stepped out to shake the hands of both. Only Sam obliged.

"Good day to you, and thank you for seeing me. I realize that a man such as yourself must be quite busy. In light of that, I do appreciate your recent efforts on my behalf," Calabrese said, somewhat quietly as he sat down. Joseph remained standing, and silent, beside him.

Preston had not met either man before, having only dealt with intermediaries during their course of business. He knew them both by reputation, though; the type of men who were the reason he had taken up real estate law, rather than criminal law. He sat down himself, already impressed at the polished manner of the man he'd heard had once made a sandwich while watching his men dismember a delinquent debtor with a hacksaw.

"I have very good news for you, Mr. Calabrese," Preston began, his mouth cotton-dry.

"The only kind I ever like to hear, Mr. Preston," Sam joked. He knew how nervous the lawyer was in his presence, and it amused him. *If only he knew the real truth*, he thought.

"The transfer of title to the Pier 33 property is all but completed. And the previous owner has asked me to extend to you his thanks at how generous an offer you made. I suspect he might have parted with the land for less, unused as it has been for so long, and in such an undesirable location."

"All the same, I prefer to pay more for my piece of mind," Calabrese answered.

Preston wasn't about to argue. He smiled, shuffled a few documents on his desk, opened a folder and passed some papers to Sam.

"Well, if you sign there and there, Mr. Calabrese, that will just about seal the deal, so to speak."

Sam scanned the documents briefly, scribbling something illegible in the three places where his name was required.

"Now, if you'll permit me, I'd like to go over the basics of the parcel one last time. Metes and bounds and zoning restrictions and all that."

Sam nodded.

"As you know, the area is really rather large, though it has sat vacant for most of the last twenty years. A lot of that likely has to do with the surrounding neighborhood, that section of the waterfront is notorious for prostitution and street crime, really quite seedy. While under-developed, considering the nearby lots, you have to remember that it is zoned exclusively for industrial use, docking and storage facilities, that sort of thing. No wild parties, in other words."

Preston laughed, but Sam remained stoic.

"Right. Well then, do you have any questions for me?" the lawyer asked.

"When do we close?"

"Within twenty-four hours. I'll meet with the bank people this afternoon and we'll settle the loose ends. All I need from you is the check we discussed."

Sam shook his head, and Mr. Preston almost wet his shorts. He was relieved when Joseph produced a large briefcase and handed it to his boss. Sam put it on the table, and snapped it open. Inside were bound-up stacks of hundred-dollar bills. Lots of them.

Mr. Preston felt some beads of sweat form on his forehead, but he couldn't bring himself to reach for his hankie.

"Are you certain you'd like to pay cash, Mr. Calabrese?"

"I am."

"Very well, it's just that, with a sale of this magnitude, well, that's just an unusual amount of cash to have all in one place."

"Are you saying I should be worried? You are *my* lawyer, aren't you, Mr. Preston?"

"Indeed. I'll see to this immediately," Preston answered, fighting back his urge to throw up.

"When can we move in?" Calabrese asked.

"Almost right away. To be absolutely safe, I'd say you

could begin moving in by tomorrow afternoon. But to be honest, no one would notice if you went over there right now," Preston replied.

"That will be fine," Sam said as he got up and motioned for Joseph to exit with him. "Not a day too soon, in fact."

❖ ❖ ❖

"Vincent? I don't see the likes of you for almost two years, then I got you poking your head in on me twice in as many days? To what do I owe this occasion?" Pat Flanagan said, with a smile on his face, as always.

He was in his office at the precinct, shades drawn, stale coffee and doughnuts on his cluttered desk. His tie was undone, as usual. The room was small, but Vince had never had an office during his time as a cop, so the mere fact that it had a door impressed him. His old buddy had made detective since their time walking the beat.

"I went by a place downtown earlier today. Thought you might know something about it," Vince answered, clearing off a pile of newspapers from the only other chair in the room and taking a seat.

"Yeah? Where's that?" Flanagan answered, offering a doughnut.

"Down in the Village, the *Bleecker Street Haven*. You familiar with it?"

Flanagan looked sideways at his ex-partner. He knew the place too.

"What the hell were you doin' down there?"

Vince said nothing. He merely stared, his face blank like a stone.

It was the same icy stare Flanagan had seen him use hundreds of times. That was part of what had made them such good partners. Vince was the quiet type; he only spoke when he had something on his mind. Pat, on the other hand, most people who knew him wondered if he was ever going to stop talking.

"Alright, alright. Yeah I know it. Flophouse, beggars and bums shack up there for a while. At least that's what they say, anyway."

"What's that supposed to mean?"

"Nothin'. Just that the place's got kind of a weird reputation, if you follow me."

"Weird how?" Vince's attention was now snared.

"Why the hell do you care about this Vince?"

"Let's say it's for a friend, huh?"

Flanagan smiled. Vince realized he might already know more than he was letting on, but he still trusted the big Irishman.

"Your friend wouldn't have anything to do with the recent *troubles* in the Calabrese crew, would he?"

Again, Vince said nothing. Flanagan knew better than to try to wait out his laconic Italian friend.

"Okay, whatever you say buddy. Bleecker Street Haven, huh? That place has a rep on the street for making people go away. People check in, so to speak, and never check out. Been like that for years now, since before the

War, easy. Pretty low profile, though, for the most part."

"I don't understand. How could that kind of thing go unnoticed?"

"This is what I mean about low profile, Vince. No one's makin' any complaints, you see. Just talk. Neighbors, bar- keeps nearby, you talk to them and they'll all say the same thing. They see stragglers and weirdoes move in from time to time, real distinctive-lookin' characters some of them, the kind of faces you don't forget. But then they never see 'em again. It's like the place just swallows them up."

"Strange, huh?" Vince mused.

"Yeah, but like I said, no complaints, no calls to the police, no missing-person reports. Nothin' we can do. Nothin' we want to do, tell you the truth. A few less bums around is fine with me, you know?"

Vince nodded. "A few less rats, right?"

Flanagan agreed, even though he didn't fully get the joke.

FOURTEEN

ALTHOUGH ONLY A FEW MINUTES HAD PASSED SINCE THE hands of the antique grandfather clock had marked half past five, several customers at the "Rock of Cashel" pub were well on their way to drowning their sorrows for the evening. Three of them sat along the length of the narrow, corridor-like bar, one sipping the last of his stout, another puffing on a cigar, and the last falling in and out of sleep as he tried to focus on his own increasingly blurry reflection in the mirror.

Vince entered through the heavy oak front door. Brass chimes clanged as it opened and closed. None of the men seemed to notice. The pug-faced bartender looked up, though, and he smiled as he finished drawing a pint from the tap. It was a grin that only ex-boxers could make, two teeth missing and a nose broken so many times it only looked straight when he laughed.

Tommy McCormick had been the only sober man in the pub. For that reason alone, he was happy to see his old friend Vince.

But neither one said a thing. No words passed between the two as Vince approached the bar. He sat himself down on a stool near the front window. Tommy served up the pint, took his money and wiped his hands on his apron. He made his way toward Vince's end. As he walked, he rolled up his shirtsleeves, revealing a pair of enormous forearms.

"You still lookin' for a beatin', Tommy?" Vince finally said when they were within a few feet of each other.

"Oh, my boy. The sun's yet to rise on the day that you could beat me!"

Vince laughed. It felt good, after the last few days.

He slipped off his coat then, rolled up his own right sleeve, and placed it on the bar opposite Tommy's. All the while pretending that he wasn't the least bit interested in the contest for which they were preparing.

"Whenever you're ready, little buddy. Unless you'd just like to admit I'm the better man ahead of time and save yourself the pain," Vince said.

Tommy did not respond, except by clenching fists with his guest. Both men locked their arms into place. Each nodded to the other. The contest began. Tommy grimaced as he tried to force his arm over Vince's. His freckled cheeks swelled. Vince didn't budge. He pushed back even harder.

"I've not seen you in here fer a while," Tommy said, between gasps. "To what do I owe the occasion?"

"I'm checkin' into something," Vince answered. "I thought you might be able help me out. Lookin' for a Spanish guy."

Tommy used Vince's pause to gain some leverage, but they remained braced in the struggle, arm in arm. Little beads of sweat congregated across Tommy's reddening forehead.

"Why're you askin' in an Irish pub? We don't get too many spics in here," he replied.

Vince squinted. His bicep burned.

"I know, but this guy's connected I think," he said. "I never seen him before yesterday. Can't miss 'em, though. Looks for all the world like a rat had sex with a spic and popped him out. Real ugly."

Tommy's grip fell suddenly limp. Vince slammed his wrist down against the bar. The arm-wrestling over, the conversation had only just begun.

"What's the matter? You're not goin' soft on me are you?" Vince chided while Tommy wrapped a wet towel around his arm.

"You know this guy, don't you?" Vince continued.

"Know who? I ain't got no idea who you're talkin' about, Vince."

"C'mon, you known me a long time Tommy, since I was a rookie on the force and you were out there runnin' bath-tub gin. You never lied to me before. Don't start now."

The Irishman's voice dropped into a whisper.

"Do you have any idea what you're lookin' at?" he asked.

"Why don't you educate me?"

Tommy sighed, still cradling his defeated arm. He looked down when he spoke.

"Okay. This guy you're lookin' for. The rat-faced one. I seen 'em. They actually call him "Rat," in fact. I don't know his last name. Or if he even has a last name."

"Who's 'they'?"

Tommy paused again, for a deeply needed breath, and for taking a nervous look around the bar. None of the other three guys seemed alert enough to either hear, or care, about his conversation. But he wasn't taking any chances.

He cocked his head toward the back of the bar. Vince understood the gesture, and with the Irishman leading the way, they took a detour to a booth hidden in the shadowed rear of the establishment.

Tommy finally looked like he was about to spill it.

"Okay, listen, Vince. You didn't hear none o' this from me, understand?" he started.

"Okay. What's the story?"

"I don't know what you been told, but this Rat fella's been running with the crew from the Sunset. Rocco Gallucci, the Vig, Paulie Tonsils and those guys."

"Right. Little Frankie Pentone's boys, the Calabrese crew. That much I figured."

"Well, here's what you might not've figured. See, Sam Calabrese's been up to some weird shit lately. I'm mean, we're talkin' real oddball here, Vince."

"I keep hearin' whispers about that. But nothin' specific. What do you know about it?"

"Well, I don't like 'em here, to be perfectly honest with you, the wiseguys and their cronies. But they been comin' in for years. What can I do? I'm just runnin' a business."

"Okay, so?"

"Here's the thing. Those guys are real tight, you know? Most of 'em grew up together in the neighborhood. Don't see too many new faces. I never seen this weird lookin' spic until just a few months back. Then one day he just shows up. Pretty soon we got a whole buncha new faces. Before you know it, it starts to look like Calabrese's been puttin' up recruiting posters in a circus tent.

"All weirdoes, Vince. Some Indian, looks like he just walked outta a cigar store. A midget with a face that looks like it's been hit by a shovel, and your man Rat. The word around is that the big guy ain't even himself anymore. I heard some guys talkin' the other day about some strange noises comin' from inside his loft. Like a bunch of dogs fighting, only no one was in there but Sam."

"I don't know what to make of that either, Tommy. But you're tellin' me that this Rat fella is one of Calabrese's guys. That's what I needed to know. Anything else you got?" Vince answered, either unimpressed by the tall tales, or merely hoping to appear unimpressed.

"Afraid not buddy. Wish I had more, but that's all I know. You want my two cents Vince? Don't get involved with this. Whatever you're lookin' at, walk away now. I don't know what's goin' on around here, but I know one thing. This ain't no numbers racket or loan-sharking. Whatever Sammy Calabrese's into these days, it's something totally different. And with a guy like him, that's never good."

"Can't really do that. Not yet, anyway," Vince answered. "Anything else you got, old buddy?"

"No. I'd tell you if I did, I swear Vince. But this is what I can do for you. You mentioned Frankie. Word around is that someone took him out."

"So I heard."

"He's not dead. Just in a hole, so to speak. I think I might be able to help you dig him out. He's the guy you need to talk to. I wish I could help you some more, but that's all I know," he replied, scribbling something on a scrap of paper and passing it to Vince.

"Don't worry. You've been a big help."

Vince read the note quickly. "Maria Torriella, 234 West Forty-Seventh, Apartment 3B." Wiping his forehead, he lit himself a cigarette, grabbed his coat, and left the bar. Tommy McCormick wished him luck under his breath as he walked out the door, even though he didn't think it would do any good.

FIFTEEN

SEAN WOKE IN THE LATE HOURS OF THE EVENING, RAM-
bling again. He was pale, almost deathly. Maggie's hand
trembled as she toweled the sweat from his brow.

"I'm sorry," he mumbled.

"About what?" she whispered. It was dark outside. A
whisper seemed somehow appropriate.

"Yesterday. Everything."

Maggie smiled. It was a grim sort of smile, the kind
made at funerals, or in cemeteries. Sean mimicked her, but
fell quickly back into his slumber.

It wasn't long before Vince interrupted.

The broad-shouldered man entered the apartment and
slammed the door behind him. He started talking before
Maggie even had the chance to say hello, or to quiet him.

"Guess where I just went? I just got back from a nice
little scenic trip all over the island of Manhattan! And you
know why I did that?

"I did that because a goddamn sideshow freak with
a face like a rodent has been tailing me since yesterday.
Everywhere I go his face pops up. I had to lead that ugly
bastard all over the neighborhood before I lost him.

"I think."

Vince stepped close to the couch, where Sean was writhing slowly in a cocoon of bloody sheets. He was clearly unconscious, but Vince talked to him anyway.

"You know what's even better? He works for Sam Calabrese. I don't know what the hell you're up to, but the word's out on you, buddy. You're in deep, old friend!"

Perhaps roused by the words, or maybe by something else, Sean wriggled. He stirred from the couch. Feebly, he seemed to be trying to prop himself up. The effort revealed the full weight of the red-stained bandages wrapped around his torso. Maggie noticed the four incision-like tears in the quilt where his *hand* had pierced the fabric the day before.

He tried to speak, but he could only manage a whisper. Maggie moved past Vince, closer to him. She knelt down to hold his head up.

"Morrigan," was all he said.

Vince took his hat off, unbuttoned his jacket and left it draped on a chair.

"What the hell?" he said. "Listen, I know he's been through a lot, and I ain't askin' too many questions. But he's gotta come clean with this much right now, forget about the rest of this crap, what's the deal with you and Sam Calabrese?"

"Morrigan."

Again, it was all Sean could mutter.

"Who exactly is Sam Calabrese?" Maggie asked.

The question brought a scowl to Vince's face.

"He used to be small time, nickel-and-dime stuff just in Little Italy. Last few years, though, he's been moving up. He's a big time operator now, even around here," Vince answered.

"Small time what? Is he a bookie or something? Is that what this is all about Sean? You came back here because you owe someone money?" Maggie asked.

His eyes were open, but his expression was strangely blank.

"Well that just takes the cake, doesn't it?" Vince said, exasperated. "Sam Calabrese's not a bookie exactly, but he does have his hands in the rackets. Bottom line, he's not a man you want pissed off at you."

He turned to Maggie as Sean slumped back down on the couch.

She'd lived in Hell's Kitchen long enough to know the ins and outs of the seedier side of things.

"He's no man," Sean muttered, and just as he passed out again, said, "Morrigan."

"Great. That's just great. You're a marked man and you're making jokes. Terrific," Vince said.

"He's lost a lot of blood, Vince. He woke up a few minutes before you came in, but he's not going to last much longer without some proper medical care," Maggie said.

"Well, there ain't no way we can take him to a hospital. Not now. Calabrese's gotta have feelers out to all the local places."

"So what do we do? Let him die here?" she demanded.

"No. Not here, anyway."

✤ ✤ ✤

It was still, and it was late. Only a few cars crossed the Brooklyn Bridge, their occupants unaware of the goings-on beneath them, as two figures approached in the gloom on the Manhattan side.

The uneven light from the street lamps left most of the lower sections of the mammoth structure drenched in shadow. Stale water dripped from the steel rafters. Dirty waves lapped along the East River shores.

Charybdis was making her way carefully down the service stairs that led below street level. In the dark, as tall and lanky as she was, she might easily have been mistaken for man, especially in her gray flannel suit and raincoat.

Her head turned at every noise, aware of her sur-roundings like a she-wolf. She stepped slowly along the wet concrete, squinting to see.

A voice as slippery as the floor rattled her from behind.

"Good evening, *madam*." There was a note of irony at-tached to the last, accented word.

The voice carried a sinister tone. Charybdis shivered as she turned to face it.

"Is that you, Scylla?" she asked, still unable to see through the darkness.

"Call me Rat, everyone else does these days."

The forked-tongued speaker stepped out from the steam-girded shadow of a steel column. Though small and wiry, he appeared threatening nonetheless. The olive skin

of his face was partially obscured by his dangling bangs.
They hung over his eyes and drooped down to his nose, a
feature that by its length and shape suggested the root of
his unflattering nickname.

"You're late. I trust that you haven't changed your
mind," Rat said.

Charybdis did not smile, but she neared, and she removed
her overcoat, despite the cold. Rat, or Scylla as Charybdis
called him, breathed deeply as the other came closer.

"Not even a question. How could you ask me that,
after all these years?" Charybdis answered.

"It has been so long," he said. "For ages now it seems I
have wandered. Ever alone, an endless hunt my only pur-
pose; thoughts of returning to you my only motivation."

Before another word could be exchanged, Charybdis
closed the final gap between them, and they kissed.

It was a long kiss, the kind between lovers who haven't
kissed for so long they've almost forgotten how. It went on
until it became two kisses, then three, or four, until finally
one merged into another.

But no one was counting.

Sean's arm was still in the makeshift sling, and Vince had
thrown his old coat over him like cloak. With the former
cop at the lead, Sean trudged out of the doorway into the
early morning light. It was the first time he'd seen the sun
in days. The dawn burned his eyes.

Maggie's hair was wrapped in a neckerchief. Most of the rest of her face was secluded behind oversized sunglasses.

"What makes you think Calabrese can't find my place too?" she asked.

Sean's breathing was labored as he stood there.

"I don't think he can't find it," Vince replied, pausing to scratch his scruffy chin. "But I'm sure they're on to me. Relocating should buy us some time. That's all."

Her car was parked about a block away, and she hurried past them to bring it around. Just then Vince realized that they should have waited inside while she did that. Any time out in the open could be dangerous.

It wasn't long before his instincts proved correct.

Sean coughed, negotiating the row of steps down to the sidewalk. Vince braced him on his good arm. Neither noticed the men approaching from across the street.

"She's pullin' the car around," Vince assured him as Sean drifted in and out of consciousness. He was as pale as a ghost.

Three men in dark coats stepped around the cars parked in front of the pair. Vince recognized them right away. It was Paulie. There was a small revolver held close to his pocket.

"Good to see ya Mr. Mulcahy. I don't know how we missed you last time. But then again, it looks like maybe we didn't miss, if you know what I mean," Paulie said. His two associates lined up on either side of Vince and Sean.

Sean was able to nod, barely. But Vince answered for him.

"What the hell is this Paulie?"

"Sorry, Vinny. It ain't nothin' personal, you know that. The boss has been lookin' for your friend here."

Without being told, the Vig gently reached inside Vince's coat. The big man relieved him of the pistol in his shoulder holster.

"Tell you what Vin'. I don't want no trouble with you. But this guy here killed one of our boys the other night, and we gotta take him in," Paulie continued. "You walk away right now, your name never comes up. Except maybe to tell Mr. Calabrese that you helped lead us to him. Which ain't really a lie, when you think about it. Since I never woulda made the connection if you hadn't gone nosin' around."

"Can't do that, Paulie," Vince began.

Before he could continue, Sean moved. He reached up with a languorous motion that was painful to watch. Gently, he rested his cadaverous hand on Vince's shoulder.

"It's okay, Vince. He's right," Sean said, in little more than a whisper.

"Let him go, Vince. He's our problem now," the Vig said.

"Trust me," Sean whispered again as he hobbled away from the stability of his friend and toward the waiting hood with the bad comb-over.

"I'm all yours," the wounded man said as he made one more step and fainted into Paulie's suddenly waiting arms.

"This sucker's half-dead already. Look at him," Paulie said as Sean slumped against his chest.

With Vince looking on, three guns trained toward him, Paulie took Sean by the shoulders. He lifted him.

"Hey! Wake up you son of a bitch!" he shouted into

the young man's face.

The noise seemed to wake him. Sean's heavy eyes drew open. Paulie tried to guide him, taking him by the wrist, as a car pulled up alongside. He hardly noticed when Sean's free hand clasped with his own. The touch was soft, and unthreatening, almost intimate somehow. That was why Paulie did not recoil right away, as he should have.

"Don't worry. I promise you won't feel a thing," Sean whispered delicately, so that only Paulie could hear.

The next moments passed very slowly for Paulie Tonsils, as though the hands of his watch had been jammed to a crawl.

At first he felt only a mild sensation. An unsettling, dull warmth that slunk across his skin. The tiny hairs on his arms and chest stiffened. A ringing in his ears drowned out all other sound.

His heart was already pounding when Sean reached out with his wounded arm, free from the sling, to touch the bare skin of his other hand. A weird lull, a strange numbness inexplicably fell over his limbs. His extremities followed, and a moment later, his entire body.

It finally clouded his mind as well.

He could still see Sean, his own eyes closed as if lost in a deep and sudden trance. But when the young man opened them a moment later, there was something familiar, *something terribly familiar* about the gaze that Paulie saw looking back at him.

The others saw it too, and for an instant, they shared a hint of the shock that paralyzed their leader.

Paulie could hardly muster a breath as he stood there in a half-dazed stupor, staring at his own face. There, as though through the pane of a magic looking glass, his perfect doppelganger stood looking back at him. The same olive skin. The same Roman nose. The same bad comb-over.

Somehow, he was clutching hands with himself. And the other him was smiling.

Even Vince caught a glimpse, the gangster Paulie standing face to face with his exact double, where Sean Mulcahy had stood only a moment before.

Shrieking tires broke the eerie calm as Maggie's Ford raced around the corner. Vince seized the arm of the assailant nearest him. In one motion he cracked Gino's limb backward. Almost simultaneously, he seized his revolver and fired three rounds at point blank range. One blasted a jagged red hole through Gino's open mouth. The other two shot directly into the face of the Vig, whose stunned expression was quickly reduced to a spray of blood and flying bone shards.

Sean, still clutched in the surreal embrace with the man whose form he now mirrored to the last detail, merely continued to grin. Paulie, horrified at the sight of his own face staring back at him, slowly slipped out of consciousness. His heartbeat slowed. His breathing fragmented. Life was draining out of him, drifting away.

After a few moments, his blood stilled. His lungs lapsed and exhaled one final time.

"C'mon, what're you waitin' for?" Vince shouted.

Sean said nothing, glaring at the limp form of Paulie

Tonsils as it fell from his grasp. Sean's peculiar juvenile features re-formed as the two lost touch, not at once, but slowly. As a ripple glides across a pond, the change moved through his shimmering, pliable flesh. In a few moments the process was complete, and Sean Mulcahy once more stood on the sidewalk.

"Let's go!" Maggie shouted from the car.

Staggering away with Vince at his side, Sean leapt toward the waiting car. They both jumped into the back seat.

Without a word from any of them, and nary a look back to the three dead men on the street behind, Maggie put the car in gear and hit the gas.

SIXTEEN

QUIET REIGNED OVER THE LOFT WHERE SAM CALA-
brese often spent the night. The man rarely slept at home.
Rumors held that he hadn't shared a bed with his wife in
years. In fact, the story was that he hadn't even seen her
since Christmas of '45, and that had been to tell her that
their marriage was, for all practical purposes, over.

Despite his less-than-savory occupation, however, he
was still a good Catholic. Divorce had been out of the
question. So he had done the only thing he could do. He
had made sure she had enough money to get along while he
entertained himself, and he had sent her to live somewhere
he knew he'd never have to go, somewhere he knew nobody
ever really wanted to go.

As far as he knew, his wife was happy on Staten Island.

He was slumbering quite peacefully, the heavy shades
drawn closed, when the man he called Lycaon, and nearly
everyone else called Indian Joe, entered and roused him.

"What time is it?" Calabrese mumbled.

"Seven-o'clock. I know you've been sleeping late these
past days," Lycaon replied.

"I need rest. The festival is especially trying for me. I

will need all of my strength."

"I know, master."

"Then why do you disturb me?"

"It's Mulcahy."

Calabrese, as if injected with a dose of adrenaline, rose immediately. He lifted his great girth into a seated position.

"I'm afraid it is not good news. Two of the men on our payroll work out of the Midtown South precinct. A few moments ago we received a call from one of them, a Sergeant Maher, who incidentally wishes to thank you for the flowers you sent his wife on her birthday last month."

The suggestion brought a much-needed laugh to the fat gangster's lips.

"In any case, he reports that they, and I quote: *Wheeled in three stiffs this morning. Shot down outside this guy Vince Sicario's place.*"

"Our boys, I take it?"

"Indeed. The one called Paulie Tonsils and his two guys, Gino and the Vig."

Calabrese scratched his chin.

"What colorful names these people give themselves. Paulie Tonsils. I've never seen the like, in all my many years."

"It looks like some of our boys took it upon themselves to locate Mulcahy."

"This Sicario again, the one Scylla's been looking at. Why does his name keep popping up?"

"I did some checking. It turns out he's a childhood friend of Mulcahy's. Knew him here before he left for what they used to like to call *The Great War.*"

"Before he learned who, or even *what* he was. This Sicario individual is likely still unaware of Mulcahy's true nature. Lucifer may be able to evade us, but if he has friends here, we can use that. I want this man. Through him we can get to Mulcahy—in whatever form he's taken."

"I'll have Scylla stay on him. We've already looked into his background a little, but not much has turned up."

"What do we know so far?"

"Vincent Nicholas is his full name. Used to be a police officer in this area, retired a few years ago for reasons we haven't been able to determine. He's been described by those who know him as *a real sonnuvabitch* and *not someone you'd want to mess with*."

"Sounds like the sort I could use on my staff right about now.

"Any family?"

"Nothing. Parents are dead, no relatives in the country. Married, but as far as anyone I've talked to can say, he and his wife haven't spoken in years. He evidently has no friends. Not the most sociable of New York's many denizens."

"Fine. Keep our people out there. He's sure to turn up eventually. When he does, keep someone on him. But do not, under any circumstances, try to snare him. Once he's located, I want to be informed. If we lose him, we lose Mulcahy, and that cannot happen again."

"He's already proven he'll kill to protect himself. Do you think he'll try to leave the city?"

"Always possible, but not likely. He's still one of us,

after all, and he can't resist the call of the season any more than the rest of us can. He'll be here for the festival, but we have to get to him before then. Before anyone else gets to him."

BOOK II

"Festival's Eve"

SEVENTEEN

DRYING SHEETS, SHIRTS, AND SOCKS HUNG FROM LINES spread across the cramped space between apartment windows. Suspended from a forest of clothespins, the laundry seemed to dance as it dried, swaying to and fro and casting jubilant shadows on the bricks below.

The pulleys usually made a squeak when the lines were rolled in, but Maria Torriella couldn't hear it as she gathered her wash. Four children, *four little monsters* as she often said, howled from the living room of their tiny third floor walk-up. Frankie and Ernie, the two oldest at nine and seven, were teasing six-year-old Ralphie. As they tossed his baseball glove back and forth, just high enough to be out of his reach, tiny little Anita wailed from her crib.

To make matters worse, the sauce on her stove was bubbling over, and the garlicky red paste was beginning to burn on the outside of the pot. Maria, curlers in her hair despite the late hour of the day, was deftly tending to all three things at once. One hand on the laundry, one on the stove, and her booming voice making every attempt to silence the kids. She might have succeeded, and might not have spilled sauce all over the front of her housedress, if the knocking hadn't erupted just then on her door.

With a slap on the back of the head to Frankie and a swat on the rump to Ernie, she swept across the length of the little apartment and unlatched the lock. She did not expect Vince Sicario to be on the other side, nor did she expect him to come busting into the room a second later.

But she was ready.

"Who the hell do you think you are?" she spat at him, holding her hand out to keep him at bay.

"I'm a friend of your brother's. You are Frankie Pentone's sister, right?" he answered, the kids still screaming. "Little Frankie's little sis."

"My brother ain't got no friends," she answered back, the wooden spoon in her other hand poised like a weapon.

"I guess he never mentioned me. That's too bad, 'cause, you see, I know a lot about you."

"Yeah, like what?"

Vince took a quick glance around the place. It was cluttered. Toys were scattered all over the floor. Wicker baskets of laundry sat on the couch. There was an old, giant radio on the mantle that predated the War. It smelled of macaroni and tomato gravy and dirty diapers.

"Let's see. You're twenty six years old, you got four kids, you hang your clothes out the window to dry."

Maria was shaking her head. He was too big to force out of the doorway, but she wasn't about to yield an inch.

"Who are you, the goddamn police?"

"No. I'm just someone who wants to find your brother."

Maria had no time for his questions. She knew what her brother did for a living, and she wanted nothing to do with it.

"Yeah? Well I don't know where he is. Nobody does," she answered.

Vince wasn't convinced, despite her apparent temper.

"Bullshit," he said back, stepping closer to her.

"Hey, no swearing in front of the children, you asshole! Now get the hell outta here! I don't know where Frankie is."

"Don't make this hard, I've had a really tough coupla days, and my patience is wearing thin, lady."

Vince moved farther into the apartment, closing the door behind him. Maria backed off. Keeping the children corralled in her shadow, she carefully moved them toward the kitchen. Vince didn't care. From under his overcoat he was slowly drawing out his revolver.

Maria turned white.

"See, it's very important to me that I find your brother," he said, lifting the pistol in a deliberately garish motion.

Her heart started racing. She felt the heat and the wetness under her arms and around her neck. Suddenly she couldn't swallow.

"Do you know who you're talking to? Who my brother is?" Boasting seemed to be the only card she had left to play. "He'll feed you your balls you bastard, bringing a gun into my place!"

He wasn't listening, and he proved it by aiming the weapon at a lamp on a small wooden table.

"We're old friends. I don't think he'd mind," Vince

chided.

He cleared his throat. His thumb brought the hammer back into a cocked position. The barrel caught a glimmer of the lamplight.

"This? Well, this he might mind."

With a calm squeeze of the trigger, a single bullet sizzled across the room. It burst the lamp like a glass balloon. The blast exploded in Maria's ears, knocking her against the wall. A ringing concussion effect throbbed through her head. Squeals erupted from the kids in the next room.

She dropped her spoon as her muscles tensed involuntarily. Gray, hot smoke burned her nostrils and stung her eyes. Shards of glass and wood were suddenly splayed all over the floor.

One shot had turned her apartment into a war zone.

Momentarily startled, the display only seemed to make her angrier. Once she got her footing back she screamed, though she could barely hear her own voice.

"You think you can just come in here and start shooting this place up! You fucking asshole! You think someone won't call the police!"

For all it did to inflame her senses, the shot had calmed Vince's nerves. The smell of the gunpowder was familiar, a rather long-forgotten sensation. He inhaled it deeply from the warm air. He enjoyed it a little too much.

After his lungs were sated, he replied with a quiet cool, like a gunfighter caricature in a John Ford movie.

"Not in this neighborhood. I used to be a cop. They won't be here for a while. Trust me."

"Gesù! Pazzo Schema!"

"The old lingo ain't gonna do it, honey. Sorry. Now, where is he? The sooner you tell me, the sooner I'll be outta your hair."

"Goddamn you!"

Vince sighed. He didn't want to go to the next obvious step, but the woman was pushing him.

"Okay."

Ralphie had poked his head in from the kitchen. Maria saw him. She screamed at him to move. But he didn't. She knew Vince was pointing the gun at him without even looking.

The other kids were wailing. She could hardly move.

"Okay. Okay. *Basta! Basta!*" she pleaded, trembling at the very thought.

Vince, quietly thankful that the lady had bought into his bluff, let the gun drop to his side. With a collected stride he stepped over a broken vase and moved closer to Maria. This time his voice was lower, but no less forceful.

"Where is he?"

Tears burst out of her fierce eyes. They were already streaming down her face by the time he got over to her.

"I don't know exactly," she sobbed.

Vince raised his eyebrows. For a moment he lifted the gun again.

"I swear to God okay? I'll tell you what I know. He's in Jersey."

"Jersey? What the hell's he doin' there?"

Maria was almost too rattled to answer. Slowly she

managed to compose herself enough to say something.

"He's resting. You want to know where? Here's the address." Hands quivering, she reached over to the table, fished out a small piece of paper from a pile of notes and handed it to Vince. "Take it and get the hell outta here."

"You gotta be kiddin' me," Vince mumbled when he read what was written on the scrap.

"What?" Maria questioned, still indignant despite everything.

"Nothin'. You've been a big help Mrs. Torriella. When I see your brother I'll let him know."

Vince slipped his gun back into his coat and calmly stepped out the door, a scattered mess of an apartment left behind him.

"I hope you rot in hell!" she shouted as he left.

EIGHTEEN

THE BLEECKER STREET HAVEN WAS ALIVE.

Though the façade remained as nondescript as Vince had found it a day earlier, within the humble confines the air was charged. Neighbors and other Greenwich Village locals already knew that the place tended to fill up with borders once or twice a year, crowded with foreign guests like some European youth hostel. But what the outsiders could not know, what they could not see behind the hand-stenciled sign and the plain gray walls was something much different.

Inside the frosted glass double-doors, and beyond the oaken paneled foyer, the atmosphere hummed with the sights and sounds and smells of a party.

Chatter filled the main library hall on the first floor, gossip and conversation made in a dozen languages. The walls there were lined with Gothic-crafted cabinets of polished cedar crammed full with old books. A series of maroon oriental rugs broke the monotony of the well-worn hardwood floor. Positioned throughout the chamber were a number of velvet cushioned, high-backed chairs and reading desks topped with Russian vases and the stark white busts of poets and statesmen.

Smoke from pipes and Cuban cigars—the kind usually reserved for special occasions—lent the air a sweet, thick aroma.

It was festive, though no decorations suggested a particular holiday. The people who mingled about were of all manners and sorts, young and old, male and female, and culled from as many different ethnic backgrounds as there were individuals circulating through the establishment. No single trait could have described them all, except that everyone present seemed genuinely happy to see everyone else.

More like a reunion than anything else.

Argus entered with his pocket-watch in hand. Lately every hour had become precious, and he was meticulous about keeping track of his time. He was alone, and he had begun to walk with a small cane, wincing with every step from some ailment that betrayed no other outward symptom. An exquisitely dressed Tiny Tim.

As he crossed the foyer and entered the library hall, he caught a look at a tall, distinguished-looking lady admiring the crystal chandelier directly overhead. Though he did not know her on sight, something about her, her mannerisms maybe, seemed familiar. The way she held her martini glass, with the pinky finger held out just a little pretentiously, or the thin stream of smoke she exhaled after a puff on her cigar.

She was slender, and appeared to be well into her seventies, with leathery, wrinkled skin and gray hair tied behind her head in a bun.

In every way she appeared to be his complete opposite.

Argus approached as if he knew her. But when he presented himself, with a deliberately old-fashioned bow and flourish, it seemed momentarily that neither one recognized the other.

"On behalf of our kind that once called Prague home, I greet you," he said.

Immediately a flash of recognition passed over the old woman's face.

"Argus?" she said. "I should have known. Who dresses better than you?"

He was dressed impeccably, as always, his miniature three-piece suit tailored in perfect proportion to his toddler's body.

"I accept your greeting, and pay you respect from my own followers, of Chaligny-Bastille," she continued.

Now Argus's face lit up with the same moment of epiphany, as though he had just laid his eyes on the woman for the first time.

"Cygnus, a pleasure, as always. How long have you been in New York?" he asked.

"Less than a day. I waited in Paris for as long as I could, hoping to gather as many of us as were left there."

"Of course, your Haven likely suffered the greatest of all of our houses. How many were you able to bring?"

Her expression was dour. He knew her response was not going to be pleasant.

"Barely more than a dozen. Before the War we were three

times that many. I had hoped that your city would fare better, but from what I've read I did not hold out much hope."

"Your feeling was correct, I am sad to say," Argus answered. "The Nazis ravaged my beautiful city, and the Soviets who replaced them are little better. Few of my followers emerged from hiding during the liberation. I come here very nearly alone. The Haven of the Three Shields is no more."

A new voice broke in then, from a third figure that neither saw.

"So the stories I've heard are indeed true, and Prague has been lost to our kind. A terrible shame, but one which very closely mirrors my own trials."

It was a child's voice, higher pitched than Argus's, but obviously prepubescent. When they both turned to see after it, they shifted their gaze and saw a beautiful little girl with blond ringlets and a fancy lace dress.

"Aeson?" Argus began.

"It is I, ever young, as I see you are as well, in this incarnation," she replied.

The girl did not appear to be any older than five, but she spoke with the diction of a scholar.

"Your followers?" Cygnus questioned her.

"Reduced to a mere handful. When the Germans starved Leningrad, I watched our kind die side-by-side with the city's inhabitants. Now there are only a few of us. Like you, we have abandoned our once great house in Peter's city," she answered, the sadness somehow more despondent when expressed on her delicate, girlish features.

"The war has left none of us unscathed. All the more reason for this new gathering of ours," Argus said. "Has there been any news from the Keeper? I must confess that I have not been much in communication of late, and I do not even know the location of our fete."

The little girl Aeson, who was sipping from a glass of Cabernet Sauvignon, shook her head. Her curls seemed to dance across her shoulders.

"The Morrigan has left word here that the announcement will be made soon. Until then she has asked us to assist in bringing together as many of our kind as possible. For the moment, we have found a refuge here at this Haven, our common ground in New York for these many years."

"Have we any idea how may of us there are?" Argus asked.

"Sadly, no one knows. So many were scattered over the past years, so many lost. This will be the first opportunity for a full accounting since the violence ended," Aeson replied.

"Yes," Cygnus followed, "but do not worry ancient one. I have been told that the plans are already in the works, and that we will soon know. The Morrigan will provide, as she always does."

Pier 33 was deserted. A deathly still hung over it, as usual. The morning hours were waning, and the almost-midday sun had just begun to throw its warm, yellow light on the city.

Sam Calabrese, Indian Joe, and a trio of their closest

associates navigated their way through alleyways of rusted iron. They were looking for one building in particular, and they had quickly found that most of the dilapidated structures on the site looked identical.

The network of scrap metal shacks and time-weathered warehouses ranged from the east end of the property, along the edges of the West Side Highway, to the unused dry dock on the west end. There the pier had been largely blocked off from the Hudson by a newly erected shipyard a few hundred yards north. It was part of the reason why no one had used the dockside spot for almost twenty years, despite its otherwise prime locale.

Indian Joe kicked at a junkie, curled up in a ball in their path. He didn't move, and the party stepped over him like a piece of trash. That was the other reason no one ever came to this part of town. No one respectable, anyway.

They finally made their way before what Mr. Preston's notes indicated was the largest of the warehouses. The corrugated metal on the outer walls was washed over in gritty shades of red and brown, and the glass panes of the windows had been shattered. A drainpipe oozed black filth out onto the pavement, which looked to have been broken, repaved, and re-broken numerous times. Each patch-up job made the place look worse, rather than better.

Inside, Calabrese threw a switch that seemed more suited to a mad scientist's lab than a dockside storage unit. It crackled like an old-time transformer, and then a scattering of the several dozen-odd lamps that lined the length of the chamber lit up. It was a long, wide place, with a high ceiling and a dusty concrete floor.

Even after decades of neglect, some of the facilities still worked. The lights buzzed an institutional, electrical sound. While only about a fifth of the total number had sprung to life, it was enough to satisfy Sam.

"Very well," he began, turning to get full a view of the empty, lonely place. "Lycaon, you may start moving our people here immediately. This place is rather spare, but we will make a home of it."

Indian Joe nodded, but his expression was not one of satisfaction.

"The trucks are all loaded at the club, master. We can begin setting up here within hours. I'm afraid we have come across one other obstacle, however," he said.

"Obstacle? Whatever it is, I'm sure you can handle it. You have my full confidence, as always. Do whatever you need to do," Calabrese said, distracted by the enormity of the desolate structure.

"I have done all that I am able to, trapped for the time being in this form, at least. This difficulty, I fear, will require your attention."

He turned from his contemplation then, and sighed.

"What is it?"

"The provisions. We have received all but the final shipment of our various narcotics from Mr. Huang's couriers. He now reports that the last haul cost him more than he was expecting. He is refusing to turn it over unless we pay an additional, undisclosed fee."

"I understand," Calabrese said. "Very well. Oversee the arrangements here; I will pay a final visit to Mr. Huang."

NINETEEN

THOUGH HE HAD NEVER BEEN TO *SUNNYBROOK GARDENS,* Vince was familiar with the place by reputation. It was way out in the rural hinterlands of northern New Jersey. In Sussex County, he thought, but he couldn't be sure since the scenery all looked pretty much the same once you got past Hackensack.

It was a hell of a drive, especially in his sputtering '37 Dodge, which wasn't in the best of shape anyway. The old girl was just about to overheat when he found the secluded hospice, guarded by a veritable forest all its own at the end of a winding country road.

There was no sign, just a double gate of black-glazed iron, connected to a fence of the same sort, which seemed to ring the entire estate. A guard in a faded gray uniform was sipping his coffee when Vince pulled up. He looked as though he welcomed the interruption.

"No, I ain't family," Vince told him, in answer to his first question.

"I ain't a friend of one of your *guests* neither," he continued.

And no, he hadn't called ahead. He was there to see Francesco Pentone. Little Frankie, as most called him.

"Nobody by that name here," the guy said quickly.

"You didn't even check the register," Vince snapped back.

"No need, nobody by that name here sir," he answered.

Frustrated, Vince retrieved the paper from his coat pocket. Atop the address were a few words, a name in fact, scribbled hastily in pencil. He had ignored it previously.

"How about a Mr. Hoover? Mr. J. Edgar Hoover? Is he here?" the ex-cop asked.

The guard unlocked the gate without another word, not even an acknowledgement of the joke. Vince let it go. With the obstacle cleared he depressed the clutch and cranked the stick into second gear. Then he motored the rest of the way up toward the imposing old Victorian mansion, slowly so that he could take in a decent view of the stately gables and the sandstone exterior.

It was getting late. The sun was starting to paint the western sky in mournful shades of red and orange. A wash of clouds had rolled in from the west during his trip. That probably meant rain. It was cold, his breath condensed when he exhaled. Still just a bit too warm for snow, though.

He didn't mention the name Little Frankie again, and he didn't have to. The nurses were waiting for him when he arrived at the main entrance.

A sour-faced blonde who looked like she wanted to be anywhere but where she was directed him through the sterile, ammonia-smelling wards. The interior felt even more ancient than it looked from the outside. Despite the oppressive sting of bleach in the air, it wasn't maintained particularly well. The windows were crusted with a yellowish film, and he felt a gentle tug on his feet as his soles clung to the invisible stickiness that coated the floor tiles.

Having passed through a series of winding beige hallways that seemed identical except for the different moans and wails that livened each corridor, the nurse led him to a courtyard. A few clearly misplaced Romanesque statues guarded the dying foliage, themselves hopelessly ensnared by honeysuckle vines and grass that hadn't been trimmed since the summer. The small porch where he stood opened onto a larger set of gardens behind the main house.

"There he is. Visiting hours end in twenty minutes. You have until then," the nurse said, leaving him for the cold bleakness of the interior. About forty feet away, standing motionless and regarding a maple tree with a little too much fascination, was a tall man.

Vince hardly recognized him. What had been a set of full, lively cheeks had turned gaunt, and his limbs had withered from their former heft. The always-fastidious dresser was unkempt, hiding under a cheap hospital gown and flannel pajamas. Several weeks' worth of scruff hung off his chin. His hair had turned scraggly and longish, unwashed, greasy and fading to gray at the temples.

His eyes were sunken, and staring outward in silence. They didn't look like the eyes of a killer anymore.

"Frank. Little Frankie," Vince began.

It produced no response.

Even looking as haggard as he did, Frankie Pentone was still an imposing figure. His diminutive moniker had nothing to do with his size. That would have been obvious even if Vince hadn't known the story behind it.

His father had been named Frank also, which would have made him Frank Jr., if his grandfather hadn't shared the name too. "Juniors" and "the thirds" weren't so odd, at least among private-school WASPs. But it wasn't so common an arrangement among old-country Italians. First-born sons usually took their grandfather's name.

Hence the double diminutive. His father had been known as Frankie to keep things straight between the first two Pentones to share the name. By the time he'd come along, the only thing left had been to attach a secondary diminutive to him. And so had the boy who would eventually grow into a six-foot-four, 237-pound frame, a boy who would kill a man with his bare hands at age sixteen, become tagged with the name Little Frankie.

"*Eh, paesano, tuo amico Paolo è morto.*"

Nothing.

"Did you hear me, Pentone? Your crew is dead. Don't you want to know why?"

Still nothing.

"Ah, *vaffanculo così*, you *testa-dura*. I'm wasting my time," he sneered with a dismissive, obscene gesture from his crotch.

But as Vince turned to leave, the man finally moved. A hint of remembrance flickered in those empty, sickly eyes.

"*Up my ass?* Nobody talks to me that way," he said, straining to see if he recalled the man in the trench coat and fedora.

"Do I know you? From the neighborhood?" he asked.

Vince smiled, which was hard to do under Frank Pentone's eye.

"Yeah, Vinny Sicario, from over on Tenth Street, used to run with Paulie Tonsils."

"Thought you were a cop." His memory seemed to be coming back, if it had ever really been gone to start with.

"I was."

"Well, you found me, whoever you are. So they sent an ex-cop to do it huh? Get it over with then, paisan. I ain't gonna give you no trouble."

"I'm not here for that. I want to talk. That's all."

Frankie didn't seem convinced. He returned his gaze to the bare branches of the maple tree.

"Talk? Right. About what?" he said, speaking to the wind.

"Sam Calabrese. The new crew at the Sunset."

The man nicknamed "Little," who was anything but, nodded.

"Got a smoke?" he asked.

Vince reached into his coat pocket. Frankie's eyes drifted off toward the tall bushes at the far edge of the gardens. Vince handed him a cigarette and lit it, cupping his hands around the end to keep the flame from dying in the wind.

Frankie savored the first drag. It seemed to bring him back. Even though they weren't anywhere near another human being, the fugitive gangster checked around to make sure they were truly alone before saying another word.

Vince had to wonder if the old wiseguy really had lost his mind.

Frankie started talking as the smoke was leaving his mouth.

"You sure you wanna hear about this shit?" he asked.

"No, but I need to," Vince answered.

Frankie took a second long drag and shrugged his shoulders. He looked like he had more questions, but he didn't ask anything else.

"It all started about three months ago. Everything was fine. Business as usual, you know?" he began, still a little more hushed than he really needed to be, given their seclusion. "Then one day this set of legs shows up in the place, dressed to the nines. Coulda been a hooker, the big guy had his share since the wife left, but this dame didn't look like that. Too classy. Real put together, you know? But, I'll tell you, a little scary too."

"What do you mean?"

"Well, she was real tall, and pretty thin. Her skin was white, and I mean real white, we're talkin' like snow here. And she had this hair. Pure black, and real long. Wearing a silk suit, all red. Really had to see it. Bride of Dracula kinda shit, you know?"

Vince nodded. He didn't quite understand.

"Anyway, that's not worth dwelling on," Frankie continued. "So like I said, this chick comes in and tells Paulie she wants to see the boss. Won't take no for an answer.

That's when I got involved.

"I come over and tell her how it is. You don't just waltz in and see Sam Calabrese, legs or no legs. You got business, you go through me. So she looks me up and down, like she's sizin' me up for a fuck or somethin' and she asks me who I am."

"And what did you tell her Frankie?"

"Who the fuck am I? She asks me that in my place? So I tell her. I tell her exactly who the fuck I am. I'm the guy who's gonna mess up her pretty little suit if she don't show some respect. So she leaves. End of story right? Nope."

"Not much so far."

"Just wait, Vin, there's more. About a week later, I come into the Sunset. It was a Friday, I remember that. Late afternoon. I ask Freddie if the boss is in. He gives me this weird look, like I'm nuts for askin'. Tells me I must be goin' soft, since I just asked that question ten minutes ago. Only I couldn't have, because I'd just got back from Brooklyn. Friday's I always made a pick-up at a bookie of ours in Canarsie. And I tell Freddie that. He says he could have sworn that he saw me go upstairs to see Sam ten minutes ago.

"So now I'm worried, and I go upstairs to check on the big guy. I knock, and I hear Sam's voice tell me to go away, he's busy. But I know somethin's up, so I go in anyway."

"And?"

"I gotta tell you Vince, I never thought I'd see anything like this in my life. Never."

"What was it?"

"Sam. And the same tall, pale chick with the long black hair."

"What were they doin'?"

"Three guesses. All's I saw was Sam with his shirt off, goddamn fat sweaty gut hanging all over the place, and this weirdo in the red silk suit with her hands in Sam's chest."

Vince knew about Sam's appetites. That part came as no surprise. But he couldn't make sense of the second part.

"What do you mean? Her hands were *in his chest*? You mean *on* his chest, right?" he asked.

Frankie shook his head. It was the biggest display of emotion he'd made since Vince had seen him.

"No Vince, this is what I'm tryin' to tell you. I coulda sworn her fuckin' hands were in him. I'm talking *inside* him."

"That doesn't make any sense."

"You're tellin' me that? I tried to say somethin', but the boss yelled at me. Told me to get the fuck out."

"And?"

"So I left. I ain't about to get in the middle of that. You know? Just to be on the safe side, though, I check up on things downstairs. Turns out, nobody knows about this woman. Nobody saw her go in that day, and nobody ever saw her leave. A few hours later, Sam comes down, all dressed, lookin' like nothin' happened. He don't mention it, and I don't neither. Still can't explain it, but as long as he's okay.

"Anyway, that was just the beginning."

Vince is still with me, he thought.

"I'm gonna guess this is around the time some new

faces started showin' up at the Sunset," he said.

"Exactly," Frankie answered. "Sam was never the same after that. He dressed better, for one thing. And he bathed a lot more. Started talkin' a little funny too, kinda like a *fanook*, to be honest. Pretty soon he's tellin' me he wants to bring in some new blood, some connections from out of town that he's got.

"He's the boss, so he calls the shots. I tell him I don't think it's a good idea, but he's got all these plans. That's when this Indian Joe guy pops in, you met him?"

"Seen him. Yeah."

"Sam tells me he's workin' on some new projects, branching out from the usual rackets. He needs his space. Leaves all the normal operations with me, tells me not to bother him with that anymore. He's gonna be workin' with these new people for a little while.

"The guys don't like these new faces around, but I tell them to leave the weirdoes alone, Sam's orders. Everyone deals with me now. But things got real strange after that. I didn't last much longer."

"What happened? No one knows where you are. Rumor is that you been taken out."

The mobster took on a dark glare then. If Vince hadn't known better, he'd have thought Little Frankie was actually frightened.

"Good. Leave me alone, that's all I can say."

Suddenly, he didn't look like he wanted to talk anymore. He began staring at the tree again, just like he'd been doing when Vince had first seen him.

"So, what sent you here?" Vince asked.

"I walked in on Sammy one time too many. And I saw shit I never want to see again."

"What? What did you see?" Vince asked.

Frankie grew very still at the question, as though the thought itself made him shudder. When he did speak, he turned to look Vince directly in the eyes.

"The Morrigan."

TWENTY

MAGGIE WAS PREPARED FOR THE WORST. VINCE HAD been away since the early morning, and he wasn't back yet. She had gone out to pick up some bandages and more rubbing alcohol, supplies for what she feared might prove to be the last hours of Sean's life.

She was even debating breaking down and taking him to the hospital, right up to the moment when she opened the door.

And found him sitting on the couch, slurping from a bowl of oatmeal.

"Do you have any brown sugar in that bag? I hate this stuff without it," he said, rather plainly.

Maggie couldn't answer. She could barely register a breath.

When she'd left only a few hours earlier, he'd been nearly comatose. He hadn't moved since the carnage outside of Vince's apartment in the wee hours of the morning. Now he was not only up, he looked *perfectly healthy*.

"I'm sorry. Where are my manners? Let me get that for you," he said, springing from the couch to take the bag out of her arms.

He carried it into the kitchen and unloaded it, all while Maggie struggled to get her coat off. When he came back into the room he noticed her dazed expression.

"What's wrong Maggie? Aren't you happy to see me?" he asked.

He was being mischievous, and she knew it. It was exactly the way she had remembered him. A little irreverent, always blissfully unconcerned, no matter what the problem seemed to be.

But whatever he was dealing with at the moment, it was painfully clear that it was no small problem.

"Happy? Happy that you're not dead? Yeah!" she answered.

"Okay, that's a start. I'm happy I'm not dead too," he said.

He was milking her astonishment for every ounce of humor, even if the joke was only funny to him. She didn't let it go on much longer.

"Sean!"

"What?"

"What the hell is going on?"

"With what?" He continued the repartee, heedless of her obvious consternation, or maybe because of it.

"With what? I don't know where to begin!" she said. The whole episode was too surreal for her to grasp at the moment; too much was going on, too much had happened.

Sean finally relented. He pointed toward the couch and gave a nod, a grudging gesture of resignation that his moment of mirth had ended. It was time for adult conversation.

"Anywhere you want. Sit down. We have a lot to talk about, don't we?" he answered.

She took his invitation at face value, but her tone remained strident.

"Yeah. Like, where you've been since nineteen-seventeen, for example?"

"Hmm. That's a long story. Be shorter to tell you where I haven't been," he replied.

She frowned, almost groaned. His outward manner had shifted, but he was still not quite taking their exchange seriously. She wasn't going to tolerate that for much longer.

He could read that in the hard lines on her face.

"Or how it is that you look exactly the same as when you left?" she continued, realizing with each question how truly bizarre a dialogue it was becoming.

"Yeah. That's an even longer story, actually. Don't sell yourself short, though, Maggie; you look pretty good too," he answered, more serious than before but still speaking as though nothing in the world were the least bit out of sorts.

"I look forty-six, which is what I am. You look eighteen, and we both know that you're not. But then again, I guess that shouldn't surprise me too much, should it? I mean, yesterday you were laying on a couch, bleeding to death. Today you're perfectly fine?"

Her last statement was more of an accusation than a query, as though he should be ashamed of his condition rather than pleased. Or at least have offered an explanation.

He knew she had gone to the edge of her patience. He couldn't push the moment any further.

"Okay, why don't we start at the beginning, then? If you really want to know," Sean said, motioning for her to finally sit down while he did the same.

"Fine. So where exactly were you? Before you showed up here I mean," she replied. Suddenly her couch wasn't at all comfortable.

"Italy. Venice actually," he said, quite a bit more sullen than he had been just a moment earlier.

She seemed impressed, nodding as though considering his words. When she answered, though, he realized she was just being snide.

"Really? Venice. I always wanted to see it myself, but I never got the chance. How very cosmopolitan of you."

It was her turn for sarcasm. Even though her tone was slightly sardonic, he knew that she really meant at least part of what she said. Maggie had always wanted to travel when they were kids. He was still curious to know if she'd done it at all since he'd known her last.

"Lovely there, yes." He really wanted to hear about her, but she was the one asking the questions.

"So what brought you back to us, after all this time? If I were living in Venice, I don't think I'd ever come back to this dump."

"I wasn't going to come back. I had no intention of it, in fact."

"But here you are," she said, that same almost sad smile on her face.

"Yeah. I ran into some . . . problems there. Couldn't stay."

Finally she looked up at him, directly into his eyes for the first time. He really was a little somber. But she was still too angry with him to let him off so easily.

"Right. Did those problems have anything to do with Orlanda?" she asked.

This time it was Sean's turn to be surprised. And he made no attempt to conceal his discomfort.

"How do you know about that?"

"You mentioned her. A day or so ago, before your recovery."

Sean sighed, but he said nothing. A slow nod was her only answer.

"So? Who was she?" she continued.

It was obvious that Sean didn't want to discuss the subject, but Maggie simply kept her gaze fixed on him until he felt no other choice. That was something about her that hadn't changed since 1917. She was nothing if not stubborn, and persistent. She was Irish too, after all.

"Orlanda Santina. She was a glassblower's daughter. I met her on Murano while I was buying a vase from her father. I came back every day for a month, until she agreed to see me again. So beautiful. She had a smile that could make you forget that you were . . ."

He stopped. He breathed. And he looked out the window. It didn't appear as though he meant to finish.

"Were what?" she prodded.

"Away from home. Alone. Pick your problem, she made you forget about it," he answered, still looking out toward the pigeons clustered on the stoop.

"What happened? You woke up mumbling her name the other day."

"She got to know me."

He still couldn't look at her.

"I'm sure she did. But that can't be the whole story. Why did you leave her?"

"Oh, you assume I left her?" he replied, his humor revived enough to bring a smile to his lips, and to turn him from the sight of the dirty birds to face her again.

"You're here. She's not. Am I missing something?" she said.

"She left. Like I said, she got to know me. Too well," he replied. An odd look came over his face just then that she had never quite seen before. It almost hinted at regret, which was obviously impossible for Sean.

"I'm sorry. For whatever it's worth," Maggie said.

The words seemed to strike a chord in him, and he reacted at first with surprise. But by the time he spoke, his tone had taken on that resigned note again, more bitter than anything else.

"Well. I finally heard you say it," he said.

"What?"

"Sorry. All these years. That's the one thing I wanted to hear."

She was about to say something, to correct him, to stop him, but he wouldn't have listened.

"Remember that day, the one when you told me about Vince and you?" he said. "It was cold. I remember that.

Raining, too. *I'm sorry, Sean. I didn't plan this. It just happened. Vince and I both care about you. We never wanted to hurt you.* That was what you said. I'll never forget it." He had taken on a dreamy gaze, as if he weren't really talking to her at all.

She answered anyway.

"I said it, and I meant it. We knew it would be hard for you to hear. We didn't expect you to smile and throw us a party. But with enough time, we thought you could learn to accept it, we thought you *would* learn to accept it."

"You were wrong," he said.

He turned from her then, got up from the chair and moved over toward the window. It was open a crack. The cold air tingled on his knuckles. He needed that sensation, just near enough to pain to remind him how it felt.

"We never wanted to lose you. We both loved you, loved you the way friends love each other. That's what hurt me," she said.

"Hurt *you*?"

He turned back to look at her, his hands were clenched hard on the railing of the sill.

"Telling you that Vince and I were in love, that we wanted to get married, that was difficult. We told you because we cared about you, about your feelings. We hoped that once you had enough time, you'd care enough about us to want Vince and I to be happy together. But you didn't. You just left."

"That's not fair, Maggie. It wasn't fair then, and it's not fair now. I left *because* of how I felt about you. Because

I cared," he shot back.

"Okay, so you left. I understand you were hurt. But you didn't even tell anyone that you were going. You just went away. Forever, we thought, until the other day."

"The war seemed like a better place to be than here. Any place seemed like a better place than here."

The pigeons all fluttered away in that instant, as though they sensed his ire and fled from it.

Maggie lessened her tone. She didn't want to raise her voice anymore. What she had wanted to say was out, though she didn't feel any better for all the effort.

"Though we did hear that you'd joined up eventually. The New York Fighting 69th, right? I even heard when you shipped out to France. But then, nothing. Never another word."

"I know. That was how I wanted it."

"That's what you wanted? You wanted us to worry about you? To wonder for years what happened? I tried everything, but all I got were form letters from the War Department. There was some talk that you deserted, but in the end all I could find out was that you were missing."

"I was. For a long time."

"So? Where were you? Other than Italy, of course."

"Russia," he said to the city outside.

Maggie was forced to pause. She hadn't expected that response.

"Russia? Whatever the hell for?"

"I guess you could say it was a trip of, *self-discovery*. Or something like that. I didn't stay long."

The view of the gray urban landscape blurred in his eyes. It faded into the vista of a hundred other cities.

"Okay, where else? Thirty years is a long time."

He rattled them off at random, naming them as the memory-pictures passed through his head.

"Czechoslovakia, Egypt, Ireland, South America, Hong Kong. You name it. Anywhere I could go to forget about you, and Vince."

"And?"

"And no matter where I went, and no matter what I did, I never could. All I could think about was you and Vince, living happily ever after."

The words hung in the air between them for a long while. The dull, heavy silence told him that he had said the wrong thing, but he wasn't exactly sure why. She told him after a painful sort of chuckle.

"Happily ever after? Not exactly."

Sean turned back from the window. The skin around her eyes was starting to swell. Red, wet splotches were forming in them.

"Sorry. I didn't mean to . . . what did happen with you two? You're not together anymore?"

"What happened? A lifetime happened, Sean. Thirty years happened. You can't walk in after all that time and ask what happened."

He nodded. He knew he deserved that one.

"You were married?" he said, in a softer voice. It felt like the only way to take things down a notch. He had no idea what to say to comfort her.

She responded in kind.

"Yeah, in 1922, after Vince got out of the Navy. He became a cop, you know."

"I heard. Never thought he'd do it. Italian cop. Guess I figured he'd end up on the other side."

"I'm not sure there were sides in those days. After Volstead half of the kids you guys grew up with ended up bootlegging. Even the cops were in on it too, from what Vince told me. He used to drink more than anybody else I knew, even then. By the time they repealed it, he was drunk most of the time. That finally did him in, but it took a while. He managed to stay on the job until they forced him out, seven or eight years ago."

"Did you have kids?"

"Two. Mary and Michael."

She almost smiled, but something was holding it back.

"Two kids. Where are they now?" he asked.

"Mary was born in the spring of 1924. We buried her in the winter of '25."

"I'm sorry. I had no idea."

"Michael was born five years later. Vince took Mary's death hard. I think he used it as an excuse to drink even more. Michael drowned, God rest his soul, in 1938. I think that was really the end for me and Vince. He stayed in our old apartment, and I ended up moving back in here with my mother. She passed away in '44."

She was right. He had missed out on a lifetime.

"You're still married, though?" he asked. There was a ring on her finger that sparkled, even in the dim, even after thirty hard years.

"Yeah," she said, as though it were nothing more than an afterthought.

"So you still love him?"

Maggie shook her head, and she sighed. Not as an answer, but merely to take a moment while she thought of one. Sean stayed still. He almost regretted asking. When she started again he was about to interrupt her, but something about her expression, the emptiness of it, maybe, told him to let her finish.

"It's hard to say. All the years between us. Everything that's happened. Sometimes I wish I could say I didn't love him, and sometimes I don't know if I ever really did. Doesn't that just take the cake?"

"No. Actually I understand that completely," he said.

Strangely, the comment seemed to come from nowhere in particular, and not from Sean's place along the sill. When she turned around, Maggie saw only the slightly open window.

Sean was gone.

Again.

TWENTY-ONE

Argus was back at his adopted cathedral. There were many others with him now. Galanthis had merely been the first to join Charybdis, Arachne, and himself beneath the shelter of the ruined Catholic structure. Through their efforts, over a dozen newcomers had now come into temporary residence there.

Even as the Bleecker Street Haven became crowded with others of their kind, his loyal followers gathered here instead, in secret, out of view of the Morrigan or any of her agents.

Some were busy at work, setting up makeshift places of rest along the walls, in the eaves and behind the confessionals. They were not using tools of metal or wood. Clear slime and sticky, plaster-like ooze were their only utensils.

Whether from that, or from something else, the place was beginning to stink. It was an almost syrupy reek, a hint of something stewing in the moist, warm air. Organic, but putrid, like crab apples rotting on wet autumn grass.

The smell didn't bother Argus in the least.

"The reunion is well along," the child-who-wasn't said,

having to rest only a moment after entering. "The Haven in Greenwich Village is already filling up with those of us who have answered the call. I spoke to the heads of six other refugee houses, Paris, Leningrad, Baghdad, Hong Kong, Cairo, and Toronto. Most report the same thing, their ranks are depleted from the War and the few who have come here are all that remain of their covens."

"And what of Lucifer?" Arachne asked, helping her master with his cane as he sat down. Yellow lesions had grown up like weeds through the soft skin of his forehead and cheeks. Some were dripping pus that mixed with sweat. His tie was undone.

"No one is speaking of him. For fear of the Morrigan, I'd guess. Many still place their faith in the Keeper," Argus answered, out of breath.

He was missing two of his front teeth, which filtered his words through a lisp. Every time he inhaled he looked as though he was going to puke, but his stomach was empty.

"They will not join with us then?" she questioned.

"No. Those of us who have gathered here will make our move without outside help," the ancient child said.

"That changes nothing," Charybdis broke in. "We've always known that if we were to do this, we would be acting on our own. We've never counted on outsiders for help before."

"Except perhaps for your beloved," Arachne replied.

"Yes. Have you spoken with Scylla?" Argus asked.

He was trying to resist the urge to pick at the scabs on his tiny fingers. One of his nails looked like it was about to fall off, undermined by the decay festering beneath.

The African woman shifted in her footsteps. Her face betrayed her uncertainty, despite the confident tone of her voice.

"I have. I cannot say what impact my words have had, however. You must remember that Scylla has spent nearly three decades bent on a single-minded course, much as I was when you first took me in. Since our parting she has hunted Lucifer like an animal, seeking any clue to his location, determined to avenge herself. It will take more than a kiss from me to turn her from that mission."

Argus gave in. He pried the hanging nail free. It came loose with barely any resistance; just a few tendrils that clung to his diseased finger like stringy, wet cheese.

"Nevertheless, if she chooses to join us, the decision must be made soon. The full season is very nearly upon us. The Morrigan will come to the Bleecker Street Haven to announce the location of her feast within a day," he advised, tossing the dead piece of his old self to the floor.

"I will try to sway Scylla to our cause. But nothing will matter if we do not find Lucifer," Charybdis said.

"Of that I am all too aware," the sickly child replied.

Pat Flanagan had gone by Vince's apartment as soon as he'd gotten word. The crime-scene guys had still been milling around when he'd arrived, measuring, photographing, and chronicling where the three bodies had been.

Bloodstains and chalk lines marked the sidewalk in a silent reflection of the morning's events. Even the stray bullets and skull fragments were marked, and there were a lot of both.

A pair of tire tracks had been cordoned off along the curb, with yellow rope draped between two squad cars.

The apartment itself was empty, which was pretty much how he'd expected to find it. There was dried blood on the couch, but the door had been locked from the outside. Otherwise, there wasn't much to go on. If Vince wasn't dead, he had to have gone somewhere, or been taken somewhere. He had an idea where, but he didn't tell anyone. He wanted to make one stop first.

✣ ✣ ✣

The Sunset Club was closed when Flanagan pulled up. But he banged on the door long enough and loud enough that someone came to open up. To his shock, it was Sam Calabrese himself.

"Salvatore, what a surprise. You here all by your lonesome self?" He had known the man for many years, and he knew exactly how to needle him.

This time, however, his gibe seemed to have no effect. Pat let himself in, but Sam didn't seem to mind. The place was dark, and empty. All the tables were pushed up against the walls, revealing the ruts of old scratches on the black and white floor. The bar was cleared out. Only a few bottles were left along the mirror, just the cheap stuff that nobody ever drank.

"I am alone, if that is what you mean. Is that what you came here to ask? Is the department suddenly concerned enough to check on my welfare? Or do you have other business this day?"

Sam was dressed in a silk robe and slippers, and he seemed to be sweating. His jowls were fuller than usual, as though stuffed with food, but he didn't appear to be chewing. Flanagan ignored the details, and took a seat at the bar.

Sam remained standing.

"Now really Sammy, after all these years, do I need a reason to come see my favorite bookie?" Again, the joke fell upon a blank stare. "Actually, I do have a business-related reason for my visit. We scraped a few of your boys off the pavement this morning."

Calabrese said nothing.

"But you already knew that, right? Should I guess that this place is so quiet because all your other boys are too broken up about Paulie and his buddies to come in today?"

Sam wasn't rattled. If Pat hadn't known him better, he might have actually believed him.

"We're in the process of making some changes. The club will be closed for the foreseeable future. Does that answer your question?" Calabrese replied.

"My first one, anyway. How about my second one?"

"Go right ahead, but please be brief."

"I'm wondering if you can help me find someone."

"Unlikely."

"Don't speak too quickly there, Sam. I think you know my friend. Vince Sicario?"

"Of course. Frequent customer. Is he lost?"

"Funny. Still got a sense of humor, good." Flanagan dropped his own feigned smile then, and he lit a cigarette. "Let me put it to you this way. We both know Vince has been in here recently, and we both know he's been *entangled*, so to speak, with some of your guys."

Calabrese remained stoic. Flanagan blew his first long puff of smoke directly into the fat man's face. He dropped his shoulder to lean in close.

"I don't begrudge a man an honest debt, and I've known Vince long enough to know he ain't exactly no kind of angel. But I'll just say this, anything happens to him, and I find out your guys are connected—then my guys are gonna come down so hard on this little operation of yours that you'll be lookin' up to see those fancy *Eye-talian* shoes o' yours.

"*Capisce?*"

Calabrese, who had seemed to inhale the Parliament smoke with unusual relish, breathed deeply in the wake of his visitor's statement. His answer was quite a bit more agreeable than Flanagan had been expecting. That bothered him.

"I understand completely. Your concern for your friend is much appreciated, but I can assure you that I know nothing of his current location. Of course, if anything were to come up, I would keep your words in mind."

Flanagan nodded.

"Now detective," Calabrese continued. "I really must excuse myself. There are other matters which demand my attention, and I have put them off far too long already."

Flanagan let himself out, more suspicious now than he had been when he'd entered.

Once he was gone, Calabrese re-bolted the door. Gathering his robe around him, he slowly climbed the stairs to his loft. He opened the door to find Victor Huang just as he had left him, naked, tied to a chair, and bleeding from the stubs where six of his fingers had been recently severed.

Calabrese closed the door behind him. There was a sound like a raven shrieking, and a growl.

Then a man screamed.

TWENTY-TWO

THEY HAD COME TO MEET IN THE WORST PART OF town. Both had made certain no one had followed them, but neither one was really positive. Every shadow could hold a danger, but when she saw him again, Charybdis didn't care.

"My love," she said, falling into his arms.

They were inside the doors of an abandoned tenement, the glass broken out of the windows. An alley cat whined nearby.

"You know I love you. I have never been able to refuse you Charybdis, but this time I almost did. It's too dangerous, we can't see each other until this is finished," Scylla said.

"Until our disgrace is absolved?" she answered.

"We're closer than we have been in so long, why risk it now?" Scylla asked.

Charybdis straightened up, and arched her back as she held him. She was serious, urgent.

"Because now is the only time. We must discuss what I proposed last night."

Scylla knew exactly what Charybdis was talking

about. In years past they had often spoken that way. With few words.

"Haven't you given it any thought?" she asked.

"I'm afraid that is all I have thought about since our last meeting," the rat-man answered.

"Then I need your answer," she said, prodding him.

Scylla shook his head.

"I don't have one. Not yet."

"We're running out of time. If we're to act, we have to do it soon."

He still seemed unconvinced.

"Why should we do anything? Why risk losing what we have waited for all these many years? Especially now, when we're so close," he said.

"Close to what?" she replied.

"To this," he said, reaching in closer to gently touch his lips against hers. "Forever. Haven't we waited long enough?"

Charybdis rolled her tongue over her lower lip. She hadn't felt that sensation in ages. She wanted it again. But she held off.

"Too many years have gone by, wasted years. That is why we must do this, so that we never waste so much precious time again," she said.

Scylla stayed close. He could still taste the cigarettes on her breath.

"Charybdis, this is all that I want. All that I have ever wanted was to be with you. Isn't that what you want too? Or have the years changed you so?" he answered, wrapping his arms around her waist.

She lowered her head from his gaze.

"I have changed, yes. But not in that way. I have learned. Learned from Argus that there are things to value more than obedience."

"Such as?"

"If we do nothing, the Morrigan will likely prevail. We will be together again, as we both wish," she said, turning back to look in his eyes.

"You speak as though that is a trifle. We will regain our lost honor, our rightful place that has so long been denied us."

"We will be servants once more. Slaves, really."

Scylla breathed heavily. He knew she was right, but he could think of no viable alternative.

"What other choice is there?" he asked.

"Freedom," she replied, plainly.

"Freedom?"

"That will last forever. You and I, free, forever. But you must be willing to do this with me. I can't do it alone," Charybdis said.

Scylla sighed. He scratched the fuzz on his pointed chin. Then, finally, he nodded.

"Together," he said. "As long as we're together."

TWENTY-THREE

SEAN WAS OUT AND ABOUT TOWN. IT FELT GOOD. HE didn't remember a lot from the past days, just a few glimpses really. But it didn't matter all that much. He wasn't about to let a few ill-timed bullets and some unfortunate blood loss spoil his plans.

No, he had come back to the old neighborhood for a reason, and it wasn't to play games with fat gangsters and odd-looking hangers-on.

His dented felt fedora slung low over his eyes, he passed anonymously through crowds of chattering, busy strangers, along sidewalks where he had once known everyone and now knew no one. He drank in the chaotic, throbbing energy of the street, listening in on a thousand simultaneous conversations and arguments and hints of music, ambling past storefronts that had changed hands many times since his days in the Kitchen, but hadn't really changed much at all.

Chestnuts were still roasting on corner vender-stands. He savored the deep burning aroma. No place else had that smell. There were street peddlers in Vienna, and Paris and Budapest, and a dozen other cities he'd been to, but for some reason, their stuff never smelled quite the same as the mélange of warm scents that was so imprinted on him from childhood.

Only in New York.

Italian fruit stands still sold oranges and apples and vegetables he couldn't pronounce. Even in the November cold, the vendors in their yellow slickers hawked their wares only a few feet removed from the stifling crush of exhaust fumes spewing out of the endless rush of taxis and buses.

Irish pubs were still Irish pubs too. Even if the pseudo-Gaelic names had mostly changed, shamrocks and beer taps and refuges from the wife and kids were the same everywhere, no matter what uncial-stenciled logo hung over the door.

Church bells gonged somewhere in the distance, muted some by the general noise of the street. They reminded him of one more thing that he had given up when he left the old West Side.

Some things were different, though.

It was brighter than he remembered; whole sections of the neighborhood were no longer strangled by leviathan daytime shadows. The elevated trains that had once rumbled so loudly above the tenements were mostly gone. Now almost everything was underground. Tubes, like in London. Finally it seemed that someone had let the sun shine down on Hell's Kitchen.

There were more ethnic folks around too. Puerto Ricans, and Dominicans and others he didn't recognize on sight. Used to be mostly just Irish and Italians, he remembered, block-by-block, building-by-building even. They had experienced enough problems getting along in his day. How all the new people fit in, he couldn't even begin to guess.

It was along the piers where he lamented the changes the most. The spot where he had spent so many sweltering summer afternoons diving into the river with Vince and Maggie was now occupied by a ventilation tower for the new Lincoln Tunnel. Nothing really was sacred, after all.

Even though he had left the place in sorrow, anger more accurately, all he could remember were the good times. As he took in the sights, sounds, and smells of his long-lost home, all he could recall was the happiness. Friends. Loves. Good times, times that now seemed so very far away.

Nostalgia didn't last forever, though. Especially not when a rail-thin blond girl wearing a raincoat on a sunny day was following close behind, watching him pass through every crowded corner and turn.

Sean didn't recognize her, but that didn't matter. She was on him, darting a little too elegantly between the pushcarts and the yammering crowds; trying a little too hard to blend in, as if she knew she hadn't been invited to the party.

He wasn't about to lead her on.

Careful to keep her at a distance, he turned into a narrow side street and pushed past a fire escape ladder that had been lowered to the sidewalk. Then, slipping around a pair of men who were arguing over a flat tire on a mint green Studebaker in what he thought was Spanish, he ducked through a torn-out section in a chain link fence that fixed the rough edges of a gravel parking lot.

He caught a quick look through the fence and the shouting men with their disabled car. She hadn't made the turn around the far corner yet, and was out of sight for a moment. The truncated lot was of the minimum size for a parking area, with about twenty-odd cars wedged in tightly between three brick-face, four-story apartment houses that stood where the grungy tenements used to wallow. Though it was no better than half-full, and by the rickety shape of most of the autos settled there, more like a junkyard than an actual lot, it was suitably claustrophobic.

Sean ducked behind a pair of Oldsmobiles parked nose-to-nose, one with the front windshield cracked on the passenger side, the other with at least a year's worth of grime clinging to the windows.

Arachne came around the corner just a second later.

She scanned the area, the empty booth, the sorry collection of junk heaps scattered around the gravel lot. No sign of Sean. But there was a noise, a yelp. It was coming from behind the two Oldsmobiles.

She neared slowly, carefully, ready for something, but not sure what. Around the bumper she came, but she ended up smiling, rather than fighting.

Two Cocker Spaniels were wrapped up in a heap of abandoned clothing. From the squeals the dogs were making as they writhed, one on top of the other, she guessed that they were humping. In broad daylight, of all things; right out in the open. She shook her head, and turned back toward the side street.

She only got a few feet, however, before she heard an altogether different kind of sound skitter up in her wake. But she couldn't turn fast enough. A large hand closed over her mouth even as she tried to whirl. Another one twisted her arm one scream and a foot-and-a-half too far in the wrong direction.

Arachne tried to struggle through the sharp surge of pain the arm-bar fired through her entire left side, but she found herself quickly thrown down against the gravel. The dogs were gone. She turned her head and found, without much surprise, Sean Mulcahy on top of her. His hands were hairy, almost furry, but she didn't have the time to consider details.

"Now, my beautiful little creature. What's your name?" he seethed, teeth clenched.

"I work for Argus. I'm no threat to you," she replied, her arm released but his hands now clenched like a vice grip around her throat. The canine hand-hair on his fingers and knuckles was receding into his pale skin, withering away with the strangest display of human alopecia she'd ever seen.

"That's not what I asked you. One more chance, honey, and then I'll have to live without ever knowing," he answered.

She tried to swallow, and tried to nod. Sean kept his hold firm on her, just enough to leave her room to breathe, a little.

"Arachne. My name is Arachne," she gasped.

"Spider-girl, eh?"

"Yes, Lucifer."

His already petulant expression turned furious.

"That's not my name."

She grimaced, choking as she fought to take a breath, but his grip on her neck finally relented.

"What's your real name?" he asked.

Arachne was puzzled.

"Answer me. Your parents didn't name you Arachne, did they? What's your real name?"

She was a long moment in wondering, but not from any intended delay. The thought had not honestly crossed her mind for the better part of six decades.

"It is, it was, Celine. Celine Lafleur," she answered, finally able to catch her breath and her memory.

"French, huh? Explains the accent. Okay, Arachne. What the hell do you think you're doing around here? Don't you people know better by now?"

She answered dutifully, like a POW offering the standard name, rank, and serial number.

"Argus commanded me to seek you, and I have done so."

Sean shook his head.

"Right. I forgot how loyal you folks are. What does that old bastard want?"

"He wishes to speak with you. The season dawns, and our feast approaches. We both know that agents of the Keeper still prowl these streets, seeking to harm you. Argus wishes to form an alliance. He wishes to help you."

"I'll bet," Sean replied as he got off her and picked up

his hat and coat from the spot on the ground where the dogs had been fucking.

The New York City subway system had been built in stages, haltingly at the start, and only later with any success. Attempts had been made as early as the mid-nineteenth century to tunnel beneath the skyline, burgeoning upward even at that early date. Those first digs had ended in failure, however, leaving abandoned, half-collapsed underground passages hidden beneath the Gotham towers.

That it was Arachne, a girl of unknown age, and of European extraction to boot, who was explaining such a history to him, was an irony not lost on Sean Mulcahy. Though he had grown up on those mean streets, under the rumbling shadows of the IRT lines, he had never been much concerned with the city's past. Since he had not been back in so many years, it fell to a stranger to explain the history of his own home to him.

"The first permanent trains were in place by about 1904. They ran from City Hall in the south up to around 145th Street. They put in a line to the Bronx around 1905. Then they added a line to Queens in 1915."

"Yeah. I think I remember something about that last one. I didn't really need to go to Queens when I was sixteen, though, so I hadn't really paid that any mind."

They had been walking for over an hour, negotiating a maze of dank tunnels with only the light of a torch to guide them. Somehow, Arachne seemed to know the way.

"Anyway, the city bought out the old BMT and IRT lines six or seven years ago, and now it's all pretty much one system. Mostly underground, as you can see. They're talking about tearing out all of the old "El" trains altogether in the next few years."

"So where are we?" he asked, a little bored.

"This tunnel was never actually used. They started building it, and got about halfway done before they realized they needed to dig farther underground. Something about the bedrock. That was decades ago. Now hardly anyone remembers it's even here."

"Except Argus."

"Well, one of the advantages to living so long is that you tend to have a memory quite a bit more extensive than most other people."

"So I see."

They climbed down a makeshift ladder, cobbled together from old rope and broken plywood. The ground beneath them was damp, but it was too dark to see. It felt like mud, or silt. She pointed the torch outward ahead of her until the soft flames revealed a glint of metal that might have been brass just ahead and to the left, an opening that looked more like a ship's porthole than a door.

"Through there. We need to take a slight detour. Obviously they built these things for trains, not the likes of us. Who knew they'd ever be used for foot traffic?" she said.

"Where does this lead?" he asked, no longer bored but a little unnerved.

She did not turn to answer.

"You'll see."

Though it went against his better judgment, Sean took hold of a very old iron railing. It was slimy with the ooze of something he preferred not to consider dripping down the old rusty pipe. He sighed when he touched it. He swore when he smelled it. It stank worse than the rat-shit he feared it to be.

With her ahead, he hoisted himself up, and crawled into the narrow tunnel.

The final leg of the passage was unlike the previous distance. Where those tunnels had been dirty, wet, and long abandoned, they were all built for trains. They were wide, with vaulted ceilings and smooth walls. As Arachne led him through their last few yards, however, it quickly became clear that they had crossed into an area of new construction. The rocky walls were rough. The frayed ends of wires and broken pipes jutted out from all sides. It appeared that a huge swath had been torn through an otherwise solid barrier, hewn *by hand*, and very recently at that.

After a few feet, they came to a light. It was filtering down from above, like a manhole cover left half-open. Arachne searched for a moment in the dim before finding a second rope ladder, hung from the dark above. She climbed it without a word, and when she reached the top, she pounded her fist against the grating.

In a few moments, the iron slid open fully. A thing that looked something like a hand reached down to pull her up.

"Follow me," she said from out of sight.

Sean had no choice but to obey.

With the hole fully open there was a great deal more light raining down from above. It was firelight, constantly wavering between glare and shadow, and very red. It was enough to illuminate the rope ladder, and to allow him to ascend and pass through the opening without any aid. Immediately, he wished he hadn't.

He emerged into the center of a Catholic Church, a cathedral really, and one he had never seen before. There was a smell about the place. That was what bothered him first. It was like soot mixed with urine, or slime of some kind, and a hint of mold warmed over it all.

It was fairly dark, the only light burning out of the braziers and torches set atop broom-handles and broken flowerpots at the edge of every third or forth pew. Occasional shards of sunlight peered through the torch-smoke, from cracks in the roof. Though it left most of the place in shadow, he could yet note enough details to make him wish he had not entered.

It was fire-damaged, but the elegance of its original design was clear nonetheless. Great arches in the ceiling, flying buttresses, and gothic columns decorated it, but they had all been fouled, and not by smoke or flame.

All along the rafters, suspended like a brood of day-slumbering bats, were things he had seen only once before. In Russia, in 1918.

They looked like cocoons, though a thousand times larger than any insect larva. Some dripped strange, luminous goo;

giant, bulging pouches wrapped in silk and slime. There were other such things, plastered against the eaves of the broken stained glass windows, and lodged like repulsive squatters in the dark recesses of the old walls. They filled the air with a dull murmur, emitting a strange buzzing, like a thousand locusts chirping a mile away.

Great webs spun from some unknown material obscured what had once been the confessional booths. Sean could see inhuman silhouettes lurking in slow languid paces behind their translucent shrouds.

About two-dozen people milled about around them, quietly, although his arrival seemed to spur them to a nervous chatter. Most of them were cloaked in heavy robes, though a few were all but naked. Those who were exposed bore hideous visages, inhuman and twisted in ways that would have left ordinary visitors both frightened and nauseous. Sean had seen their ilk before as well, though. He turned away without paying them much heed.

"Most have already entered the first stage," Arachne said, fairly stating what was, to him, already very obvious. "The wise one has not yet done so, however. And he is waiting."

She led him down the main path between the pews, toward the area at the far end, where he knew the altar should be. Instead, he saw only a virtual wall of velvet tapestries and veils suspended from the rafters.

Through the barrier they passed, to find a "room" on the other side, lit by dozens of hand-made candles jammed into every nook and crevice in the walls. What had once been the consecrated altar sat, half-broken in the center of it all.

Against the far wall there were two figures. Charybdis with her sharp West African features was just entering the chamber from a side door. Beside her stood the wizened toddler. Both were dressed impeccably in men's suits. They were clothed almost too well, considering the squalor of their confines.

To Sean's as-yet unknowing eye, the child Argus looked like a leper, deathly sick and covered in untreated sores. But he knew well enough after so many years that mere outward appearance meant so very little among a gathering of those with whom he now kept company.

"Lucifer. I believe you've already met my master and his servant, Charybdis," Arachne stated, by way of introduction.

The black woman stepped forward at the mention of her name. Sean half-bowed out of courtesy.

"Charybdis, huh?" he said, not really surprised, but making an effort.

"I believe I was in the process of shedding the appearance of blond Northman when last we saw each other," the black woman replied, Argus beside her stepped forward.

"And that, of course, is the wisest of us all. The eldest of our kind, Argus," Arachne continued.

Sean moved farther into the chamber, acknowledging the child-who-wasn't.

"So, you're Argus now?" he began, not sure if it was appropriate to kneel down to the small figure's level.

"I am. My appearance has changed since last we met, as it always does with our kind. Never fear, soon I will be my old self again, and you will see me as I was when we parted company so many years ago," the wise old toddler replied, cordially. He seemed to have trouble getting up from his seat. Pustules and scabs were festering all over the exposed skin of his face and hands. Sean ignored them. He already knew what the child was suffering from. "But, outward bearing aside, I remain the same as I have ever been."

"And what is that?" Sean asked.

"Your friend?" the un-childlike boy replied. Sean also noticed that his eyes bore a weird red glow, just like he had remembered them from those many years ago in Czechoslovakia when he had come to know Argus in a much different form. What the old creature had told him was his *true* form.

"We were never friends," the wanderer sneered.

"Then let us start now. There has never been a better time. The season of changes is upon us again, as my present condition so testifies. The feast draws near. I know you can feel it, as we all do. A momentous occasion it will be, if you let us help you," Argus said, an urgency present in his voice that belied his carefully chosen words.

"Help me? Help me do what?" Sean asked.

"To fulfill what is written."

Sean threw up his hands. He had come all that way for this? To hear the same old thing he had rejected those many years ago?

"Christ. You never give up, do you? That goddamn

book again, huh? That was bullshit in Prague. It's bullshit now," he said.

"No less uncouth despite the decades, I see," Charybdis snickered, from the shadows beside the altar.

"Screw you," Sean answered, turning to look at the woman in the man's suit. "Come to think of it, I might just have to do that. Last time I saw you, you were some big Swedish lookin' guy, but you got yourself in a nice little package this time, nice rack, probably some nice gams under that suit. And I've had a lot of women, but never a black bitch."

Charybdis did not take the insult lightly. She quickly brandished a blade from within her coat. In a moment she had crossed to where Sean stood, the knife poised in front of him.

He did not budge from his place, staring her down with a face that was as implacable as a statue.

"Come and try it," she seethed, and turning to Argus, "maybe he isn't worth all the effort, after all."

Argus, as always, remained the coolest temper in the room. Though tiny and faltering in his stride, he managed to step between the two, growling Charybdis and the stoic, bemused Sean. Neither wished to anger the ancient sage, and both stepped back.

"You must forgive my associate, Lucifer. Charybdis has always been sensitive to his appearance, especially when he has taken a form that is perhaps not as manly, as he prefers."

"I told your errand girl, and I'll tell you. Don't call me Lucifer. You know better," Sean snapped.

"But how can you still deny the obvious? I think you most certainly are him. The one who's coming Galatea, scribe of Nestor, recorded all those ages ago. In fact I have no doubt."

"I don't think so."

Argus smiled his chapped, split lips. Several teeth were missing from inside his mouth.

"Of course, it may not matter what you think. The Morrigan believes in you. That's why she tried to kill you in the city they now call Leningrad, and later with your unfortunate lady friend in Venice."

The suggestion caught Sean off-guard. He grimaced. The face of beautiful, lost Orlanda intruded for a moment upon his thoughts. Argus was clever, he remembered that well enough. The old creature was willing to go to any length to sway him, even dredging up his most private pain. He clearly had no qualms about rubbing salt into that deep, secret wound.

Sean shrugged it off. He had no intention of discussing the subject. Telling Maggie had been enough, and she was the only person he had spoken to about it. He looked back at Argus, staring him down, peering at him for any hint of a reaction.

Sean realized something in that instant. Argus shouldn't have known about Orlanda. He'd killed all three of the agents sent to snare him, agents of the Morrigan, he had believed. How did Argus know about her?

He didn't have time to consider it. As he had so many times before, he took a breath, and forced the image out of his mind.

"That's why she continues to hunt you. You are the greatest threat to her in centuries. She fears you. She wants to eliminate you before you can realize your significance."

Argus was coughing while he spoke. A brownish drool seeped from his gaping mouth. He made no effort to stem the flow.

"My significance?"

"Perhaps you were not ready for the full truth of it in Prague, those many years ago. And perhaps I erred in expecting you to understand then. But now we do not have the luxury of long contemplation," he said.

Argus lectured as best as he was able in his weakened state.

"You will be the next Keeper. And with my help, you will be the greatest Keeper in all of our long history. Once our kind were led by such a king. Once the Children of Nestor knew the rule of a benevolent protector.

"To the Greeks he was *Eosphorus*. To the Romans, *lucem ferre*. He brought the gift of light, as the morning star banishes the darkness. He was wisdom. He was peace. But as the old ways died, ancient secrets became dangerous superstitions. The heirs of the pagans vanquished him, he who they called Lucifer, the enemy.

"Now their descendants know that name as an evil moniker. They demonized him as they demonized us. But for all these many ages, while we have hidden from the outside world, we have held fast to the hope that the light bringer would one-day return. And now he has.

"You will lead us back to where we once were. You will lead us out into the world from which we so long ago retreated. You will return us to our rightful place in the open, into the light. The time is coming when humanity will be ready to accept us again.

"The next grand gathering is on the horizon, the fifty-first since the Morrigan slew Apollo. *Sated from fifty feasts, the tyrant will fall.* You are the one, a trickster from the north, across the western ocean. You will topple the Keeper. You are Lucifer, the dawn bringer reborn."

Sean snarled. He had heard most of it before, and he had thought he would never have to hear it again.

"I've told you, I am not what you want me to be. I never will be."

"And I have told you. The prophecy remains, whether you choose to acknowledge it or not. The Morrigan believes that you are Lucifer, and she will stop at nothing to keep her throne. She will kill you whether you believe in the Book of Nestor or not. If you ignore that peril, you merely aid her in her quest."

"She'll try. She has tried. I can handle her."

"Look around you, my son. Look at all of us. Our own people. Our own kind. They await you. They will follow you. You need only to step forward. The words have already been written. They are beyond dispute. The Morrigan knows this. That is why she fears you so. Why she hates you so. The mantle of the Keeper is yours to claim. Speak to your flock."

Half a smile on his mucus-stained lips, Argus lifted the

veil and opened the curtain that separated the antechamber from the great hall of the ruined cathedral. His face
invited Sean to step up with him. Outside, the strange and
hideous figures had gathered.

Sean did step forward. All in the cathedral fell still.
Even the chattering and the wheezing from the things
cocooned in the church eaves, and suspended from the
rafters, quieted.

"Lucifer. Lucifer speaks," someone, or something in
the crowd whispered.

But no words came to him in that instant. Standing at
the edge of the broken altar, Sean saw the teeming masses,
strange and weird beings of every size and shape. Human
mingled with beast, and with things even stranger.

He had seen them all before. In Russia, when he had
first learned the secret of what lurked within him. And he
had seen them in the myriad forms under which he himself
had traveled the world, those many years since.

He saw himself. And he despised the image.

Argus, noting his trepidation, moved closer to him.
He reached out his tiny hand toward the arm of the un-
naturally young man. But there was no arm to touch.

In a moment of horror, a sight that even the gathered masses themselves could not bear to watch, the body
of Sean Mulcahy fell to pieces. As though shredded by
a thousand unseen scythes, the flesh of his skin split and
ruptured. His blood spilled to the floor. His bones tore
themselves from their joints.

Like a heap of human scraps, the sundered pieces of

his flesh collapsed into a sopping pile, his clothes left to fall to the church floor.

Gasps and screams from the assembled broke the silence his arrival had heralded. Argus fell to his knees to see after the grisly remains. Charybdis was at his side in an instant, and Arachne as well.

"What has he done?" Arachne questioned, never expecting an answer.

One came anyway, disembodied, eerie, but the voice of Sean Mulcahy nonetheless.

"What I must do."

A moment later, the pile of bloodied clothes sprang to life. Hatched from a nest of mire, sent forth within a spray of loose, gray feathers mixed with blood, a dozen birds darted upward. They were pigeons, or so it appeared, they moved so fast it was hard to be certain. The birds surged toward the rafters, one after another until there remained on the floor only a vacant heap of red-stained clothes.

The broken boards of the ceiling afforded them an exit, one and all. Then there was no sign of Sean Mulcahy left in the cathedral.

"Now what shall we do?" Charybdis questioned of her master, stunned as all the rest by the incredible display of the man they sought for their savior.

"What can we do? He is beyond our powers," Arachne said.

Argus remained pensive. Undaunted, as ever.

"No. We must persuade him," the child-who-wasn't answered. "And perhaps his friends will help us."

TWENTY-FOUR

VINCE'S CAR WASN'T GOOD FOR LONG TRIPS. JERSEY wasn't even too far, and the *old bucket of bolts*, as he called her, only barely made it back to Manhattan. Night had already fallen over the city by the time he parked, three blocks away from Maggie's, for safety's sake. Some of the street lamps were out along the roundabout way he took to get over to her block, but he preferred it that way.

The darker, the better.

The things he had heard from Frankie, cloistered away in that "hospital" out in Sussex, half-insane and scared of his own shadow, had bothered him for the whole ride back. It couldn't all be true, that would be too much. But there *was* a kernel of truth in it. There had to be. Too many weird things had been going on lately for it to all be demented raving. Sorting out the fact from the fiction, or whatever you wanted to call it—that was the trick.

One word stuck in his head. One word connected everything.

Morrigan.

That was what Sean had said, himself half-dazed

and muttering at the time. What the hell was Morrigan? Something that had scared the hell out of one of the toughest wiseguys Vince had ever known, and something Sean kept repeating when Sam Calabrese's name had come up.

Vince wasn't a pencil and paper kind of guy. He preferred to think things out in his head, or sometimes, to think out loud. He did that as the events of the past days tumbled through his mind. Maybe it was because of such, or maybe it was just fatigue, but for whatever reason, he didn't see the figure that lurked behind him as he turned the corner to Maggie's.

"Morrigan. Morrigan," he repeated, right up until he heard the rustle of leather.

He turned, and he cursed himself for an instant that he had let his guard down.

The figure darted out from behind a row of parked cars. Even in the tricky evening light, Vince could make out his distinct features. It was Rat.

The ex-cop wasted no time. He was outside Maggie's place. He had led the bastard right to them. His revolver flew out of his shoulder holster. He cocked back the hammer with a twist of his callused thumb.

Rat moved quickly, lithe and slinky like his namesake. He was between two cars, then behind another. Vince could hear him breathing, heavy and wheezing. He could see the shine of his shoes, reflecting the cold streetlights, and he couldn't miss the glint of sharpened steel in his grip.

It was that deadly blade that lunged at him a moment later, once, then twice. Both missed, but only by inches.

The dark man moved so fast, a strike, then a feint. Vince tried to get a clear shot, but he was like a whirlwind, in three places at once.

His next cut sliced open a gash in Vince's leg. He let loose a scream from deep in his belly. He turned, determined to shoot at the next thing he saw.

But there was nothing.

For a terrible, long moment, Vince scanned the block. Rat had vanished. He listened. He heard nothing, just the usual groans and chatters of the city at night.

For a second, as he turned toward Maggie, he caught a wisp of a high-pitched whine. It ended quickly, though, when a dart pierced the wet skin at the back of his neck, and he fell to the pavement.

From behind a pile of cans and bags there arose the being some called Scylla, and others knew as Rat. The one some knew as a woman, and others referred to as a man.

There were two more such darts still in his hand. Despite his speed in eluding Vince, he stumbled as he approached the fallen man. A colorless drool seeped from his mouth as he breathed. Dark, crusty film infested his hands, like a fungus that had also spread to his face.

"Worthy foe, I have to say," Scylla whispered, lifting the body from the pavement and easing it into his own car. "Another few minutes, and you'd have outlasted me."

TWENTY-FIVE

Scylla was breathing heavy. He could barely open the door when he heard the knock. He opened it, heedless of the fact that the slumped and unconscious body of Vince Sicario was on the floor in full view.

"Charybdis, my dear. I haven't the words," he sighed, the tall woman slipping through the doorway.

"Have I not always been there for you, Scylla?" Charybdis answered, seeing her long-estranged lover for the third time in two days. The rat-faced man was coughing. He looked drained.

Charybdis had received the call almost an hour ago. Scylla had stalked and stunned his prey, the man known to be the friend of Lucifer. The man he had been hunting for days. But his symptoms had overcome him before he could finish his task. He had made it to the small and dingy Times Square flophouse where he'd been sleeping of late. Now he needed help.

"The master bade me seek out and snare this Vince Sicario individual. I have done so, but I am no longer able to carry on. The molting has overtaken me. I must rest,"

Scylla said, collapsing to the floor next to Vince.

"I will watch over you," Charybdis said.

Rat tried hard to shake his head and raise his hands.

"No. You mustn't," he said.

Charybdis knelt down, stroking her hand over his pus-drooling face. She felt his ear start to come loose and so aborted the gentle touch with a sigh.

"I will not leave you, not after we've been apart for so long. The Morrigan can wait. Lucifer can wait. Let them all wait. We have," Charybdis replied.

"My love," Scylla muttered, smiling. "I have not done this for the Morrigan, or anyone else. Do you not see? This is my answer. I have done what you asked me to do. For us. But you must finish the work that I have started. This is the trickster's friend. This is the key to finding Lucifer. To freeing . . ."

Scylla fell unconscious, in his lost lover's arms.

"I will do as you ask, my cherished," Charybdis said, her hand on his heavily crusted face.

In a moment, the rodent-featured man fell fully into slumber, content to rest in the cocoon that would soon grow over his entire body.

Charybdis merely smiled. She laid a soft kiss on the raw, ooze-slathered space where his ear had been.

✤ ✤ ✤

Vince awoke as he was being set down. It was gentle, but even a gentle move made his sides hurt, and his head throb even more. The scarf that had been his blindfold was pulled off by a woman, he thought, but his eyes needed a moment to adjust.

He was in a small room. It was dark, and his bearer was lighting candles in several places. The floorboards looked charred. There were piles of musty clothes lumped in the corner, beside what appeared to be a dresser of some sort.

There were no chairs, but he had been set against a wall, on a part of the floor that appeared to have been swept clean. As his eyes became used to the lowlight, he made out the figure of an African female. She did not speak and went about seeing after the place. He was about to say something when she turned for the only door and exited.

"What in the name of . . . ?" he exclaimed, to an empty room.

It did not remain so for long, however.

As if in response to his expletives, the door opened from the outside. The child Argus entered.

"Who the hell?" Vince began.

"Please do not be hostile Mr. Sicario. We mean you no harm," came the response, strangely accented and spoken in the peculiar voice of a youth.

When Argus neared, Vince could see that he was addressed by a mere toddler. The boy did not appear well, though. He was naked, and he limped along with his weight almost totally supported by a cane, as though both of his legs were broken. The child's skin was covered by hundreds of cancerous growths, interrupted in a few places by massive tumors that completely distended his flesh. His little eyes gleamed a strange reddish hue.

"What the hell is goin' on here? Who are you?" Vince managed.

"Many questions, not very much time. You owe us a debt, do you not? My people have done you a service. That man who stunned you, he was under orders to bring you into the custody of others who would ultimately have killed you," Argus answered, though with much trouble. He appeared to be in pain. Even drawing breath seemed to drain the strength from his tiny body.

"Rat?"

"Is that what she was called here? Her actual name is Scylla, though she was known by many names to your kind. I am called Argus, by the way."

"She?"

"Yes. I know. She appeared quite masculine to you. Merely an illusion, I assure you," Argus said, coughing.

"This doesn't make any sense," Vince replied, heedless of the introductions, his head still throbbing.

"You may be surprised to learn that I agree with you, but now is not the time for that discussion. You are in no danger here, I assure you. The poison in your system is mild, but it has not yet worked its way out. Sleep. Tomorrow we will talk again."

Vince wanted answers, despite the ache in his gut, the cut on his leg and the pain in his skull. Argus, however, did not seem up for the conversation. His words finished, he trudged back out of the room, and closed the door behind him.

Vince passed out before he had a chance to protest.

Outside the door, in the altar-room, Argus fell. Charybdis rushed to his side, calling for Arachne.

"It would appear that my time has finally arrived," Argus muttered, through a mouth that was almost obscured by the dead skin flaking away from his lesions. "Please take me to my chair, my place is all prepared."

Charybdis did as she was told, lifting the toddler for the last time and setting him down on his confessional chair. The surreal child sighed. He closed his tiny little red eyes just in time for a large sheaf of lifeless skin on his neck to harden, and fall away from his body.

Arachne called out from behind a moment later. "You startled me. I was not aware that he had entered the molting."

"Just now," Charybdis replied.

"Have you brought Scylla back with you as well?" Arachne asked.

Charybdis did not answer, she was faltering as well. Arachne noticed for the first time that her skin had begun to swell like Argus's.

"No, she remains where I found her, in a small hotel just outside of Times Square," the African finally managed. "She has entered the cocoon, and could not be moved. I will go back to look after her until she has emerged."

Arachne still appeared healthy, with no sign of the malady that had overcome her master and was now beginning to plague her fellow servant. When Charybdis tried to straighten herself up, she stumbled and fell to one knee.

"You can't go anywhere. Not right now," she said. "You're only hours away from the process yourself."

"I must go. I cannot leave Scylla again," Charybdis protested.

"I will go. I will watch over her while you rest. Once you have emerged, you can re-join us," Arachne offered.

"But you will enter it as well, soon enough," Charybdis replied.

"True, but you are no good to anyone right now. You can't even travel in public like this. Let me help you."

Reluctantly, Charybdis agreed. She set herself down to rest.

"I have to say Charybdis, though I have known you for some time, I do find myself a little surprised," Arachne remarked as she helped her friend recline beside the ancient one.

"How is that?"

"You're known for your loyalty, renowned for it, really. So I'm a little surprised that you'd betray the Morrigan so completely, after so many years. And for Argus's sake, no less," Arachne replied.

Charybdis kept her expression cold. She adjusted her torso by shifting her weight to her back.

"Not for Argus. Not for him at all," Charybdis answered, putting her head down to rest.

✛   ✛   ✛

Arachne had taken the directions and gone to the hotel

without delay. She had found Room 115 just as Charybdis had told her it would be: dusty, dingy, and empty. There was only one thing in the room that didn't seem to belong there. Stepping around the bed and its cigarette-stained sheets, farther around the nightstand with an unread King James Bible on it, she came to a broad canvas sheet. It was covering something large.

With a motion like a circus ringleader, she lifted the sheet and snapped it off. A cloud of dust spilled into the staid hotel-room air.

Beneath was the figure known to the local underworld as Rat. He was frozen it seemed, in a swath of hardened, translucent ooze that covered his entire naked body.

"So that is the legendary Scylla?" Arachne said, sounding impressed, despite the fact that she was essentially alone.

Arachne moved a little closer, to get a better view.

"So many stories about you," she continued, knowing full well that Scylla was in no position to hear, much less respond. "Strange to see you in a man's form. Somehow I pictured you differently. Scylla the Slayer. Kali the Black."

Arachne probed the sticky husk that had now grown fully over the rat-faced man's skin.

"I suppose I will see soon enough," she said.

TWENTY-SIX

SAM CALABRESE AND INDIAN JOE WALKED UNDER cover of night, through the ghost town of rust and ragweed that was Pier 33. Their car had been parked within the warehouse nearest the western edge of the property, as had all of the cars of those who were now gathering there. It was important for the place to continue to appear deserted. Secrecy was now paramount.

The things that were to follow could not be witnessed by outsiders.

"Has Scylla contacted us?" Calabrese asked as they walked, his aide lagging a step behind for the first time in recent memory.

Indian Joe did not answer. He yawned instead, looking as though he hadn't slept in days. Gray circles had begun to fill in under his eyes. Anger was clearly etched across his boss's wide face, though. The fat man's eyes seethed.

"Tell me again. How long has it been?" the bloated gangster continued.

The Native American lifted his left arm slowly, as though the simple movement hurt him. With a scowl, he pulled back the sleeve of his suit coat to reveal his watch. The skin around his wrist had become dry, speckled white and black rather than reddish-brown. Long bristles of hair, or maybe fur, were poking through in places. The nails of his fingers had grown unusually long as well. They were beginning to turn black.

"Her last report came in nearly twelve hours ago," he managed. "She had spotted Sicario again after nearly a day of searching. She was about to move in. There has been no contact since then."

"Perhaps she has begun the change," Calabrese replied.

"Possible, but we spoke of that. She was under strict orders, if the molting were to come over her suddenly, she was to contact one of our agents. None of our people have had any word," Joseph replied, his breathing slow and difficult as he walked.

Calabrese did not seem at all worried by his friend's condition.

"Disturbing, to be certain. We'll need to send someone to her refuge. Make sure that she has not begun the change. If she has, she might be there," Calabrese said.

"There is another possibility," the Indian said.

"Argus."

"Indeed. Scylla reported the ancient one's followers were tracking Sicario as well. If they got to her, she may already be dead. And Argus may have Sicario, or even Mulcahy by now," Joe said.

"I must speak with our old friend," Calabrese answered.

"Argus? No one seems to know his location, since he

arrived in New York, he and his followers have hidden themselves from us. None of our agents have been able to learn their whereabouts."

Calabrese did not appear concerned.

"The ancient one is cautious. His many years have taught him the value of privacy. I don't begrudge him his secrecy. If he is indeed plotting against me, he will not tip his hand even a moment before he acts. And he will not act until the moment is right.

"I know that he has visited the Bleecker Street Haven, and spoken with those of our kind in residence there. I have told them that I will appear there personally tomorrow, to announce my intentions. Argus will be there.

"I will speak to all of our flock that has gathered, to welcome those who remain loyal to me, and to gauge the treason of those who may not be."

They stopped their trail when they came before the same enormous structure that they had inspected only a few days earlier. This time neither man entered. Indian Joe rapped on the aluminum door, and both awaited a response.

It came quickly, but not in the form of a person to greet them. As if by unseen hands, the door opened from the inside.

"Many of our folk have gathered within. The molting continues. Some have already emerged. They will expect the festival to begin soon," Joseph said.

"And your time is fast approaching as well, is it not?" he replied.

"I shall take my rest within, this night. By your leave,

of course."

"By all means, Lycaon," the boss answered. "The time for this charade is now over. Salvatore Calabrese dies tonight. For the second time."

Both men entered, and the door soon closed in the same way. They were plunged into total darkness. It was cold, and it was quiet. A reddish light shone from the distance ahead of them, but it was impossible to know how far away the glow burned.

"Come forth, children. Your master has arrived to see after the feast," Calabrese said, but in a different and altogether softer voice than the gangster had ever used.

The reddish hue blossomed then, but strangely, it seemed to cast no light upon the figures of Calabrese and Joseph. From its center there stepped forward three silhouettes. They were cloaked, but clearly feminine in shape. The two on each flank held lances high. The blades beamed reflected firelight like steel torches.

The one in the middle, unarmed, lowered her veil and revealed her face to the pair. It was canine. Part hound, part lady. She was strangely beautiful, with sharply angled features, a round black nose and delicate whiskers that flared from the sides of her snout. Her eyes were black slits set in green crystal.

When she spoke, the words growled from between deadly fangs.

"The Daughters of Cerberus bid you welcome, Keeper. The preparations proceed as per Lycaon's direction. May the festival meet with your expectations," she said.

Their message given, the three receded, and their peculiar glow with them. In moments they were once again absorbed into the shadows from which they had appeared. A second door opened, only a few feet in front of the two men.

The sounds of chatter, and the bright light of lamps and braziers, spilled onto them.

Indian Joe turned. Sam Calabrese was no longer beside him.

A new figure had replaced the slobbering hood. Presiding among the smoke and the darkness, there stood an elegant, towering woman. A shroud that glittered deep crimson swirled around her like a pool of blood. Black tresses flowed from her crown in a waterfall of shadows, and her pallid features exuded a delicate glimmer.

"Shall we enter, Queen Morrigan?" Joseph asked.

✥   ✥   ✥

Vince did not know that the night had passed, or that morning now dawned upon the city. But he did know that something sinister lurked just out of sight.

The room in which he was held was dark. When a noise roused him from sleep, his mind immediately began imagining what might have made it.

Something entered through a concealed side door. Vince tried to look, but for all his straining against the dark, he could not see more than a hint of movement. The figure moved through the shadows along the wall, nimble as a cat.

Vince shuddered.

"You need not fear, my friend. As I told you yesterday, you are safe here. I assure you."

The voice that greeted him was familiar. It was that of the child with the weird red eyes. The one who had named himself Argus. But when the figure emerged into the candlelight, the child was nowhere in sight. It was a new, and utterly peculiar being, which had presented itself. Unlike the truncated, diseased frame of the boy he had met a day earlier, the Argus before him now was long and lean of limb, but he resembled a man in that respect only. The remainder of his features were, to Vince's sight, utterly hideous.

Three gleaming eyes were set like a triad of ruby stones upon a face that seemed carved from white granite. A long, thin nose almost merged with his stark, ladylike cheeks. His lips were full and rounded like a woman's, but eerily bluish and hypothermic against the pallor of his skin.

Combed back from his temples, waves of shimmering, blood-red hair gathered the candlelight in deathly sparkles. It fell thick over his bony shoulders and clung so close to his skin that it seemed to drip across his androgynous breasts. His limbs were stringy, the musculature pulled tight beneath his cold flesh. His hands grew uncommonly long.

When he lifted them, they turned to reveal the palms in a fluid, dancer-like motion. Nestled in the heart of each was a crimson eye staring outward with its own conscious gaze, just as the three atop his forehead.

Then he lowered the shiny leather belt that held fast the

layered, silken folds of his skirt, which fell to the floor and hid all of his lower quarters. There, a sixth eye, brilliant and scarlet as the others, peered forth from the navel. As a single, bizarre concession to vanity, a silver ring pierced the skin of his lower belly. It was the only jewelry the ancient creature ever wore.

"The one you call Sean. He is your friend, is he not?" Argus began.

"He was, once. A long time ago," Vince answered, truly frightened for the first time he could remember.

"And you care for him still?"

The question was simple enough, but Vince waited a while before answering. He wanted a drink. His lips were so dry. Argus merely stood before him. He seemed as patient as a statue, unmoving but for the scarlet flickering of his half-dozen eyes, which did not blink together, but rather in an endless, unnerving sequence. One after the other, on and on. Five of the six were always open.

"He came to me for help. What was I gonna do? He was my best friend. I lost him once, and I never had . . ."

"Never had?"

"Never had a friend like him again," Vince finally said, unable to look upon the extreme visage any longer.

"Then if you care for him, you must help us find him," Argus said, sensing his *guest's* anxiety, moving closer to place his bony hand on the ex-cop's shoulder.

"I don't even know who . . . what . . . you are," he said, still unable to look upon the strange being.

"We are the only ones who can help him. You must

know by now, there are very dangerous people looking for him. They *will* find him, sooner or later. And when they do, they will kill him. Of that I can assure you.

"Help us. Help us help him."

TWENTY-SEVEN

THERE WAS AN ENVELOPE DANGLING FROM HER DOOR-knob. Not so strange a sight, perhaps. But given the events of recent days, Maggie wasn't sure what to make of it. It stirred a moment of hope in her, but that optimism was quickly overwhelmed.

She had only been out for a short while, looking for Sean or Vince. Anyone really, though she'd somehow known she wasn't likely to find either one. It was now drawing past noon. There'd been no sign of either once since the previous morning.

The envelope was yellowed. The paper seemed delicate, aged like old newsprint. It was sealed with a glob of red wax that had been imprinted with a round stamp. She didn't recognize the design. For a moment she guessed it to be Greek, but didn't give the matter much thought.

It wasn't addressed to anyone, so she snapped it open. A single sheet of parchment, dry and ancient as the envelope, was folded inside. Text was inscribed in scarlet ink across its face. The script was elegant, a little archaic even. The first letter of every word was oversized and each "S" was rendered with a long tail like an "F," which lent the message a classical air, but only complicated her reading of it.

Was it a joke? The thought crossed her mind for a moment.

When she read it, brief though it was, all ideas of humor slipped away. She felt a chill crawl over her. Her fingers trembled as she fiddled with the keys in her purse. They clattered against the lock as she clumsily unfastened it.

The apartment was dark. She wanted to call out after Sean, but she couldn't muster the voice. Instead she tore through the place in silence. As she suspected, he was not there.

She thought about staying, waiting for him to return, but she couldn't do that. Vince was in trouble. She needed to find Sean. So she left, venturing out into the neighborhood like she had so many times as a child, looking for Sean Mulcahy.

It was almost as if the last thirty years had changed nothing.

✤　✤　✤

The afternoon had passed, and the evening was growing late. Long midday shadows were threatening to spill over, stretched out and tired in the wake of endless rows of brown brick and age-stained iron. A dark tide seemed poised to wash fully into the narrow, dirty streets as the sun failed in a red-orange haze somewhere beyond the west. Alleyways and vestibules and alcoves had already flooded, shallows submerged by the first lightless waves.

Maggie had tried all the old haunts. She'd poked through most of the midtown after-work joints around Eighth Avenue and the West Thirties, but saw no sign of Sean amid the chattering throngs of lawyers and accountants and insurance salesmen dulling their senses just enough to stomach the commute home.

That hadn't really been a surprise, but it was worth making sure.

She'd fought her way through the hive of worker drones circulating in and out of Penn Station like a swarm shuffling about a subterranean nest, then around the big post office as it closed down for the night, and over toward Tenth. The bars there were a little less upscale, if that was saying anything, and a little more local in the way of patrons.

Most of the swill consumed in those pubs was chugged on tattered stools under lowlight by grizzled, hard-faced rail-yard men still stained with their daily mess of black dust and grease. The chatter was rougher too, a blend of accents throwing up guttural laughter and tossing around casual, working class vulgarity. More Vince's kind of place.

She had no luck in any of those dives either, barring the four or five drinks she had been offered in as many locations or the slightly incoherent marriage proposal whispered in her ear at *O'Neil's Aran Isles*.

So she'd scrambled through the tunnel traffic that always clogged five or six blocks in each direction around that time of the day, north toward the lower forties. She

was still fairly certain from her memory of Vince's old hab-
its which places she could rule out without physically going
in. That cut down on her options quite a bit. Personally
checking every Irish pub in Hell's Kitchen would have
taken days.

By half past seven on her grandmother's pocket-watch,
she had already covered just about everyplace she could
think of, and still hadn't found a trace of Sean Mulcahy.
Now she was reduced to checking inside every liquor store
and bodega.

The sun was down fully. Night had fallen over the city.
Maggie knew that she was passing through a part of town
that wasn't safe after dark.

Some teenagers were loitering on the corner as she left
a Spanish-run newsstand, passing a bottle between them.
Local Irish kids, she figured. All of them sported short-
cropped hair in identical military fashion, but they were
far from clean-cut. Several wore similar jackets, the black
leather beaten and creased. Dirty, threadbare clothes
clung to the rest of them, knees ripped out of their trousers
and holes dotting their shirts. None of them looked to have
bathed in days.

As Maggie approached, a kid named Gerry stirred
from their circle. He was nineteen, but the scruff on his
face added a few years, making him look more like he was
in his early twenties. The others followed behind him. He
was the largest of them, which was more than enough to
qualify him as their leader.

"Hey, hey pretty lady. What's doin'?" he said.

Maggie growled under her breath. She was no stranger
to the bands of restless delinquents who roamed the Kitchen.
She tried to stay calm, even as she felt her hands trembling.
They were probably just drunk, she told herself.

"Get lost kid," she sneered, stepping past the group as
if they weren't there.

His friend, a younger kid named Brian, stepped in
front of her. Despite his evident youth, Brian had a nasty
gray scar snaking across his chin and jaw, and he spit out
a wad of chaw that landed inches from Maggie's foot. A
slight brown stain remained on his lips.

Even though it wasn't late, the street was empty.

"Hey, now. That ain't a very nice way ta talk to my
buddy there," he said, through a mouthful of yellowed,
crooked teeth.

He was near enough for her to smell him. His breath
was like a dog's. Shit mixed with yesterday's trash, warmed
over with a hint of cheap whiskey.

"Yeah, 'specially fer a lady who just come outta that
spic joint," Gerry added, moving shoulder to shoulder beside his friend.

The others were drifting into a circle around them.
One of them fingered half a broomstick handle. Another
made a show of cracking his knuckles.

"What are you talking about?" Maggie said, obviously
impatient with the delay.

"Valencia's. That's a spic name, damn PRs are takin'
over," Brian replied.

"Yeah, 'cause this used to be a nice neighborhood till

them greasy slimeballs started movin' in," Gerry said, without even a hint of irony.

"You got a helluva mouth on you for a little boy," she scolded.

"Whoa, there! Maybe you don't get it, honey. See we don't like them spics too much, but the lousy Americans who go with 'em are worse," Gerry said, his voice raised and his hand outstretched.

From behind her a third one stepped up, a gangly red-haired kid named Brendan. His shirt was two sizes too small; his wardrobe had not yet caught up with latest growth spurt.

"Yeah, she's prolly sleepin' wit some slimy Rican!" he said. It was the wittiest thing he could think to say, but it won him a laugh from his buddies.

"Why don't you lemme show you what a real American man is like!" Gerry offered. He was joking, but the joke brought on a raucous cheer from his cronies.

"Alright, you're all very tough," she said, exasperated.

She tried to push past Brian, but to no avail.

Finally, she shifted her handbag from both arms to one, and put her free hand on her hip, the schoolteacher expression crossed her face again. She turned her attention toward Gerry, if for no other reason than he appeared to be the most vocal of the four.

"Okay. What do you say you and me take a little walk over there and talk this over?"

Excited by the offer, but cautious, Gerry slowly stepped backward toward the alley behind the store. His eyes remained focused on Maggie, however, who followed him with a careful glide.

"What do you have in mind?" he whispered, once they were out of earshot of the other guys.

"You'll see."

She bridged the gap between them and they continued to wander farther back into the alley. Then, she neared, and placed her face right up next to his.

He stank of the same cheap whiskey and old cigarettes. Bad, but not nearly as foul as she had expected under the circumstances.

"I'm sure you'll remember this . . ."

With as much calm as anyone raised on the streets, Maggie let her handbag fall to the ground, her keys remaining in her grip. Gerry was still staring into her eyes. He never saw the swing.

The smash of the jagged makeshift weapon, chased by a howl-like scream alerted the others. They turned from their awkward guarding of the street and rushed into the alley. She tried to run, to push by them as they came toward her, but they reached their arms out and closed off her only avenue of escape. Brian caught her. He shoved her back into the alley.

Gerry remained on the pavement, holding his forehead with his hands. A healthy stream of blood was slipping between his fingers and dripping into his face. He felt the tear on his scalp. He bottled his rage up with a snarl.

"You fiery bitch!" Brian shouted as he grabbed hold of her, clenching her arms hard in his grasp.

"Yeah! Nail her right here, Bri!" Brendan shouted.

Kevin, the tallest of the group, with dark hair and a large pale face, said nothing. He merely nodded, looking Maggie up and down as the others laughed. Then he opened a switchblade.

"Make sure Ger' is okay," he told Brendan. Then he turned to Brian, who had Maggie held fast in his dirty hands. "And you make sure you don't let go of her."

He waved the knife in front of her face. Maggie spit at him, but it was a feeble gesture. The tip of the blade stroked her throat and sliced open her blouse. She wanted to scream, but she felt her chest tense and her voice failed her. A tear formed in her eye as the knife pricked her flesh.

Then everything froze.

A cat squealed in the shadows.

Something rattled a chain-link fence in the dark, just out of sight.

Someone cleared his throat.

"Now, boys. Play nice, eh?" a voice scolded from the ether.

It wasn't clearly male or female, but it was authoritarian; commanding in a weird way, like a mother talking to her children. It seemed to have no source whatsoever.

"What the hell is that?" Brian questioned.

"Whoever you are, scram! This ain't your problem." Kevin shouted into the dim.

He was answered with a deathly still. A quiet that was unusual for Hell's Kitchen.

Thinking his words to have scared away any interlopers, Kevin continued to trace the blade along Maggie's exposed chest. Gerry smiled as he got up.

A tin can tumbled out from behind a dumpster, rolling in the awkward end-over-end fashion that only happened when someone kicked it.

"I've warned you once. Now go away *boys*," the peculiar voice intoned again. For an instant, the last word resonated through every corner of the cramped space.

"Take her over there," Gerry said.

Brian dutifully obeyed. With some of the others, he tugged on Maggie and forced her to walk behind a second dumpster, beneath a fire escape.

"Whoever you are. We're gonna make you sorry too," Kevin said, Gerry and Brendan at his sides, fists bared.

They waited for an answer.

A scream was all they got.

It was horrible. Ghastly. The wailing of a boy frightened beyond his understanding, shaken to his young, delicate heart.

It was Brian. His cries were mixed with pleas, rendered through a voice that quivered with every breath. The boys found themselves momentarily stopped, unable to move. When Gerry did finally step forward, toward the dark and slimy place where Brian had secluded their victim, he screamed too.

From the cold, thick evening shadows, yelping like a dying cat, *something* crawled out into the alley. A chattering, clicking buzz accompanied him, *accompanied it*. And the boys who saw it felt their limbs go numb.

Roaches. A thousand of them. Ten thousand, maybe. They teamed and crawled in a feeding frenzy, circulating like a hive over the prostrate form of a small human. The figure, covered head to toe by the ravenous insects, tried to lift an arm toward the boys, and then a head. When he did, some of the giant, brown bugs fell away from his face, and the once-fearless gang saw the bloodied remains of their friend's features beneath. All that remained of Brian were blue eyes and gently freckled cheeks, barely visible under dozens of discreet, blood-soaked bites.

Before the boys could catch their breath, the pestilent horde moved off what had once been their friend. It left behind a naked, gnawed-on husk thrashing about beneath the fire escape. Then, as though mustered by some unseen master, the carnivorous horde clambered toward Gerry and his pals. The sound of a hundred thousand insect limbs striking the concrete raised a clatter.

Bravado aside, the rest turned and ran. They didn't stop until they reached the Hudson.

Maggie, shaking still, finally opened her eyes when she was sure the screaming was done. She found herself in the damp, rancid corner between the dumpster and the fire escape, but the alley was deserted. All but deserted, anyway. The soft meow of a cat caught her ear. Out of the corner of her eye she saw a black feline leap from the dumpster, and flit across the alley.

Slowly, she stepped into the burgeoning moonlight, and she couldn't believe her eyes.

"Sean?"

"Hey, Maggie. You alright?"

He was sitting, dangling really. Perched, like the cat she had heard a moment earlier, on a ledge atop a ten-foot wall across the way.

"The neighborhood's getting better, I can say that," he said, shaking his head. "But these kids? When I used to run the streets with little punks like them, we never acted like that. Damn hoods have no respect anymore."

Maggie just stood there. She was still shaking.

"God, I'm sorry. You're probably pretty shaken up, and here I am musing about old times."

"Christ, Sean!" she finally said, looking down at the man-gled, still-breathing body of Brian on the sticky pavement. "I've been looking all over! What the hell are you . . . ?"

She stopped her sentence in mid-thought, because when she looked up, Sean was no longer perched on the ledge. He was standing a few short feet in front of her.

"Go ahead, what were you saying?" he answered.

She ignored the impossibility of how fast he had moved, for the moment.

"I thought I told you to keep your head out of sight. You know how much trouble you're in?" she scolded.

He merely smiled, placed his hand on her shoulder, and tried to fix her torn blouse.

"I know, but this is still a pretty rough part of town. Funny, even after all this, you're still worried about me."

"What happened here doesn't change anything. Not for you," she said, looking up at him as he adjusted her coat. "But I am glad you were here. Vince is in trouble, I think with some of *your friends*."

Sean nodded again, and smiled.

Looking directly at him, near enough to kiss him again, Maggie couldn't help but marvel at how young he looked. It was as if he had just stepped out of 1917, or the last thirty years had vanished in a heartbeat.

She suddenly felt self-conscious.

"You hungry?" he asked, as though there had been no mention of Vince at all.

"What? I just told you . . ."

"Are you hungry? You wanna eat?"

"I . . . I can't . . . what are you talking about?"

"Just trust me. C'mon, you'll like this, trust me," he said, and she couldn't help but follow.

TWENTY-EIGHT

THE FRONT DOORS TO THE BLEECKER STREET HAVEN were old. They had been installed during the only renovation in the building's 113-year history. That had taken place during the tenure of the first man named Roosevelt to occupy the White House.

When the hinges creaked and rattled from the outside, none of the people socializing in the foyer or the library room paid any attention. The wind usually caused that kind of sound, especially in the late fall and winter. Generally, though, it didn't last long.

When the rattling grew louder rather than softer as the moments wore on, however, some among the gathered noticed it. Argus was there, speaking again with his old friend Cygnus, the latter now fully molted into the human-swan hybrid that suggested her ancient namesake. Both paused when the wind outside drew up a gust that sent the doors swinging open.

A rush of cold air tumbled into the entranceway and the antique-furnished sitting room beyond. Argus stood from his chair. He extended his all-seeing hands.

A hush fell over the parlor.

"Welcome," he said.

For a moment there was no answer, just the light from the outside flooding into the tobacco-smoke and candle glows. Then, a figure emerged from the evening. The doors closed behind—this time without protest.

"Honored Argus. It has been too long," replied a smooth, mellifluous voice.

Argus recognized the speaker, as did most of the others milling about the Gothic study. A collective shudder came over them, the once serene ambience suddenly made anxious.

She was nothing less than a goddess, a presence of terrible, powerful beauty. Long black hair cascaded around her face, falling about her shoulders like the hood of a crow. The deep red gloss of her lips captured a sparkle in her eyes, a shimmer like the reflection of blood. Her porcelain features lurked in half-shadow beneath the locks, soft and delicate and somehow menacing for all their innocence.

She wore a cloak of shimmering fabric that was several colors at once, midnight black, Roman purple and deep scarlet in succession.

"Morrigan. It has truly been a long time," Argus said. "Even by our standards."

"It warms my heart to see so many of our kind gathered here, under your capable aegis, and that of our other Haven masters," the glimmering figure replied as she slipped like a feather through the Oriental-styled foyer and toward the stately Baroque confines of the library.

Her words sounded more like music than a human voice.

"We have been hard at work, seeking out and protecting all those of our ilk we have been able to find since the War's end," Cygnus answered in squawking fashion from beside Argus, a little uneasy at the Keeper's sight, but composed.

Hints of stolen candlelight sparkled about the Phantom Queen, captured and cast off in her wake.

"The human conflicts have ravaged our ranks. Terrible, terrible times we have seen. Some among my own circle wondered if we'd lost your followers entirely when your Haven was destroyed," the Morrigan answered.

"We were very nearly finished, I am afraid. Little was salvaged from the Nazi occupation of Paris," Cygnus replied.

"Too many of our kind were lost," Argus added. "As it was in my own city."

"So I was told. Will you return there? Can you?" the Morrigan asked.

Her voice sang in softly melodious tones, so hypnotic that many of the gathered found themselves drawn to her sight. Most were soon unable, or unwilling, to pull their eyes from her shadow-glittering figure.

"The remains of my Haven have re-formed here. Though we are only a handful. Your former associate Charybdis is among us, as you may have heard. I think that Prague may be beyond our reach now," Argus said.

He was aware of the trance into which many of the others had fallen, but he ignored it, focusing his attentions completely upon the Keeper.

"Tragic, for it was beautiful," the Morrigan replied.

Her ivory hands slipped across the carved sandstone of the fireplace, a flawless reproduction of Tsar Nicholas II's heraldic-crowned Bremen masterpiece. She moved through the smoky chamber like a sun shimmer at dusk, glistening a harsh red on the embossed bindings of the shelved tomes and sparkling like dour rain on the crystal chandelier.

"So it was," Argus said.

The Morrigan glided to the center of the room. The candles all went out when she raised her hands. For an instant, darkness fell upon the hall. But the blindness reigned only a moment.

Light cast outward from the Keeper's strange cloak lit the whole of the sitting room. Cygnus had to step backward, and shield her sight.

Argus, his eyes so very more capable than those of the others, was able to look upon the Morrigan. The war goddess was no more.

Born anew from the ephemeral darkness, the menacing, deathly aspect of her had faded from sight. The Morrigan yet stood in the center of the chamber, suddenly timid and shrinking beneath her fantastic shroud. Yet recognizable, she seemed more phantom now than queen, as though malice had flown away with the shadows, leaving nothing more threatening than a beautiful, gentle girl.

She spoke with the same voice, however, as though nothing about her had changed.

"Very well. So we are here, many gathered for the celebration. Let me welcome you all then, to New York

and to the Festival of the Molting. I have arranged our
place of celebration. Pier 33 along the Hudson waterfront,
there I have purchased numerous warehouses for our use.
The location is private, and secure. My servants have been
working day and night. They have set our stage within the
largest of the buildings."

Argus nodded. The Keeper gestured to him with a
discreet wave.

"For those who have yet to enter the change, there is
ample space for cocoons, and for quiet slumber. For all
the rest, however, those who have passed into their natural
forms, this shall be the greatest of all our grand feasts.

"Everything has been provided for your pleasure,
Chinese opium, fine tobacco, hashish, all manner of alcohol, even that rare and increasingly hard to obtain treat,
absinthe. Come, indulge your fantasies. Let loose the demons that lurk within you all.

"This is your time. Time to put aside the worries and
the sorrows that plague you. Time to forget the cruelty and
the horrors of humanity. Under my protection, you can be
carefree again."

Those assembled cheered. Argus was forced to smile
with them, all the while fuming under his strange skin.

The Morrigan was beside him a moment later. She extended a hand toward the secluded corner of the study. He
knew to follow without a word. Then the two spoke apart
from the rest.

"No doubt you have heard the rumors," she began.

Argus considered his response, but not for too long.

Anything out of the ordinary could provoke suspicion in the Keeper.

"I have heard that Sean Mulcahy is present in this city," Argus answered.

He settled himself into a leather chair as he spoke. When he looked back over to the Keeper, also seating herself, the lovely young girl was gone. He now conversed with an old crone. He did not let the change startle him. The Morrigan appeared in many aspects.

"The one some have dubbed Lucifer evaded my hands once, and he is now on the run. I will find him soon," she said, her voice yet unchanged, though it now issued from the lips of a withered hunchback.

"Of that I have little doubt. I know Charybdis is especially anxious for an end to the trickster's flight, having not seen her beloved all these many years," Argus replied.

"Nothing would please me more than to see Scylla and Charybdis returned to my side," the Morrigan said.

The mention of Charybdis spurred a slow tilt of her head. It was a gentle move. Argus guessed that she really did mean what she said.

"What is it that you wish, my queen? Why do you come to me about this?" Argus asked.

He did not know what, if anything the Morrigan knew of his plotting. Until he could learn more, he would have to play his hand close to the vest. It was possible that the Keeper already had cause to suspect him, and she was now fishing for confirmation. But fifteen hundred years worth of small talk had prepared him well.

"I seek your counsel, as the oldest and wisest of us all. I know that many among my flock have sought guidance from you, and that most have inquired about the prophecy. I am merely the Keeper of our lore, you are the most knowledgeable in the writings of the ancients," she said.

The flattery was wasted on the six-eyed figure, but he pretended that it wasn't. He acknowledged the wrinkled old woman's comment with a polite smile.

"What I can offer you is only this. The words in Nestor's book were written ages ago, and they are nothing if not vague. The prophecy does not mention a specific place, time or person. Some do believe that Mulcahy is the light bringer reborn, but in the end, that may not matter," Argus said.

"Why is that?"

"Prophecy is a strange art, some would say it is no art at all, but we can leave that discussion to the philosophers. The only really true thing that can be said about any prophecy is that it is never evaluated with foresight. Only in hindsight does anyone ever remark about it having been accurate.

"So I would counsel you that the truth of whether our fugitive Mulcahy is indeed Lucifer depends less upon what is written, and more upon whether you prevail in your search for him," Argus said.

The Morrigan nodded.

"If he overthrows me, then the people will accept him without question. But if I kill him, then he could not have been Lucifer," she answered.

"That is, in any event, what the great masses of our folk will believe," Argus said.

The Morrigan gazed up and away toward the ceiling. There was not a hint of cruelty in her eyes or her voice. She seemed oddly serene.

"So that is what I must do," she said, as though she had not even considered the decision until just that moment.

While the shriveled Morrigan spoke with a sad confidence, Argus sighed. He did not seem convinced.

"Must you?" he asked.

The Morrigan turned. She knew what Argus was alluding to. They'd been having the same conversation for three centuries, off and on.

"They are not ready for us. Not yet," she answered.

"But the superstitions we feared for so long are mostly dead. No one burns witches anymore. No one looks to demons to explain the noises brimming in the dark of the night." Argus was more animated, almost passionate in his plea. "Science rules their minds now. Maybe they would want to study us, learn from us."

"Maybe they wouldn't kill us, you mean."

"In so many words," Argus answered.

The Morrigan nodded. Her face told Argus that she was truly considering his reasoning. For the first time in many decades, the Keeper was not merely dismissing his argument out of hand. But her tired, haggard visage spoke more of regret than anything.

"I wish for the same thing, old friend. Secrecy is a burden our people have endured for far too long. But now is not the time to lower that veil. The outside world is not ready for us. Not yet."

Argus's crimson-boiling eyes opened wide with a surge of feeling, all six charged with life in their own, eerie way.

"But they've come so far," he said.

"They have. Even in the space of my own lifetime, the flowering of the Renaissance, the works of the Enlightenment. The Rights of Man. But they're not far enough yet.

"For proof of that we need only look back a year. They're still slaughtering each other *en masse*. Tens of millions of them lay rotting in fresh graves.

"No. They're not ready for the likes of us yet. Attitudes take generations to change, ideas sometimes require longer. Someday, maybe by the end of this century even, their actions might finally converge with their ideals. Then it will be our time."

"And if we emerge before?"

"Then I have no doubt that our kind will vanish forever. I intend to make certain that never happens. Prophecy or not, my duty is to protect the Children of Nestor. Everything I do is to that end."

"Even if that requires the death of Lucifer, the death of the prophecy that gives us all hope?"

The Morrigan nodded.

"Even that."

Now Argus was certain. The Keeper's intentions were clear, and so then was the course that he would have to take.

The old one did not answer.

The Morrigan smiled. She offered a hand to her

ancient friend. It was a congenial gesture, but Argus had been acquainted with her long enough to know that everything the Morrigan did, even the smallest motion, could be threatening. Her smile was no exception.

"Thank you, my old companion. Your counsel has been a great help to me, as always," the Morrigan said, leaving the pale, thin figure to wonder if he had somehow just revealed himself.

TWENTY-NINE

GIANNI'S TRATTORIA CAMPAGNA WAS CLOSED. THE SIGN in the storefront window said so. **CLOSED** in big red *sans serif* letters. It was dark too, and the doors were locked. Sean didn't seem to care.

"We're going here?" Maggie asked.

He didn't answer.

"Do you know the owner?"

Again, there was no answer.

Sean rummaged around in his coat pockets, and finally produced a set of keys. He played with them, trying each one in succession in the lock, until he found the right one.

The doors opened.

"Did you steal the keys to this place?" Maggie whispered as they entered.

"I most certainly did not," he replied, feigning indignation.

"Then how did you . . . ?"

"The manager gave them to me, if you must know."

"But why would he?"

"I suppose you could say he mistook me for someone

else," Sean replied.

A slightly impish grin curled his mouth as they stepped into the darkened, steam-warmed place.

"I don't understand; how could he do that?" she asked.

Sean was no longer beside her by the time she finished her question.

She was alone for only an instant before the house lights flashed like a series of Broadway spotlights. The restaurant was cozy, long, and narrow, with replica frescoes of Pompeii and Herculaneum painted on the walls. Freshly polished hardwood lay underfoot. A liquor-lined bar with a pair of cappuccino makers occupied the far left corner. Dozens of tables, almost too many for so small a space, covered the area, chairs turned upside down on top of them. All but one, and it was that one which drew her attention.

In the very middle of the floor a single table was prepared, two chairs turned down with a rather stereotypical red-and-white-checkered tablecloth. The gleaming silverware of two place settings rested beneath a glass vase crowned with a single white rose.

Music played, yet another scratchy old record, and another familiar old song. But she didn't have a moment to think about it. Suddenly Sean was behind her again, though she had not heard him approach. Without a further word, he led her over to the table like a *maitre d'*.

"A lovely flower for a lovely lady," he said, presenting her with the seat.

"Roses of Picardy" was the tune, another John McCormack recording. The music was haunting, all the more so because she knew every word.

Roses are shining in Picardy
In the hush of the silvery dew
Roses are flowering in Picardy
But there's never a flower like you.

Having seated her, Sean moved to his own chair. He wasted no time lifting a bottle of prewar Pinot Grigio from a bucket of ice and pouring it.

"Where did you?"

"Questions, questions, just relax. You said you always wanted to see Italy, right? Well this isn't quite Italy, but it's as close as I could get on short notice."

Once both glasses were filled, he raised his own for a toast.

"To old friends, and more. *Salute*," he said.

Even though she wasn't exactly sure what he meant, Maggie lifted her glass, clanged it against his and sipped the wine.

"I used to hate this song," he said. "Do you remember? But you loved it so much. I could never quite figure out why, but it grew on me after a while."

"I remember."

"That one time when I talked you into going to the Hippodrome with me. Must've been the summer of '16. We snuck in through the service entrance and saw that band with the white hats and bowties. They were playing this just as we got inside."

She knew exactly what he was talking about. That humid, sweltering August night had been the first time they'd kissed. It had also been the last time.

And the roses will die with the summertime
And our roads may be far apart
But there's one rose that dies not in Picardy
'Tis the rose that I keep in my heart

"I hate to spoil your hospitality Sean, but don't we have a few things we need to talk about?"

"I should think that we do," he answered, leaning in across the table as though he meant to repeat the seminal event of that long ago evening.

Her response was not what he had hoped. Instead she pulled herself back and put down her glass.

"What's the matter?" he asked.

"It's Vince," she answered, momentarily relieved to have changed the subject.

"He intrudes upon us again," Sean sighed.

He drained the contents of his glass before putting it down.

Maggie grabbed her bag and sorted through some things. She produced the parchment envelope with the broken wax seal.

"There was a note on my door this afternoon."

"From who?"

"No signature. Here, take it. It doesn't make much sense, not to me, anyway," she said, handing it to him. "It says your *old friend* has Vince in his care. If you don't return to church soon, Vince will never come back."

THIRTY

THE SKY ABOVE MANHATTAN WAS BLACK. STORM CLOUDS gathered, blotting out the stars in the west and battling with the moon. Cold mist loitered over the city. Frost crystallized on windows and exposed steel. Snow threatened.

From the north, a brood of crows split the fog in a ghostly descent of black feathers.

There were ten, then twelve, or perhaps only nine. The dim made it hard to discern. Whatever the number, the flock turned and dove when they came close upon the broken cross that crowned the spire of an old church. All moved as one, and all landed in unison upon the iron and brick steeple—the highest point in the area.

Though no one was looking, and no one would have seen the change, the birds waited in silence. Until a bank of clouds swept briefly over the moon, robbing what little light there had been from the city.

When the clouds passed, and a scattering of moon-glows once more lit the steeple, the birds were gone. Sean Mulcahy rested there, naked but for a tattered black over-coat. His bare skin was drained of color, bone white and stark against the night.

Like the ghost of a failed saint, he clung perched atop the fractured church spire, haunting a domain he had long ago rejected. Though his form was nearly normal in other respects, his face was still. His eyes gazed forth in emptiness, sunken deep into an alabaster visage that was only vaguely human.

Fingers that stretched absurdly long wrapped themselves like twine about the rusted iron base. His beaten coat flapped in the wind, a dark and ersatz flag over a dark and grim neighborhood.

What little remained of the cross that had once presided over the cathedral heights cracked and fell away when his unnatural grip loosed. His skin, his limbs, and his face all shrunk and grew paler until the whole of him seemed almost transparent. Then, like glacier ice melting into the dark of the sea, his feigned humanity dissolved into pure liquid. In a matter of moments, the stuff of Sean Mulcahy ran in streams down the side of the steeple and over the church roof like rain.

Once it had seeped through the ashen-cracks in the ceiling timber, all which remained upon the spire was the once-elegant overcoat. Snagged upon the jagged metal, it continued to flap in the wintry air.

Argus rested upon the chair he had built from the remnants of a confessional booth. The frame was oak, but the lacquer had been singed during the fire of '41, leaving the legs and arms pockmarked and charred. The violet cushions had rather amazingly survived the fire intact, and their stitched velvet was still quite comfortable.

He was alone. Beyond his "room" where the altar had once been, on the other side of the tapestries and veils, the cathedral was already half-empty. Word had spread of the Morrigan's announcement at the Bleecker Street Haven. Most had left to follow the call of the Keeper. Argus had been forced to repose, and to consider his next move.

How much did the Morrigan know? Had she somehow learned of their plot? Most importantly, had the Queen already dealt with Lucifer?

Resting like a Buddha statue, hands lifted upward in the lotus position, the eyes of his face and navel were gently closed. Those on his palms, however, gleamed bright red. They reflected the candle-glows as they peered upward, knowingly.

When the white, luminous liquid fell from the rafters like rain, his hands saw it. They knew not to be alarmed. Argus merely waited in silence as the strange fluid pooled upon the chalky floor, churned within itself, and arose into a human-looking form. Then he opened the rest of his eyes. And he spoke. His final question now had an answer.

"Lucifer. I have been awaiting your return. Interesting choice for an entrance. But given your exit, I expected no less," the ancient shape-shifter began.

Sean waited to respond as the remainder of the liquid around his naked form swirled, and replicated clothing.

Soon he stood before the six-eyed being fully "dressed" in black. Only his overcoat and fedora were missing.

"Where is Vince?"

"You have nothing to fear, Lucifer. Your friend is confused, understandably. But he remains as we found him. We merely needed to bring you back into the fold. We wish to harm no one," Argus said.

His voice was silky and whispering, all the better to match his ghastly visage.

"I want to see him. Then we'll talk," Sean replied.

"Very well. There is no need for hostility," the changeling hissed.

His gestures imbued with an awkward panache, more like an amateur magician than a sage, the ancient being unfurled his stringy arm like a flag. His gleaming fingernails pointed toward a small door at the edge of the altar-room.

Without another word, Sean moved toward the door. His gaze never left Argus, those red eyes blinking one after the other, until he had turned the rusty knob and entered the room that had once been the dressing chamber for the church's priests.

It was dark. His eyes needed a moment to adjust. A brass candelabrum rested on a table at the far end, where a figure sat huddled against the wall. An empty chest of drawers stood silently beside him.

"Vince?" Sean began, in a half-whisper.

At first there was no answer. He was about to try again when the man lifted up his head and looked directly at him. His gaze was cold.

"You're one of them, aren't you?" Vince asked, but it was more like a statement than a question.

"One what?"

"Don't play around with me Sean, not after the crap I've seen lately."

Sean nodded. He stepped fully into the room, closing the door behind him. The scorched hinges creaked as they swung shut.

"I'm sorry Vince."

He wasn't sure what else to say, apologies seemed to be his forte lately.

"Sorry? You're sorry? That don't even come close."

"I never meant for you to get pulled into all this," Sean interrupted, moving closer. Vince remained slumped against the far wall. "You may not believe that, but it's true. If the Morrigan hadn't interfered, I never would have gone to your apartment that night. You never would have known I was here."

Vince dropped his head. He didn't seem to care. Sean kept talking anyway. He needed to keep talking.

"It was all going to be so perfect. Maggie would just disappear. You'd hear about it, of course, but by then there'd have been nothing you could do. You'd never have known how, or with whom. And you'd never have heard from me again."

"Monkey-wrench got tossed into your plans, though, huh?" the ex-cop muttered, without looking up.

"Nicely put. Truth be told, I didn't just show up the other night, I've actually been in New York for several months now. I've been watching you and Maggie both. Quietly. Following you; to the liquor store in the morning, to the bar in the afternoon, back home at night. Watching you squander your pension money. Laughing at you, honestly."

The insult piqued Vince's attention. Insults usually did. Sean remembered that much from the old days.

"No way. Even drunk I could smell a tail a mile away. Just ask these friends of yours who tried to follow me."

"First off, these are not my friends," Sean replied, smiling. "And second, you never saw me because I never wanted you to see me. But I saw you, every single day."

"Yeah?"

Sean made eye contact with his old friend. He found himself enjoying their repartee, it had been a long while since anyone could argue with him the way Vince always had.

"Don't believe me? Try this. You used to buy your morning paper each day from a lanky Italian guy named Joe, then a few months ago there was a new kid on his corner, a Puerto Rican you called *buddy*, there on Thirty-Ninth and Eleventh. Every day he said the same thing."

Sean swallowed, and gathered his breath. When he spoke again, it was in a markedly different voice, a voice all too familiar to Vince.

"Gracias, Meester Vince, good day now."

Vince shook his head. How could he know that? How could that be the same voice, the exact same voice?

"When you were inside the Rock of Cashel pub, you noticed a new fella there, an old Irish guy sitting in the corner. You asked Tommy his name; he told you it was

Whitey Pete. You offered to buy him a beer about three weeks ago, but he just shook his head and walked away."

Vince was getting agitated. He got up from the ash-stained floor.

"How the hell do you know that?"

Sean continued, undeterred.

"Or how about the bum outside the bank where you cashed your check on the third Thursday of every month?"

Sean stepped back then, into the thick of the shadows beyond the reach of the candlelight. Vince could hear him clear his throat again.

A voice that was not Sean's again echoed from the dark.

"Hey sonny, could you spare a dime fer an old fogy?"

When he looked, a tiny old man with a flea-bitten beard poked his head out from the dim into which Sean had retreated only a moment before. Hunched over, but smiling his crooked teeth, he only paused for an instant before slipping back into the gloom.

"You see? It was me. They were all me," Sean's voice said from the dark into which the old man had vanished. A few seconds later, Sean once more stepped out of the void.

"I don't expect you to believe that, of course. I never would have, if I were you. But I really don't care," he said, clearing his throat one last time.

"This doesn't make any sense," Vince was standing beside the table now. His legs were quivering, but he was trying hard not to show it.

"Doesn't it? You have no idea how much sense it makes, old friend. I spent thirty years trying to forget about you, and about Maggie, living a hundred different lives, in a hundred different places. But you know what? It was never the same. It was never me. It was always someone else's life, someone else's love. The only time it was ever real was here. Home sweet home."

"What are you trying to tell me? You want your old life back, after all these years?" Vince replied.

"Not my life. That was never worth much of anything in the first place. No, Vince. I came back for *your life*."

Sean's smile was gone now. His look was deadly serious. Vince's whole body felt faint. It was all he could do to keep standing up. He couldn't even wipe the sweat from his brow.

"I have to admit, I was a little hesitant. Even me. Once I got back here, and I saw what you were doing with it, though, I didn't feel so bad anymore. I mean, hell, if you're just going to piss it away, why shouldn't I take it?"

"You're all nuts. All of you. Frankie was right. I really thought that guy was out of his head, but he wasn't, was he? *Crazy, Vince*, that's what he told me. Guys in robes, dancing in circles around candles like savages or witches or something. A man who looked like a woman, turning into a *thing* with the head of a snake and the body of a wolf, eating a human alive. Then laughing out loud as it became Sam Calabrese? A thing called Morrigan!"

Sean remained unmoved by his friend's outburst. Vince nearly fell down as his emotions overcame him. He was halfway between laughing and crying. Or perhaps he was doing both.

"You're a bunch of sick, twisted *things*!" he finally shouted, collapsing to his knees.

Sean nodded, and he placed a hand on the weeping man's shoulder. He regarded his old friend for a long, quiet moment, his gaze alternating between his own hand and the bare skin of his friend's face.

Finally, he lifted his touch away, as though the contact itself was painful. Then he turned to leave.

"Goodbye Vince," was all he said.

✠   ✠   ✠

"You have had your time with your friend. Now, are you prepared to join with us? We haven't much time. The Morrigan has already gathered the flock. The festival commences as we speak," Argus said as Sean stepped out of the inner chamber.

There was a grim look across his face. He did not even look at the old, old being when he addressed him.

"Go to hell, Argus."

The words came as a shock to the creature who had thought his many ages to have rendered him immune to such a feeling.

"Excuse me?"

Sean did turn to face him then. His own eyes glowed like a leopard's. Feral. Angry.

"You heard me red-eyes. Go to hell."

Sean pushed past him, toward the veil between the altar-chamber and the main hall of the cathedral. Argus rose from his chair. He threw his long, skinny arms outward in disbelief.

"You fool! You can't leave us. Don't you know what the Morrigan will do! What I will do!"

"I do."

"Turn around now, Lucifer. Don't make me harm your friend. Stay with us, or I promise you, your friend will die! He'll die a slow, horrible death."

Sean turned back from the wall of ancient tapestries, and to Argus's terrible chagrin, the ageless Irishman was unmoved. In fact, he was smiling. With both hands outstretched, he opened the veil and called out to the gathered masses. Despite his previous rejection, half of them bowed on sight. The remainder hushed to hear him.

"All of you! Brothers. Sisters. I know that we are of the same kind, in some way at least. And I know that you seek a leader. You seek me," he called out.

"But I tell you today. You do not need me. You do not need the Morrigan, or even Argus the all-seeing. Your lives belong to you! Go out and live them. For that is what I have come here to do. That is the lesson I have come to give you. Argus is wise, but he is not your master. You must find your path on your own, as must we all. That is your true liberation. That is where you will find the freedom you seek. Not in exchanging one ruler for another."

He was greeted by quiet. Not reverent, worshipful quiet. Stony, deafening silence.

"Hear me! I declare this to you now, and forever. I will not take the Keeper's throne!" He turned his back on the gathered, and he faced Argus again. The six-eyed, white-skinned figure was irate. All of his eyes blazed his anger.

"Your friend is doomed," he seethed.

"You still don't understand, do you? Kill him. Do whatever you want. Whatever thrills your deviant little heart. The only thing you'll accomplish is to save me the trouble of doing it myself.

"Good luck, *old friend*," Sean said, his body dissolving into a rising plume of smoke.

The words were spoken in Vince's voice.

BOOK III

"Mysteries and Revelations"

THIRTY-ONE

HE ENTERED HER APARTMENT QUIETLY. THE HOUR was late. The place was dark, and it was still. She might have been asleep, had this been any other cold November night. He half-expected to find her so as he slipped through the crack of the door, somehow heedless of the chain that only allowed it to open six inches wide.

The living room was empty. The shades were drawn shut. The radio was off. Even the bloody sheets were gone from the couch. Carefully, he crept in deeper, toward the kitchen that adjoined it. A moment after he moved from the carpet to the tile, he heard the click of a .38 from behind.

He froze.

"It's me," he said, breathless.

Those two words, that familiar voice, it was all Maggie needed to hear. In a single frantic motion, she lowered her pistol and reached her hand out to his shoulder, spinning him around to look once more at his craggy, stubbly face.

"Vince!" she all but shouted. "Where have you been? What happened! What's going on?"

They were questions, but she threw them at him rapid-fire, like statements in an argument. That way she didn't need to think, because she wasn't sure she'd want to hear the answers.

"It doesn't matter now. It's over," he answered. His stoic calm made a natural contrast to her pure, raw display of emotion. In the long history of their relationship, that was their usual routine.

"What do you mean? What's over? Where is Sean?"

Her words just kept coming. But they seemed to bounce off him. He didn't actually answer any single question.

"Sean got involved with some very unpleasant people. Some very dangerous people. There wasn't anything I could do."

She knew what that meant. He didn't have to say it. But she wanted to hear it anyway. After everything she'd seen over the past few days, or thought she'd seen, because she wasn't really sure of anything anymore, she had to be sure.

"He's . . . ?"

Vince nodded. He sighed as she neared. Saying the words somehow made it official. At least between them.

"Sean is gone."

Maggie wanted to ask a thousand more questions. Why had he come back? Who had gotten to him? What had happened at the church? Those were only the start. But as Vince wrapped his big arms around her, she knew there was no point in asking even a single one.

"We can't stay here," he whispered.

She didn't reply, but he felt her move, felt her lift her head against his chest. He knew she was listening.

"It's still dangerous here. The men who were after Sean aren't finished yet. We'd best get out of their way."

"How long?" she asked.

"Until things cool down. A while, I think, but maybe not so long."

"Where?"

"Does it matter?"

She knew that it didn't.

"I thought I'd lost you, again," she said.

Tears were welling up in her eyes. Vince felt them. They were warm and wet on his dirty shirt.

"I know. You'll never have to worry about that, not anymore. You know I always loved you, through everything. All that I ever wanted was to be with you," he said.

For the first time in a long time, longer than she could recall at the moment, Vince actually seemed sincere. Without smelling of liquor, to boot.

"I never stopped loving you. Promise me you'll never leave me this time," she said, nestling deeper into the folds of his coat, against the hard edges of his chest.

A lump stuck in his throat. He was a long moment in thought before answering, almost long enough for Maggie to notice.

"I promise. But we have to go soon," he finally said.

"How soon?"

"As quickly as you can pack. We can't waste any time."

She lifted her head. She kissed him. They hadn't done that in ages.

"I won't spare a minute," she said.

THIRTY-TWO

THOUGH IT WOULD HAVE SEEMED LIKELY, FOR THE myriad shapes and forms taken by his race, there had never before been a Lycaon recorded on the ancient rolls of Nestor. Not until the Morrigan herself suggested the feral name for the pitiable child-thing she had found wandering along the forested edges of Ghent, in 1814.

It had been the autumn of that year, and the dark queen had been in the Belgian city for nothing more than curiosity's sake. Fortunate for the shaggy young boy, but a stroke of luck for the Keeper as well, as it turned out.

In the guise of a European gentleman, she'd come to observe the mingling "big-wigs" from both sides of the English-speaking Atlantic. Men who had, by that date, only just recently discarded the powdered coiffures that had given rise to such a nickname. The Morrigan had rather lamented that fact, disdainful in general of burgeoning nineteenth-century sensibilities, including the growing distaste for such wonderfully decadent styles as she had worn in her own youth.

Perhaps it was for reasons of that sort that she had

quickly found the negotiations between Britain and her filial realm rather more boring than expected. Thus had she wandered out of the city proper, venturing among the nearby woodlands. There she had stumbled upon a disheveled, growling child, scavenging for food and mumbling in Flemish through pointed teeth.

The boy, she later learned, had been turned loose by his kin like diseased livestock, run out of his village, and cursed as a devil for the peculiar changes that had overcome his pubescent body. That he had not been put to the fire, or impaled by the stake were the boy's only fortunes. Luck of his own making, on four legs he had proven far swifter than the two-legged villagers who had tried to slaughter him. Fodder for one more superstitious European werewolf story, drawn from the tragedy of one more misunderstood dissident of her persecuted race.

At first, it may have been pity that had moved the Keeper to kneel beside the half-molted waif. Sympathy for one of her own kind, in need of her aid. But that was not why the Morrigan had kept the wolf-child close for all the many decades since. In Lycaon the Keeper had found a man-beast of a sort unseen in centuries, a protector for the Protector.

Under the queen's tutelage did the youngster then walk, passing through many forms, every one a powerful incarnation. Unlike his peers, never certain of what form the next year's molting season might bring, the boy Lycaon sprang forth from the cocoon every year strong, never as a child or an elderly person like so many others of his ilk.

But while it had been that raw power which had initially snared the Morrigan's attention, it had been the events of one dark night that had cemented the Phantom Queen's undying trust.

Winter 1827.

The ranks of Nestor's Children had gathered amid the Ottoman splendor of Istanbul, the Morrigan indulging her yen for harem girls and the life of a sultan prince. The grand fete had been marred, however. A plot from within, a scheme hatched by her trusted aide, the erudite Ovid.

It had been the third, and ultimately final, attempt to assassinate her.

The conspiracy would have done her in, had it not been for the loyalty of a single man. The beast Lycaon, by then a fully-grown adult, and a fearsome canine to behold.

When the conspirators had come, they had come prepared. They had not initially struck the Keeper herself, instead trapping her deep within the palace, rising from the harem shadows to attack her renowned guards, Scylla and Charybdis.

Once those two most feared of her protectors had been occupied, and the queen had been cut off from her white-robed Maenad servants, the assassins had turned to the Morrigan. Lycaon alone had remained with her in those moments when the others of her cadre had turned. So it was that in the halls of a dead Turkish king he fought the usurpers to a bloody end. He had nearly perished that night himself, nearly given his life for the being who had once saved his own. For that, he earned the Keeper's undying trust, at her side in a hundred different incarnations through all the many years that followed.

Finally, he had even come to supplant both Scylla and Charybdis, in the wake of their disgrace in the cold Russian winter of 1918.

Now, his time had dawned once again, and Lycaon had sought the refuge of a quiet, shadowy corner of the main warehouse on Pier 33. While the beating of drums, the shouts of revelers and the scents of pungent opium had wafted around him, he had rested.

Rested for all of a single day, and most of the following. Behind a veil of slime and hardened ooze, secreted from his pores like gallons of sticky sweat, his shape had altered. His skin had shriveled, his human face had fallen away, and his true form had begun to emerge.

Then, as night fell again over the shivering city on the Hudson, Lycaon the beast was reborn.

With hands that were more like paws now, he cut through the translucent cocoon that held him suspended against a cobwebbed nook in the wall. He thrust his forelimbs forward and backward, up and down, left and right until the shell cracked and fell away. Lycaon came forth in all his savage splendor.

Something like steam, though utterly foul-smelling and tinged with a yellow glint, huffed from his nostrils. Drops of the urine-like liquid clung to his wet, black nose and dripped from the end of his slender snout and whiskers.

His gray fur was speckled black beneath his eyes and at the edges of his pointed canine ears. Atop his head it grew long like his human hair had, and it fell upon his shoulders, merging with his bushy mane.

A long, fat tail wagged lazily behind as he stood half-erect on his hindquarters. His arms were nearly human, though lined with tufts of fur.

What had not changed were his eyes. The fearsome glare of Indian Joe remained within those dark pupils. Coming forward, he was greeted by a silent figure in a pristine white robe. It was one of the Keeper's personal attendants, the faceless Maenads who stood by the Morrigan's side at all times.

"Lycaon. Are you rested?" the messenger inquired, her features hidden completely beneath a broad mantle.

"I am, thank you," the wolf-thing growled. His fangs were drooling into the sticky, wet fur of his snout. The Maenad did not seem to mind.

"The master has sent word. Scylla remains missing," the servant continued.

Lycaon was still getting his footing, stretching his legs and reacquainting himself with some of the more bestial foibles of his natural form. He had almost grown too used to looking human, acting human. It was going to feel nice to let some of his less-domesticated inclinations run amuck for a while.

"Have we attempted a search?" he questioned.

The mere fact that the Maenad was before him suggested that they had not, and Lycaon felt his heart begin to race with the thought of the hunt. Nothing spurred the desires of a wolf like the thrill of the chase.

And he was hungry too.

"Our human agents have set about the task, but to no avail. There is only one place that we have not been able to check. The Morrigan said that you would know where."

Lycaon snarled as he shook off the last remains of his cocoon, brushing some of the heartier patches of hardened slime from his fur.

"Is it night?"

The messenger nodded, her entire hood moving as she did so.

"Then I will see to it at once," he answered.

THIRTY-THREE

ARACHNE SAT SILENT, ALMOST TRANCE-LIKE. SHE could feel her heart rate slowing. Her skin had become coarse. Every time she ran her hands through her lovely blond hair, clumps of it came loose.

Across the room there rested the body of the one called Rat, partially covered over by the dusty canvas sheet. It did not move, except on the very rare occasions when something seemed to be attempting to poke out from under it. But those episodes usually lasted only a moment or two.

Arachne kept her gaze fixed upon it, as the hours passed slowly, one upon the other, ever so quietly. She knew it would be her turn soon.

She watched the largely still cocoon; she fought hard against it. She regulated her breathing, and made every effort to stay awake. Anything that could maintain her consciousness could help forestall the inevitable. Singing songs out loud, reciting Byron or Shelley, counting the number of water-damaged beige ceiling tiles, and then the number of undamaged ones, and then the number of ones that were only half-stained.

"Just a little longer," she told herself. If she could only hold out until Scylla emerged, she would have fulfilled her promise to Charybdis, and kept safe the one person her mentor cared about more than anything in the world.

"Just a little longer."

Inside the shell, the legendary hunter-killer slumbered for a second day. What had once been a translucent outer husk had clouded during that time, and turned nearly brown in color. Whatever waited within could no longer be seen from outside. Arachne knew what that meant. The molting cycle was almost done.

It was when the layer of gray dust that had settled over the sheet fluttered and shook off that Arachne knew the time had finally come. Scylla was stirring.

It hurt to walk across the room, as though her legs had fallen asleep and would not wake, but she forced herself to endure it. At last, she came to rest on the edge of the bed, directly in front of the cocoon. Tearing the sheet away, she could see that the hard surface of it had already begun to fracture.

Arachne reached into the largest crack, and she pried open a wide break in the outer shell. Underneath, there was a face, but it was not the scraggly visage of the man called Rat. Instead, peering with eyes that were opal-black and sparkling, there stared the face of a beautiful young woman.

She was conscious, but swathed in ooze and muck that radiated a slightly yellowish glow.

"It is an honor to make your acquaintance, great

Scylla," Arachne began. "Allow me to introduce myself."

"Arachne," Scylla whispered before the other could say it herself. The spider-named girl seemed startled.

"You know my name?"

"Charybdis told me," Scylla answered, groggy from her brief hibernation. "We expected you might come into play here, eventually. You are Argus's chief protector, are you not?"

Arachne leaned back, content to allow Scylla to work her way out of the chrysalis. She was so tired. Her extremities tingled with the pointed touch of a thousand pins and needles. She needed to rest.

"I am honored that my reputation precedes me, especially to one as ancient and powerful as you," she replied.

Scylla coughed up some greenish phlegm and cleared her throat. It smelled like rotten meat, which was perfectly normal.

"You are a rare specimen. I'm anxious to see your true form, I've heard it's quite breathtaking," she said.

"Soon," Arachne continued. Scylla pushed out from the inside of her shell. "Did Charybdis tell you that I have modeled myself on your example for years? I have always wanted to meet you. I'm only sorry it happened under these conditions."

"She mentioned that," the bronze-skinned woman replied, slowly working her torso free of the dry husk—with the use of six fully formed arms.

"Only a mention?" Arachne seemed genuinely disappointed, but also too exhausted to make much more than a trifle complaint.

Scylla did not notice. Despite her efforts, she was finding that her lower limbs had become entangled with the dried slime. It was known to happen on occasions when one put off the change too long and fell into the slumber without proper preparation. As Arachne seemed to drift away, sprawled out and exhausted across the bed, Scylla tried to stretch her legs.

They did not come loose. She cursed a very ancient god.

Frustrated, but having not yet lost her patience, she flexed her multiple upper limbs and attempted to force herself out. It appeared that Arachne had become momentarily self-absorbed, having settled into a comfortable position. She didn't even seem to realize Scylla was in a predicament.

"For all my life, since entering my name on the rolls, I have heard the tales of your deeds. How you and Charybdis served for centuries as the twin guardians of the Morrigan. Scylla to her left. Charybdis to her right. Deadly to any who dared defy the Keeper."

"Those days are long gone," Scylla said, with a wince.

"Always I thought that one day I will be as great a warrior as she," Arachne continued, almost as though she were talking only to herself. "But the times of old are long passed away. There are no more empires to rule, and no more primitives to worship us as goddesses."

"They are long gone," Scylla agreed.

Arachne turned from her dreamy state then, and she finally saw Scylla twisting at the waist like a hula dancer, furiously trying to shed the lower half of her cocoon.

"Oh, how foolish of me. My apologies," she said.

She got up, with great difficulty, and slinked over to where she had been sitting earlier. From her coat, set down on the chair, she retrieved a blade. It was like a long hunting knife, or possibly a very short sword. The single edge of it glinted, obviously sharpened to a razor-edge.

Arachne turned back to Scylla, dreading the return trip across the little room. Every moment left her more and more drained. *If she kept talking,* she thought, *maybe that would keep her awake long enough to free Scylla.*

"I have watched over you, so that you might molt without harm, and soon I will take my own rest, but before I do, might you indulge me one thing?" she asked, dragging her legs in Scylla's direction like they were tied to boulders.

"Whatever you wish."

"Your fall from grace. Charybdis would never discuss it. You two were once the greatest of us all, next to the Morrigan herself. Inseparable and glorious. Yet you have not seen Charybdis for decades, and you no longer occupy the guardianship of the Keeper."

"Is your single wish to torment me in this captive state?" Scylla joked.

Arachne was too tired to appreciate the humor.

"No, I would like merely to know *how.* How came you and Charybdis both to fall so far from the favor of the Keeper?"

Toweling off her exposed torso with her lower arms, Scylla raised her four upper limbs, and breathed deep and long. She spoke while her legs continued to squirm, with anger that had nowhere to go.

"We failed the Morrigan. And we have been punished for it ever since. Forbidden to speak, or to even see one another until our failure has been remedied, for all these long, long years."

"And now you mean to do so? To correct some old mistake?"

"No." The reply was simple. "It appears that our failure will go un-reconciled. I only fear that Charybdis has not now led me to some new mistake which will eclipse our previous transgression."

Arachne was now before her, the gleaming blade poised.

"You don't believe in the Prophecy of Lucifer?" she asked, cutting at the hard substance that entombed Scylla's legs.

"On the contrary, I think no one believes it more than I do. I've lived it. For the last thirty years I've hunted him, the most elusive man in the world. But now that I am within reach of my goal, I have yielded to the whim of my lost-beloved."

"I suppose we'll do almost anything for love," Arachne answered.

She had made a cut, but needed to chop at it to break the crystalline material.

Just then, however, a furry claw gripped the outside windowsill, and then a second. Neither Arachne nor the preoccupied Scylla noticed the intrusion. A moment later, Lycaon's snout poked in through the open window, right at the moment that Arachne hacked her hardest into the lower section of Scylla's imprisoned form.

The beast raged. He did not pause for a moment to consider.

Teeth bared, paws outstretched, Lycaon surged from the open window with a growl. Arachne saw him, but her reflexes were slow, the change had dulled her senses. She did not react in time to defend herself.

His swipe caught her across the chest, tearing her flesh and drawing blood. The blade went flying out of her hands.

Scylla screamed.

A second slash landed on Arachne's jaw. Spared the sharp nails by only a fraction of an inch, the force of the blow was still enough to send her reeling.

Her head tilted backward as she fell. When she struck the floor, a long cut opened, spilling red onto the dirty carpet. She was out cold before the blood really flowed.

Satisfied, Lycaon turned, but he found even his own bestial heart sink when he saw Scylla.

Arachne's blade had flung loose, and plunged deep into her gut.

✤ ✤ ✤

The sun had been set for some time. The city had once again fallen into a shadowy freeze when Charybdis returned to the lights of Times Square, and the room where she had last seen Scylla.

Her middle-aged, West African features were gone now. Only her lanky, thin frame remained to suggest her former attributes, and she had already taken a few moments to shave the hair from her head when she had emerged from the slumber. Other than those details, her appearance, like all those of her kind, had altered radically in the space of little more than thirty-six hours.

Now she was pale. Her skin wasn't snow-white, although the blood surging beneath it lent her a rosy shade, which was especially evident in her eyes and her fingernails. Her face was angular, with a hard chiseled jaw-line that looked more male than female, although her anatomy was certainly of the latter. That aspect of her current form was a bane she had long ago learned to tolerate, but had never embraced.

She opened the door without a key. It was a skill she had learned in Vienna, during the time before she had come under Argus's sway, prone in those younger days to life on the fringes of the law.

It was immediately clear upon entry that the place had been ransacked. The nightstand and its Bible had been overturned, and the one chair in the room had lost two legs. The bed was soiled with some dark liquid, maybe blood; the filth of the sheets made it hard to say. In the middle of the carnage, the sticky remains of the cocoon sat empty. It was as though the shell was waiting, patiently, undisturbed by the violence that had evidently erupted all around it.

Of Scylla and Arachne, though, there was no other sign.

✤ ✤ ✤

She had traveled back to the church quickly, but in her heart, Charybdis sensed that her long wait might finally be over. Perhaps the end had now come for she and Scylla.

Argus was watching for her. He approached as soon as she entered.

"Has something gone wrong?" Argus asked. If she weren't already deathly pale, he might have noted how sickly she looked.

"I've lost her, again," was the only reply she could manage.

"Scylla? What do you mean?"

"I should have been there; I should never have let Arachne stand in my place. We are the cursed Argus, all of us cursed by this damned affliction!"

It was not the first time in his long life that Argus had heard such sentiment. But never from Charybdis, one of his most studious pupils. He attempted counsel.

"Settle yourself, you must explain."

They sat down then, out in the open of the cathedral, like penitent and clergy. In all the centuries of her Church, however, no such figures as these had ever conversed under the sanction of Rome.

"I ventured out to the hotel where I had left Scylla in her cocoon. Arachne had volunteered to watch over her while I underwent the change."

Charybdis was clearly upset, but she maintained her poise. It was the way she had been taught that a man always acts, many years ago, when she was still a child.

"And?"

"They're both gone. There were signs of a fight, furniture overturned, broken glass from the lamps. Some blood was left on the floor, and stray tufts of Arachne's hair as well. But other than the remains of Scylla's cocoon, there was nothing. No way to tell where they had gone, or why they had left."

"The Morrigan must have known of Scylla's whereabouts. And if she has Arachne, she may now know of ours."

"What shall we do, master? It would seem our plans have come to naught. Lucifer has left us, and now we may have been exposed to the Keeper."

The wise old creature did not appear nearly as upset as his younger protégé, and he answered with a calm nod.

"Speak with Mr. Sicario again."

Charybdis shook her head.

"Why?"

"Lucifer may be done with us, but I do not think we are entirely finished with him yet."

THIRTY-FOUR

THE CATHEDRAL HAD ALMOST CLEARED OUT. THE IN-
vitation of the Morrigan, and the rejection by Lucifer had
drawn many of Argus's followers away. Most had already
departed to the announced gathering place, leaving only
the stragglers to keep the ancient one company in his fire-
ruined palace. Among the eaves and the rafters there hung
the remains of their strange transformations, cocoon shells
and dried slime interspersed between the masonry.

Perhaps because there were so few of them still left in
the place, or perhaps simply out of frustration, Argus had
now released Vince from his "prison" in the room beside
the altar. The wounds from his encounter with Scylla still
hobbled him, though. As much as he desired to flee, he
could barely yet walk.

In any case, the gaze of the pale figure who sat day and
night on that chair atop the altar was on him at all times.
Even if he could have run, he knew that Argus would see
him. Somehow, the bizarre creature never seemed to
sleep. At least two of those glaring red eyes were open at
every hour.

So Vince found himself left to watch the few figures that remained in the church. Some were still in the process of emerging from their slumber, others simply milled about, gathering their things and periodically coming and going through the hole in the floor at the cathedral's center.

One in particular caught Vince's attention as she wandered through the aisle between emptying pews. Unlike the many, many strange things he had seen since first being brought to the surreal place, she was human-looking, and eerily statuesque, as though some hidden god had breathed life into a forgotten Bernini or Canova, liberating the form from its marble confines. She was, like many others, bare as a newborn, though utterly careless of the fact as she walked in plain sight. He marveled as he watched her every move, walking with a delicate, smooth stride as fluid as the river waters that rushed along not so far away.

For a long time he stood idle at the foot of the altar, in the shadow of the half-toppled Eucharistic offertory, studying her, captivated by her every gesture. So enrapt was he in fact, that he neither heard nor saw the mollusk-like creature that slithered up beside him.

"You should find your place, my friend. The last of us will be leaving soon," it said, in a voice that was deeper than any he'd ever heard before, though enunciated with the accent and diction of one well versed in the King's English.

Vince did not respond. He had already grown immune to the very bizarre things that circulated through the church. Or maybe he'd just become numb all over, he didn't know. Whatever the case, he wasn't the least bit startled by the slimy, gray-skinned being that was now beside him. He was a bit sickened, however, by the pair of flittering stalks that grew from his face, each one crowned by a disturbingly conscious eye.

"Hmm. I know him. His name is Medea," the British snail-thing said, his soft yellow underbelly distending as he spoke.

"What? No, I'm looking at *her*," Vince said, pointing toward the woman.

The shell-less mollusk laughed. He nodded the best he could with his oversized and altogether unwieldy head.

"I know. That's who I'm talking about. He's lovely isn't he?" it replied.

"I'm sure I don't know what you mean. What are you trying to say, that *that is man*?" Vince answered, forced to hold back the nausea in his gut when he finally looked full on at the slug-beast.

It laughed, and placed a flipper-like appendage on Vince's shoulder, unaware that its very sight repulsed him.

"You must be new. I'm sorry. I remember my first one too. Quite a shock isn't it?"

Vince stared back blankly.

"I'm called Glaucus. And you are?" it said smiling, sort of.

"Vince. At least that's what my friends call me. My parents named me Vincenzo, but no one's called me that in years."

"So it is your first time then. Well, we'll have to see to it that you shed that human name, and take one among your own kind."

Vince ignored the statement; he was too fixated on the *woman*.

"Medea, you say? Why do you keep calling her a man?" he asked.

"Because that's what he is, or at least was, and likely will be again," Glaucus replied. He was clearly enjoying his chance to tutor someone unversed in the ways of his folk.

"She used to be a man?"

Charybdis joined them then, from behind. Nearly naked herself, the peculiar albino beauty of her true form was laid bare for all to see. She was tall, with lanky limbs that seemed to dangle off her. A soft white aura, pure as new-fallen snow, radiated from her skin, perhaps cast beneath a perpetual spotlight. And while clearly possessed of the delicate features of a young woman, her black hair was close-cropped and manly.

"In a manner of speaking, I suppose you could say she used to be a man," she said, careful to step between Vince and the slime-trailing thing. "Gender is a very dicey subject among our kind. Honestly, most of us really don't consider ourselves one sex or the other, but I always found that a little too shifty."

"Charybdis? Is that you?" Glaucus interrupted.

His eye-stalks arched to get a good look at her. He was a little startled by the ashen-pale woman who wore only a folded gray cloak.

"Indeed, old friend," she replied, with a wave of her very long hand. "My true self has returned."

"Very well. Vincenzo, have you met our master's chief aide, Charybdis?" Glaucus asked.

"We have met, yes," Charybdis said, answering for Vince. "But I'd doubt that Mr. Sicario would recall. I had not yet entered the cocoon at the time. He saw me as the African female I had been since the last molting."

Glaucus gave the best nod he could with his strange head.

"But, my own image aside, you were speaking of Medea, were you not?" Charybdis said.

"Oh yes," Glaucus continued. "Medea happens to share my own view of things. He was born male if I'm not mistaken, and if I remember correctly, he ends up male more often than not at the end of every molting season. It's just during this time of the year, when he reverts back to his *natural form* that he appears female. And quite beautiful, as you've obviously noticed."

"So he was born a man, but he changes back into a woman every year?" Vince questioned.

"Exactly. His name is female, Medea was a woman in the old Greek tales, but that really has no significance here," Charybdis answered. "I suppose he could consider himself female, but I believe he had much the same experience as I had. Both he and I formed our identities as males before we entered our first molting, in our late teens. Like him, I still prefer the trappings of manhood, despite my present appearance."

"I never woulda guessed that," Vince answered.

"Don't worry, you're new, you'll get used to it," Glaucus

answered. "Look at me. I'm much the same."

Vince cocked his head at the suggestion, somewhat bemused. His grotesque new friend was hardly offended.

"I don't mean literally, of course," he chided. "I too have spent several years, 1937, 1921, 1886, oh yes now *that* was a good year, all as a woman. The point is that I have been female many times myself. Most of us have been at one time or another.

"And I was quite a lovely little lady too, if I do say so myself," Glaucus said.

Charybdis laughed, but her mirth was not long lived.

"My friend, I wonder that I might have a word alone with this new one?" she offered.

"Of course," Glaucus replied, obviously deferential to the stern-looking albino. "I shall take my leave then, and wish you the best of luck Mr. Vincenzo. Perhaps we will meet again."

"Right," Vince answered as it skulked away, leaving a glistening, sticky film in its wake.

"I do apologize for that. This must be very strange for you, I realize," Charybdis said, offering him a seat as she reclined on the altar steps. Her legs were as long and skinny as her arms. She seemed to stretch out over half the steps when she leaned over.

"You could say that," he replied, still fairly numb, even in conversation.

"Perhaps I should attempt to explain," she said.

"Explain . . . this?" he asked, smirking.

"That may be a little much. And to be honest, the less

you know, the better it will be for you. You've already seen far too much as it is," she answered.

"Then what?"

"Your importance to us, to Argus. We have no wish to harm you, despite what you may have heard Argus say. He has only kept you here for your own safety, and to bring Lucifer closer to us."

"Okay," it was all he could think to say, pretty much anything sounded reasonable under the current circumstances.

"You have known Lucifer for a long time, yes?"

Vince stared back blankly. Charybdis understood his puzzlement.

"Of course, he's not Lucifer to you, is he? Sean, then. You have known him for many years."

"You could say that, I guess. I knew him years ago. I thought I did anyway. We grew up together, same neighborhood, you know? But he left during the War, the first war. I hadn't seen him since, not until a few days ago."

Charybdis smiled, and she laughed.

"Somethin' funny about that?" Vince questioned.

"No. He was one of us once, as well. Many years ago. But he left our fold too. Lucifer does not like to stay in one place for very long."

"Lucifer. Why do you call him that?"

"That is his name among us, among his kind."

Vince again did not respond, except to furrow his brow and fix a silent stare into her eyes.

"Surely by now you must have guessed that you are not

among ordinary folk."

"You don't look so strange, a little pale maybe, but noth-in' compared to that last guy or the fella with all the eyes."

"Argus, yes. He is truly an unusual specimen, even among us. As for myself, however I appear to you now is merely a phase, a temporary form. In a matter of days, this will pass away again. Not a moment too soon, as well, I can assure you."

"What the hell are you people?"

The comment was half-intended as an insult. But to Vince's surprise, Charybdis took no offense. In fact, she grinned.

"That's debatable. Depends on who you talk to," she answered. "Argus believes that we are a noble and ancient race, banished from our rightful place in the world, and destined to return to our former glory one day. The Mor-rigan on the other hand, she seems to think that we exist only to serve her."

"And you?" the answer had hardly satisfied Vince's curiosity, but he still wasn't sure if he wanted to know any more.

Charybdis sneered, and she sighed.

"No one has ever been much interested in my opinion, except perhaps for Lucifer. If you care then, I'll tell you what I told him. I say we are a cursed lot, the damned walking si-lently among the saved, to put it in the Christian vernacular."

"And what did he think?"

"When I knew him I suspect he might have agreed with me. He was a wretch in those days, lost and more scared of himself than anything else. Argus and I found him, *rescued him* according to the ancient one. He stayed with us, at our Haven in Prague, for almost a year."

"Prague, huh? As in Czechoslovakia? What the hell was he doing there?"

"Wandering, drinking, causing trouble."

"Sounds like Sean."

"As closely as were able to discern, he came to Europe in 1917 as a part of the American Expeditionary Force, but he left his unit during the War. He first came to our attention in St. Petersburg."

"Florida?"

"Russia, what they're calling Leningrad today."

"Guy got around, didn't he?"

"Indeed. He left quite an impression as well, as you might imagine. I sit here today because of him, in fact," Charybdis said.

"Really?"

"Again, a rather long story. In any case, after Russia we lost track of him ourselves for nearly six years, until he wandered quite accidentally into Argus's jurisdiction, which used to be Prague."

"He'd just been walking around in Europe since 1917?"

"Apparently so. He was never willing to discuss it much, and I was perhaps the closest person to him at the Haven."

"Haven? There's that word again, as in the Bleecker Street Haven?"

"Yes, our safe-house in New York. We have them all over the world, places for our kind to rest, and to do various other things."

"What *other* things did you do there?" Vince asked, with a wink.

"Nothing as sinister as you may be thinking, my friend," Charybdis answered, a smile on her own lips. "We tried to teach him the ways of our kind, our history, and our traditions."

"What happened?"

"He was reluctant at first, then he seemed to accept some of what we had to show him, but it always seemed to me that he never really wanted to be among his own kind, he never felt like one of us. Argus ignored my worries. I thought we were becoming close, he and I, but then one day, he simply vanished."

"Vanished?"

"Yes, Lucifer you see, has some rather, *unique* abilities."

Vince laughed. This time it was Charybdis's turn to be confused.

"Do you know something about that?" she asked.

"What you're talkin' about? Not a clue. But unique is the right word for Sean, you hit that one on the nose."

"Tell me."

"It's kind of a long story."

"Have we anything but time?"

Vince could not argue.

"Well, okay. Sean was always a wild one. We used to fight all the time, when we were kids, you know? Our buildings were close to each other, about a block away. But his was on Thirty-Eighth, which was a mick block, and mine was on Thirty-Ninth Street, at the time one of the few Italian areas of Hell's Kitchen. So naturally, we hated each other."

"Oh, naturally," Charybdis replied. She didn't quite understand, but the logic seemed to make sense to Vince.

"He was kind of a small kid, we were about the same age, but I was much bigger than him. Anyway, there was always a lot more micks in the Kitchen than guineas like me, especially in those days; we're talking about 1910 or so here. They didn't like us movin' into their neighborhood, and we had it out with them guys almost every day. Sean, even though he was a little punk, he was a loudmouth, and he took a beatin' all the time. From me personally quite few times, in fact. Stubborn little jerk never gave up, though, didn't matter how much you pounded on his ass one day, he'd be back the next day still calling you a dumb dago right to your face."

"Yes, difficult man to discourage, isn't he?" Charybdis echoed.

"Right. So then there's this one day, we've got to be about eleven or twelve by then. My mother, God rest her soul, was sick, couldn't leave the apartment. But she couldn't miss lighting a candle at the church every day for my grandmother, who had just died back in Sicily. So she had me go all the way over to Holy Cross every day after school to light one for her. Problem was, I had to run through a big mick neighborhood to get there and back. And every day, there's Sean, chasin' after me, callin' me names with all of his little shanty Irish buddies from the corner.

"So one day, I'm just fed up, and I stop runnin'. They catch up to me in an alley, and me and Sean have it out. It's just me you know, and him with all his dirty mick friends, but we fight one on one, fair fight all the way."

"How honorable of you," Charybdis interjected. Vince ignored him, since the sarcasm was lost on him anyway.

"Funny, I remember that no matter how hard I hit him, he just kept comin' back at me, and damn if he didn't hit hard for a little twelve-year-old potato-eater. Crazy thing is, he was smilin' through the whole thing. I'd whack him as hard as I could, and he'd shake it off, laugh, and then wallop me right back.

"This goes on for almost an hour. Finally, I'm dead tired. I catch him off-guard. I get him once in the gut, and while he's doubled over, I crank him across the jaw. He goes down in a heap.

"That's when his buddies jump in. Three or four of them, all older and bigger than me. One gets me wrapped up with a chain, right around my neck, and another's got a broken bottle. They're passin' some swill around, laughin' as they try to decide how they're gonna mess me up. I'm chokin', I can hardly breathe, and they're about to cut me.

"That's when Sean got up. I'll tell you, I still don't know why he did it, but I never much cared. In about a minute he had all of those micks off of me, and Sean told me to get lost. I didn't waste any time."

"Interesting story," Charybdis said.

"Yeah, but there's more. The next day, Sean comes down my street. Anybody else, any other time, and me

and my paisans woulda killed him. But I owed him in a
funny sort of way, and I let him talk. He actually apolo-
gized for his friends, and told me that he always fought fair
and that if I wanted to take a free shot at him, that was
okay by him."

"And?"

"And we've been friends ever since."

"So you didn't take a shot at him?"

"Of course I did. But like I said before, that little mick
was so tough, nothing could ever really hurt him.

"We were buddies for years after that, he even intro-
duced me to the girl I ended up marrying."

"Margaret."

The fact that Charybdis knew her name snapped
Vince right out of his nostalgic funk. A slap of cold water
right in the face.

"How did you know that?" he demanded.

Charybdis sensed his discomfort. She tried to calm him.

"Lucifer told me, in Prague. He said that was why he
left."

"Yeah. I bet he did. But now he's back, isn't he? And
now he's got Maggie all to himself, finally."

Charybdis looked up. She saw Argus gesture toward
her from the altar. Politely, she excused herself from Vince's
company, dazed though it was, and made her way to the
ancient one's side.

"I would allow you more time, but we haven't the
luxury," Argus said. "What were you able to learn?"

"Very little. He's not entirely coherent. I think he

believes Lucifer has run off with his wife," she replied, with a wry smile.

"Don't dismiss him too quickly, Charybdis. Perhaps there is something to that," Argus said.

"What do you wish to do?"

"Lucifer has called my bluff. That leaves only one option. You'll need to make contact with the Morrigan. I had hoped to avoid a repeat of the events in Venice, but now it seems we are left with no other choice."

"What have you in mind?" Charybdis asked.

"Go to the Morrigan. Tell her of my betrayal. Tell her that you once thought me wise, but that you have now seen the error of my course," Argus said.

"But master, I can't . . ." she answered.

"You must. Doubtless she now realizes that I am aligned against her. This is the only way. You must regain her trust. Despite our young trickster's belief, the Morrigan will not stop her pursuit until one of them is dead.

"I suspect that she has plans in the works as we speak. You must learn what they are, insinuate yourself into them and protect Lucifer from harm. If we can show Sean Mulcahy the folly of disregarding the Morrigan, we may have one last chance to use him for our ends."

THIRTY-FIVE

THE "THRONE OF THE KEEPER" WAS A FIGURATIVE seat. There had not been a literal, honorary chair as such since the true throne had been lost amid the chaos of the early Holy Roman Empire.

Yet as the day dawned across Manhattan, the Morrigan presided like a dark queen, perched upon a seat that was of her own crafting. It was a high-backed chair of bronze and iron, sunbursts carved beside the headrest, with white Chinese silk sewn over the cushions. Coated in gold from the cache of a Sultan, studded with gems from the vault of a Tsar, it was a testament to the many lives she had led among the human world, and a statement to those *others* who were her subjects. She was their lord. Both king and queen, emperor and empress, powerful, watchful, and above all, beautiful.

With eyes that were flame-red and gleaming, she regarded the festival beneath. Her thin, lithe frame draped in a silken mantle, the being who had now shed the bloated form of Salvatore Calabrese rested atop a broad platform at the far end of the warehouse, which itself had been utterly transformed.

The empty ruin was now a raging, bacchanalian paradise.

Joyous mayhem reigned through a haze of hashish smoke and squeals of deep delight, the blissful chaos the Morrigan so loved. Hedonistic excess spilled out in every direction. Figures both beautiful and hideous cavorted in orgiastic glee, spread among the many gatherings scattered throughout the cavernous expanse.

At the center of it all, a brood of naked celebrants slithered amongst one another, their skin oiled and slick. Limbs and fingers, legs and tails intertwined in fluid entanglements, dreamily captive to the rhythm of a hypnotic dance. Their every lascivious gesture called out cheers from their fellows, as the pace of their waltz ebbed and flowed to the notes of a twisted orchestra.

Stationed at the base of the Keeper's stage, they were the strangest collection of musical talent ever assembled. A pair of headless violinists joined their melodies with the notes from a trio of faceless cellists. A woman with four arms and four hands played two string instruments in unison, producing delicately interwoven sounds the likes of which no human ear had ever heard. A green-skinned woman who had no hands played the flute together with a yellow-skinned man who had no mouth. At their lead was a leonine creature who fiercely plucked the strings of a lyre with his spotted tail.

A snarl from the left broke the mood of the party, however, alerting the Keeper to a sudden disturbance. A moment later it came again, more like a howl the second time, a familiar sound to the glowing Morrigan. It was the growl of Lycaon, and it was not a pleasant sound.

The wolf-faced aide appeared amid the crowd, having just passed through the dark gates wherein the fearsome Daughters of Cerberus stood endless watch. The Morrigan took note of him at once, even before he reared on his thick hindquarters and bounded to the pinnacle of the Keeper's platform in three great leaps.

It was only then, as Lycaon came to rest on one knee before the black-haired regent, that the Morrigan saw he was not alone. Clutched among his hairy forelimbs were two unconscious figures. On his right he clung to the bloodied, half-molted form of Arachne. Her body, while partially covered in hardening self-secreted slime, looked to have already been ravaged.

His left arm held Scylla, free from the cocoon and clearly a woman of surpassing features. She was unclothed, her skin bronze and flawless, her pose elegant even braced limply in the arms of the beast.

For all the beauty of her thin frame and her soft face, however, those were not her most striking attributes. What garnered the Keeper's attention were her arms, all six of them, arrayed from her shoulders like a Hindu goddess.

A swatch of blood-soaked linen was tied hastily over the wound in her middle.

The Morrigan arose from her seat with a start. She recognized Scylla at once, for though she had last seen her only a few days earlier, it had been years since she'd seen the changeling's true form.

"Scylla, lovely Scylla. What has befallen you?" she said, though only Lycaon could hear her.

"She is not dead. But I fear her time may be short," the wolf-thing answered as he set her down.

A wave of his clawed hand brought forward a cadre of the white-robed adherents from the foot of the Keeper's platform. The forms of the Maenads, however hideous or lovely, were all hidden by their heavy woolen shrouds. In a silent march they took up a circle around Lycaon and the Morrigan, turning their backs and shutting out all view of the Keeper, her trusted aide, and the two fallen women.

When the Morrigan placed her graceful hand over her face, a warm light illuminated her features. Scylla's opal eyes opened slowly.

"My apologies, master," she began. "I have failed you again."

"Unnecessary, but accepted nonetheless. Can you tell us how this terrible thing befell you?" the Morrigan asked.

"Lucifer . . . I have sought Lucifer . . ." she answered, delirious. Her midsection was swathed in Lycaon's poorly wrapped bandages. The blood loss had rendered her senseless.

"I believe Argus is to blame," Lycaon said.

"Argus?" the Keeper inquired.

"You sought proof of his treachery, now we have it. The ancient one has betrayed us," Lycaon said. "When I came to her, this other one, Arachne was attempting to kill her. A younger member of our fold, she was Argus's most recent aide and guard."

Their attention turned for a moment to the body of the motionless blonde.

"Do we know of the ancient one's location?" the Morrigan asked, her hand stroking Scylla's brow gently as she fell out of consciousness.

"He is not at the Bleecker Street Haven, and appears to have been gone from there for some time. We still have no idea where he has set his lair within the city. We do not know where he hides, or how many of his followers hide with him."

"And Charybdis?"

"I have no information about her, only that she has been with Argus since he arrived here. Of her part in this plot I cannot say, though I have my suspicions."

"Indeed, we must locate her now."

"And of this one?" Lycaon asked. He was itching to sink his claws into Arachne's flesh. "I would take it as a personal honor if you allowed me to kill her myself."

"No," came the quiet reply.

"My queen!"

"Take some pause, loyal servant," the Morrigan said, the light faded from her touch, as the life continued to ebb from Scylla's wounded belly. "This one will suffer, of that you need not worry. But her agony will be for my gain. If she is Argus's trusted aide, she may prove useful to me. Even if she doesn't know it just yet."

THIRTY-SIX

Maggie's doorbell rang, and she jumped.

Vince was in the bedroom packing a suitcase. He appeared in the foyer a moment later. His gun was already drawn from his shoulder holster. He cocked it slowly, with minimal sound.

They did not speak. Both knew, of course, that few killers were in the habit of ringing the doorbells of their prospective victims. But it was prudent to be cautious. With a nod, he eased her behind him. She receded toward the hallway that led to the bathroom.

Vince cleared his throat with as little noise as he could, and he stepped up to the door. He did not unlatch it.

"Who's there?" he began.

The voice on the other side seemed to recognize him.

"Vince? It's me, Paddie. Let me in, we need to talk."

"Paddie?" he responded, suggesting he'd never heard the name before.

Maggie kept watching, wondering what Vince was doing. She hadn't seen Pat Flanagan for years, but even she remembered his gravely, two-pack-a-day voice.

"Paddie? What is this? Very funny, Vince. Detective Flanagan, maybe? How'd you like that? What did you go soft in the head since I seen you last?"

Vince did not answer. Instead he looked back at Maggie. She nodded, though she couldn't imagine why Vince was seeking *her permission* to let *his* ex-partner into the apartment.

Finally, he unfastened the deadbolt, leaving the chain in place. Then he slowly opened the door as far as it would go. Pat's ruddy Irish face was peering in.

"See? It's me old pal. Just me."

Vince exhaled deeply, closed the door enough to undo the chain and allowed the man to enter.

"Sorry. But we can't be too careful these days," he said, closing the door behind Pat only a moment after he stepped inside.

"You're tellin' me? As bad as it is now, it looks like things are about to get a whole lot worse. It ain't safe for you and Maggie here anymore."

The door closed and relocked, Vince stepped past the others and sat down in an armchair near the window. As Maggie offered the detective a seat on the couch, he kept one eye on Pat and the other on the street beyond.

"That's what I've been trying to tell her. We need to get outta here," Vince agreed, the silvery steel of his revolver still displayed prominently in his hands.

"Mind if I smoke?" Pat asked.

Maggie shook her head.

"Vince, you want one?" he offered.

Vince lifted his head away from the street below, took a glance at the open pack of Parliaments his ex-partner was holding in his direction and nodded. He took out a cigarette and let Pat light it for him.

"Has something happened?" Maggie asked.

"Somethin' is always happenin' around here, Maggie," Pat answered, after a long first drag. "This is different. Some of my guys went by the Sunset Club this morning. Place was deserted. Sam mentioned somethin' about making some changes last time I saw him, but the joint is closed down completely now. No sign of anyone from the Calabrese crew."

"Isn't that good news? If they're all gone, I mean," Maggie asked.

"Not necessarily," Vince said.

"Especially if you two are mixed up with them somehow. Whoever's after them might be lookin' for you too."

"I thought this was about Sean," Maggie said, her words clearly directed toward Vince. The ex-cop said nothing.

"And Sean would be that friend you keep *not talkin'* about, Vince?" Pat chided.

Again, Vince said nothing. Pat turned back toward Maggie.

"Whatever's goin' on, we know this. It's bigger than any one person. Calabrese's people have been disappearin' for months now," he continued. "Little Frankie Pentone was the first to go, rumor is Rocco Gallucci ain't comin' back anytime soon either. Then we got this mutilated, still unidentified corpse from a few days ago, plus Paulie, Gino, and the Vig—all dead outside your place, Vince.

"And here's somethin' else that's funny. I talked to the Medical Examiner this morning. He says he don't even know what killed Paulie Tonsils. Can't pinpoint a cause of death. Says the guy just stopped breathing, all his organs just shut down at once. Like somebody sucked the life right out of him. Any idea how that happened, old buddy?"

Vince continued to sit quietly. His expression remained as stoic as always.

"Must've been havin' a really bad day," he answered, almost smiling.

"Right, you can say that again. Anyway, we gotta get you two outta here, ASAP."

He pronounced the abbreviation as though it were an actual word.

"What did you have in mind?" Maggie asked.

"We got a safe-house up north of Rockland, 'bout an hour, hour-and-a-half from the city. DA uses it from time to time to keep witnesses under wraps before big trials. Sometimes we use it too, bring guys up there for a little, off the record interrogation. Right, Vince?"

"Sure. I'm always up for a little sight-seeing," he joked, getting up from the chair and walking back into the bedroom.

"How soon can we leave?" Maggie asked, ignoring Vince's sarcasm as he left the room.

"I'll set it up down at the station. We can be on the road by late tonight," he replied.

"Fine. I'll let Vince know, but he's been anxious to

leave. I'm sure he'll be ready," she said.

"Okay, I'll make the arrangements," Pat said, getting up to head for the door. He stopped just before exiting. "If you don't mind me sayin' Maggie, I can't remember the last time Vince even tried sayin' anything funny."

"So what?" she replied.

"Nothin', I guess. He just don't really seem like himself tonight, that's all."

Charybdis was nervous. She knew Argus's plan was nothing more than a last-ditch gamble, and one that required her to expose herself to their enemies.

To that end, she had come to the appointed meeting place. It was a West Side rail yard, deserted at night, but near enough to the river that the clanking from the docks made it anything but quiet. Wrapped in a tattered blanket, she would have looked like any other homeless woman, were it not for her stark white skin and jet-black crew cut.

She smelled the Morrigan's messenger coming before she saw him, or even heard him. The stench of canine feces and dog-breath assaulted her.

Finally, Lycaon sprang into view. A litter of stray cats hissed and scampered away when he landed.

"I have bad news," the wolf-man began, wasting no time. "Scylla is dead."

Charybdis breathed heavily, several times. She wasn't sure how to respond. She wasn't sure how much Lycaon knew, or how truthful he was apt to be under the circumstances. The grip on her dagger tightened beneath her makeshift cloak.

"I'm sorry. I know how much she meant to you," the wolf-beast continued.

"We were close once, for many years. As close as two of our kind can possibly ever be. Had we been human we might have grown old together by now," she replied.

"She was killed by Arachne. We caught the spider-girl in the very act of it. We believe your friend Argus tracked her down and ordered her to kill Scylla while still in the cocoon.

"She did so, and by my hand she lost her own life in the process," Lycaon concluded.

"Argus is not my friend," she said, explained the details that the ancient one had fabricated for her. She hoped her tone was convincing. The news about Scylla had shaken her.

"Did Scylla manage to tell you how Arachne had subdued her in the first place? She was one of the most resourceful killers I've ever known, anyone has ever known," Charybdis questioned.

She cursed under her breath. Was it a ruse? Had their plan somehow been betrayed? Or had their gamble failed, and her lover truly was dead? Ever in control of her emotions, her face betrayed none of her feelings.

"She did not live long enough to tell," Lycaon reported. "But we do know this: before she was lost to us, Scylla had tracked and captured Vince Sicario, the human friend of Lucifer."

"Did you find him as well?" Charybdis already knew that they hadn't.

"No, but we think we know why. The Morrigan's agents are in the process of correcting that as we speak."

"I don't understand," Charybdis replied, the first honest thing she'd said since their conversation had begun.

"He likely escaped while Arachne and Scylla fought. A source among Sam Calabrese's associates has informed the Morrigan that Mr. Sicario is now in hiding with his estranged wife, Margaret. Together they are planning to flee from the area."

Now Charybdis was puzzled. She knew Vince was safe and secure in Argus's lair. How could the man be in two places at once?

Almost as soon as the question occurred to her, it practically answered itself.

"And you believe that if you apprehend Sicario, you will soon find Lucifer?" Charybdis answered, the absolute truth of that statement now utterly clear to her, if not to Lycaon.

"The Morrigan is convinced of it."

"What does she ask of me? My blade is at her service."

"She expected that you might wish to have a hand at avenging the death of Scylla," Lycaon answered. "The Keeper is assembling her death guard, to hunt down and seize both Sicario and his wife. We could use one more reliable warrior. If you wish, of course."

Charybdis paused. Was it a set-up? She still had no idea how much the Morrigan knew, or whether Lycaon's report of Scylla's demise was true.

"I would consider it an honor, and I would extend my humble thanks to the Keeper for the opportunity," she finally replied.

"I will pass your sentiment along," Lycaon said. "Though I believe you will soon have the chance to do so in person."

THIRTY-SEVEN

THE WAREHOUSE HAD FALLEN STILL. IT WAS DARK; A moody, sullen dim of spent pipe-smoke and ashes. Only the Keeper's throne dais felt the warm touch of candlelight, from flickering tapers arrayed upon its steps and near to the Phantom Queen's great seat.

An interlude had been called amid the debauchery, a brief repose for the revelers to consider the solemnity of their occasion. So had the orgies and the sex games settled out into casually entangled clumps of celebrants, three or four or sometimes more, still intertwined in licentious jig-saws of flesh, lulled for a time from their carnal pursuits.

And so too had the glassy-eyed, stumbling, inebriated denizens halted their binges to allow their senses to return to them in some small measure.

None dared disobey the command of the Morrigan to call a pause in their indulgence, contrary though such a suggestion was to everything that they had gathered to celebrate.

All eyes in the vast expanse focused their attention on her platform, though the pleasure seeking had not fully ceased. Some among the deviant throng continued to puff gently on their opium pipes. Others stroked one another sensuously as they huddled.

The occasional squeal from some shadowy corner passed largely unnoticed.

The Morrigan stepped down from her gilded chair when six figures in white shrouds stepped into the circle of candles. She had again assumed a guise that was much more the innocent girl than fearsome goddess of battle. Her delicate face beamed golden, as though reflecting the light from an invisible sun.

"Children of Nestor," she began, her voice high-pitched and melodic, but echoing clearly. "This is a special night. You have come here from every land of the world, across oceans and seas, to be with others of your kind."

Prompted by the drums and the lyres of the Keeper's orchestra, the gathered recited a phrase. It was in a language that had not been spoken by humans for centuries.

As the tide of chanting ebbed, the Morrigan slipped through the shadow of her own chair. She emerged from the brief, dark interlude once more a wrinkled crone.

The withered old lady she now was raised her hands to the crowd. Her voice was unchanged.

"The time has come for us to join. We must unite, become one. One people. One Haven. Beyond these walls, there are those who would destroy us, the humans who refuse to acknowledge us as their ancestors did. We must continue to be vigilant against them. But now there is a new threat."

Again they chanted in their hidden tongue. Again she

passed through light and into shadow.

"Some among our own seek to scatter us, to betray their own kind. It is my pledge to you, as Keeper and Protector, that I will not allow that to happen."

In the center of the circle, the six lowered their hoods, and dropped their shrouds.

The gathered chanted once more.

"Here stand your guardians. Those who have sworn to fight to the death against the enemy, those who have offered their own lives to protect yours," the Morrigan continued.

Standing before the Keeper were the fiercest of all the changelings, their faces lit by the candles. Horus stood farthest to the left, bearing the regal head of a falcon upon a body that was split between bird and man. He rested in a menacing perch beneath scarlet wings. His talon-arms both clutched swords.

Beside him hovered Tisiphone. Her reptilian features and wild eyes fumed beneath a tangled mane. Claws extended from the scales along her arms. She held them before her like a pair of scythes.

To their right stood the eternal pair, Icarus and Anubis. The first was a slender, beautiful youth. Snow-white wings grew out of his shoulders. The elegant, strange feature both suggested his ancient namesake, and marked the only malformation to his near-humanity. He wore nothing but a tunic and chain belt, a long sword slung at his side.

The second of the two was a canine with heavy jowls. Recalling his Egyptian predecessor, he yet bore a largely human form, though jackal-headed and carrying elongated, fur-lined forelimbs.

Standing a step apart, but together within the circle, were Lycaon and Charybdis.

The Morrigan stepped out a second time from the shade, her aspect yet again altered. War goddess once more, her visage a storm cloud of blood and shadows and anger, she stepped forth in a threatening stride. She lifted her arms, and her waving cloak twisted into the wings of a black raven. They spread wide as her face grew to crown them with the terrible glower of the death-bird.

"I hereby dispatch you six slayers," she announced. "Avenge your sister Scylla! Hunt down and bring forth the traitors!"

✢   ✢   ✢

It was a clear night, chilly but not too cold. Typical for late fall in New York. Flanagan was at the wheel, and no one had said a word since they'd left the city. That silence, combined with the endless rolling of the tires and the whistling of the autumn wind, made it seem like they'd been on the road for hours.

When they saw the sign for a hamlet ahead, Pat suggested a brief rest stop. Vince and Maggie agreed without discussion.

The town was small, just a main street along a ridge overlooking the Hudson. The grocery store was already closed for the night, as were most of the other places, the barbershop, the post office and the church. There was a bar, though, with a couple of flickering signs outside and some cars parked in the vacant lot next to it.

That was where they pulled in.

"I'm gonna get a cup o' coffee," Pat said. "We still got about a forty-five-minute drive to the place. Anyone else?"

Maggie shook her head. She hated bars, even ones that served coffee. And she didn't much like Vince going near one either. Under the present circumstances, however, that seemed like the least of their problems.

Vince tapped her on the shoulder, asked her if she'd be okay, *if she was okay.* Then he disappeared inside with his ex-partner.

Maggie spent a moment peering upward then. You really couldn't see the stars very well in the city, too much light pollution from the buildings, the cars, and the street lamps. It was only when she made it out into the country, upstate some, that she ever got a chance to see the real night sky.

Her father had often taken her up near West Point as a child, to where her aunt and uncle lived in Highland Falls. *They were near there now,* she thought, *farther up the river than she had figured Flanagan was going to take them.* Close to where she had first learned the names of some of those constellations many years ago.

With all the strange things she'd seen lately, she relished the chance to take a breath, and stop for a moment with something so familiar, so reliable.

When the others exited the bar a few minutes later, she heard them behind her, Vince's coat rustling, and the small talk between him and Flanagan. The wind snapped the branches in the bare trees, occasionally drowning out their talk of old times and old faces. But she didn't take her eyes off the sky.

Not until she heard a series of footsteps, fast-moving and heavy. They snared her attention, and that of the others. Maggie spun her head, to the left, away from Vince and the car. Then she saw them.

There were six. All dressed the same, beige raincoats, belted at the waist, collars lifted above the neck. Black hats, broad-brimmed and flat, sat low over their heads, hiding their faces in the evening shadows.

"Maggie . . . !" She heard Vince's voice, but she couldn't move in time.

The half-dozen strangers were on her in a heartbeat. One had a blade. Maggie felt the steel cut through her jacket. It pierced the soft skin of her belly with a hard, stinging slice. She gasped, and staggered. A clammy grip braced her on the back of her neck.

Vince grabbed Pat Flanagan by the shoulder.

"You son of a bitch! You sold us out!" he shouted.

Flanagan stumbled backward, looking for cover behind the car. He reached for his gun under his coat, suddenly unsure if Vince was going to shoot him for trying.

"Vince, I swear. I didn't!" he shouted back.

The calls drew four of the intruders, who peeled off from the circle around Maggie. Three aimed their focus at Vince, while the fourth dashed toward the sedan, and Flanagan.

"Vince, you gotta believe me! I don't know what's goin' on!" he continued to shout.

His cries stopped abruptly a moment later, when a figure lunged at him from the darkness. He fired, several times, but the bullets clanged against the side of the car.

Vince's gun was drawn as well. Three men rushed toward him. He fired, emptied the revolver's six shots in a hot blast of smoke and fire and sound. He hit all of them, or so he thought.

But they kept on coming, faces hidden. There wasn't even a hint of blood from under their coats.

Maggie screamed. The blade of the one in front of her rose up for a second cut. A splash of her own blood already trickled along the edge. The grip of the one behind her tightened on her neck.

Vince charged the three while Flanagan struggled with his own attacker. His gun was now empty too.

The big Italian led with his left. The target intercepted his fist, catching it in a hand that was black and scaly, altogether more like a claw than anything human. His right hook met with the same fate. In a moment, the two flankers had him held fast, pulled down against the hood of the car.

The one in the middle bore down on him, face still obscured by the malevolent shadow. He could hear Flanagan fighting for his life behind him, and he could see Maggie struggling just a few yards away. She hadn't given up, but the two figures on top of her had nearly swallowed her beneath their girth. There was blood on the dirt at her feet. It glimmered dark red in the starlight.

He tried to call out to her. He heard her muffled cries just as he finally got a look at the face of the one in front of him, the hold of the two beside him too powerful for him to break free. The eyes were serpentine, and the face was reptilian, though vaguely human nonetheless. It was one of his own kind. The one called Tisiphone, if he recalled.

Again they've trapped me, he thought. *Just like in Venice.*

This time he wasn't going to be nearly as gentle.

For an instant, he smiled. But it was a sad kind of smile. Sad like the way Maggie had smiled when she'd first seen him on the couch. The sentiment was lost on his attackers.

As they looked on, as Tisiphone reached out for his throat, even, Vince's face changed.

His eyes contorted. They bulged, swollen from within. Then they shrank, receding deep into red, open sockets. His skin seemed to wither, the color suddenly drained as though sucked inward from something underneath. In a moment, it was gone too.

Exposed muscles, pulsing arteries and blue veins stared down at the four. Tisiphone felt the skin dissolve from under her grip, the liquid flesh seeping over her arm. A skull was now facing them. It was laughing.

She recoiled, gripped her arm in sudden agony. The stuff that had leaked off Vince's neck spread over her like hot tar. It bubbled, blistering her skin. Burning. She fell shrieking.

If he had needed to, he could have slipped out from under the hold of the others, but it wasn't necessary. They stepped back when their leader collapsed.

Gone from in front of him, Maggie was afforded a clear view, horrified by what she saw. The two assailants eased off her. The one with the blade stepped away. The one behind her, however, did not. She heard a woman's voice in her ear, whispering.

"Fear not Margaret, I am a friend of Sean's."

She could only watch as the bastard-thing that had been Vince suddenly burst out of his clothes. Flames incinerated his coat, charred his hat. His decomposing body suddenly, violently combusted.

A scream erupted within the rush of fire, like the call of a hawk. From the core of the raging human pyre there sprang forth a phoenix. It soared into the night, a golden-blazing firebird; wings spread wide and trailing cinders.

"Lucifer," the one behind her mumbled.

Maggie shivered.

Tisiphone writhed in the dirt. But Horus and Icarus threw off their clothes, revealing their inhuman forms. Lifted by their own wings, they flew to challenge the fire-storm that had been Vince Sicario.

Maggie could only gasp when the attacker in front of her dropped his own hat. The face of a jackal stared her down, his pointed ears trained upward. Anubis growled. He brought his blade to her throat, heedless of the chaos above.

Before the cut could be made, she felt the hands on the back of her neck edge her aside. She watched as the bony, albino figure of Charybdis, herself fallen out of disguise, sidestepped the attack. The jackal-man was taken by surprise, for only a moment, but it was long enough.

Her own curved steel bared, Charybdis passed the blade once across the middle of the beast, opening a gash that immediately surged blood. In a fluid motion, before Anubis could even howl, she sliced the dagger through his thick neck. Then deeply into his snout.

A final, cruel pass across his groin was unnecessary, but it felled the monster a moment quicker than he would have dropped otherwise.

Maggie dropped to the dirt, her face and hands splattered with canine blood. Her side ached with a deep wound. Charybdis was next to her an instant later, but her eyes were fixed on the deadly display overhead.

The phoenix figure darted left, then right, burning a trail of orange and red across the night. Horus, talons bared, climbed in a high arc and dove upon the firebird from behind.

His claws caught the other in the wing, piercing its flame-swathed flesh and jerking it backward. Icarus saw the attack. He circled, his long saber drawn before him. Horus, momentarily ensnared by his own falcon claws, fought to pull his talons loose. His feathers burned in his skin.

The long blade lifted, Icarus swooped down, carried by his lofty white wings. His cut split the heated air, but the phoenix bird suddenly flailed. The sword sliced clear through the talon claws of Horus. It severed the bird-hybrid's legs from under him.

He wailed in a voice that was neither avian, nor Homo sapiens, but something torn between the two. Agony sounded much the same, no matter the species.

Flanagan managed to break free of his assailant, for an instant. He dragged himself from behind the car, pulling his heavy, aching self forward with desperate, bloody fingers. From the shadows, he emerged into the firelight, beaming down in random cascades from overhead.

Jagged, fleshy wounds hobbled his thighs, staining the fabric of his torn trousers a slimy wet-black. Claw-scratches had robbed his torso of any human dignity; his muscles and tissues were little more than raw meat now, wounded prey ripe for the kill. His coat was shredded. The remains of his cheap oxford shirt were hanging off him in a mess of bloodied rags.

He felt it breathing behind him; snarling and slurping blood from its teeth, savoring his salty taste. It was not yet pursuing. He had a moment to get away, or maybe not even that long. But his legs would not oblige him.

As hard as he pushed, as much as he willed them, the bones would not obey. They just lay there, clinging to his waist, cruelly disconnected. All he could do was rake his hands against the cold dirt.

He screamed. It was anger mixed with fear. A last, dying hope for pity.

The beast Lycaon reared on his hairy haunches and leapt forward.

Flanagan felt his bowels release as the wolf's jowls seized the soft, fatty skin of his throat. Then everything went cold.

Icarus circled. Scalding embers sparkled in the smoke

around him. His eyes watered. He tried to look through the tears, but he no longer knew which way was up.

A hand reached out when he turned. He never saw it coming. He did see the face of Sean Mulcahy, however, as it took shape upon the phoenix, replacing the bird-form entirely in a matter of moments.

Sean's hand clenched his larynx. It squeezed the delicate cartilage like a vice. Icarus tried to fight off the pressure, even as he felt the skin of his face swell and his lungs burn.

Horus, squealing horribly, dropped from the sky, landing in a splash of his own blood. The last sound he heard was the crack of his spine, as every bone in his back splintered apart.

Sean now hung aloft, suspended by the wings of Icarus. The bird-man struggled desperately to breathe through the grip that was collapsing his throat. The pair of them fell together, Icarus unable to break the vicious hold, or to maintain consciousness.

They landed in a heap only a few yards from Flanagan's car, in plain sight of Maggie and Charybdis, and the now roaring, kill-maddened Lycaon.

With hands that were uncommonly gentle, despite the chaos, Charybdis moved Maggie behind her. She slowly guided the wounded lady backward and away from the fight.

Now Lycaon stood alone. From the pile of flesh and shattered bones that had been Icarus, Sean rose. There was not a scratch on him. His skin glowed.

"Your friend is dead, and now your time has come, Lucifer," the werewolf snarled, exposing his yellow, blood-stained fangs.

Flanagan's insides were strewn about the dirt beneath him, savaged human detritus steaming in the cool night air. Spongy little pieces of him clung to the animal-man's whiskers.

Sean did not respond. He passed a slow gaze over the desecrated husk that had been Pat Flanagan, barely recognizable for the monster's butchery. Then he returned his eyes to the growling visage of Lycaon. But he did not approach.

Instead, his sight stayed locked on the beast, and the wolf-thing kept his own wild eyes trained hard on his foe. Sean stepped gingerly over to where Tisiphone continued to toss and turn through the dust. She was still peeling in agony. Her skin was blistered and singed all over her body, as though doused with acid. Careless of the sight, Sean laid his hand on her arm.

She squealed one final time, and the pox seemed to leave her, drawn out into the touch of the changeling. Her moment of relief passed, she smiled with a last notion of sweet release.

Then her heart gave out within her feral breast.

Seeing this, the wolf-beast roared and leapt upon him, claws held high. Sean remained still, however. He made no attempt to evade the creature. A second later, Lycaon learned why.

The huge paws of the creature struck the bare, unde-fended chest of their prey. Instead of sinking through the flesh and tearing into the muscle beneath, as Lycaon fully expected, they shattered. Lycaon howled, his paws fractured. He recoiled.

Sean's skin had turned to stone.

Wounded, but not swayed from his rage, Lycaon was not finished. He whirled his massive tail, and used his rear legs to spring to the side of Sean. He moved with the speed of a wild predator, and his long tail wrapped around Sean's neck like a noose.

Again, the attack had little effect.

Lycaon found the man's throat as inflexible as the rest of him. The pressure he exerted did nothing but constrict his own tail.

Sean shook his head. He wrapped his fingers around the tail, and as Lycaon looked up, momentarily helpless, he yanked the appendage so violently that it tore away from the monster's rear.

Lycaon tumbled to the dust. His mangled front claws throbbed. His hindquarters quivered, raw and bleeding from the severed vertebrae. Still he snarled, but his defenses were lame. Sean approached, slowly. He extended his right arm. His flesh congealed. As though his skin was more liquid than solid, his fingers merged, forming a single, long appendage where his hand should have been.

The beast staggered backward, yelping. Sean pursued at a pedestrian pace. He allowed Lycaon to feel every terrible second of his demise.

All color had vanished from his arm. From under his torn sleeve a serrated dagger menaced in place of a limb.

He raised it, and Lycaon was blinded momentarily by the glint of moonlight reflected off organic steel.

But the pursuit ended without Sean laying a finger on him. Lycaon howled his last when he limped backward. It was one step too far. The blade of Charybdis was waiting. It plunged deep into the soft flesh between his shoulders.

The beast put down, Sean turned his attention to Maggie. She was on her knees, looking up at him with eyes that were wide like a child's.

"Sean?" she stammered. "What did . . . how could . . . how?"

He had returned to a passably human shape.

"This isn't the time to explain," he replied.

"The hell it isn't!" she shouted back.

He knelt beside her, looking at her ripped jacket and the blood on the dirt. Her blood.

"You're cut, you need to get help," he said.

She ignored his concern. When he tried to place his hand on her exposed side, she batted it away.

"What have you done to Vince?" she demanded.

"I haven't done anything to him."

He feigned ignorance, knowing full well that he was telling the truth. She didn't care for his irreverence.

"Don't lie to me, damn you! I saw the whole thing, whatever the hell it was. I saw him standing there! I saw what happened!"

Sean merely stared back at her, stoic, almost like Vince used to do.

"I did see him, didn't I?" she continued.

"You did," he assured her.

"So what happened to him? Where'd he go?"

Sean breathed heavily. He knew where the conversation was going; it was a talk he had intended never to have. This especially, was not the time. Regardless, he answered.

"He was never here."

"But you just said . . ."

"You saw what you thought was Vince. An imitation of him. A reproduction."

It made no sense to her, and he knew that.

"But I talked to him. I sat with him. I kissed him," she said, more to herself than to him.

Sean shook his head slowly. His own memories of those brief moments played out in his mind.

"It wasn't Vince," he finally said.

Her expression was befuddled. Even though he hated the very idea of it, he knew he needed to explain.

"It was me," he said.

"You?" she replied, exhaling. "I don't believe you."

Sean nodded. He'd expected that response, even with all that Maggie had just witnessed. He was going to have to show her. He just kept thinking how badly that same attempt had gone with Vince.

"Watch carefully," he whispered.

Stepping back a few feet, Sean craned his neck. He loosened his joints and breathed deeply. He seemed tired, and the change that came over him this time was slow. But Maggie saw every second of it.

First the color faded from his skin, leaving it looking

more like wax than living tissue. Then, as though they were no more than temporary, his features dissolved. His eye sockets widened. The bone beneath was soft and malleable, shaped by some unseen sculptor. His nose lengthened and his mouth expanded in the same way. Greasy secretions from his scalp dampened his hair like black sweat. The strands were becoming darker and heavier.

In a few short moments, Sean's face was gone. Maggie found herself staring at Vince Sicario again.

"Mother of God," she gasped. "That morning in front of the apartment, with Paulie . . . the other day, when you were suddenly better . . . the alley with the kids."

"I know it must be hard to understand," Sean attempted, though she did not allow him to finish.

"Where is he?" her expression suddenly took on a fierce glimmer.

"What?"

"Vince. If he's not here, then where is he?"

"He's alive," Sean replied, his face grotesquely re-forming as he spoke. The change did not seem to bother him, but for a slight shiver.

"Where is he, Sean!" she shouted. "Enough lies, tell me the truth for once, damn it!"

She winced when she yelled. The pain was evident in her eyes.

"He's with my master, at a church on the Lower East Side. He's safe, I assure you," Charybdis answered, suspecting that Sean might not.

"I want to see him," she said.

"That's too dangerous," Sean answered.

"Dangerous? After what happened here you're telling me that's too dangerous? No Sean, you're going to take me to Vince, right now. Understand?"

He looked at Charybdis. The pale figure nodded.

"Fine."

"I don't know what the hell is going on, and maybe I don't want to know. But this charade has gone on long enough, and you better have some goddamn answers," Maggie said.

Sean looked away, to the pool of her blood in the dirt.

"Not now," he said.

She was about to yell something back at him, but Charybdis intervened.

"He's right. You are owed an explanation my lady, without a doubt, but not here. The locals hide now, but they will be out soon to investigate. We must get back to the city, back to a safe place. Then there will be time enough for answers."

THIRTY-EIGHT

FLANAGAN'S CAR HAD TAKEN THEM AS FAR BACK AS Harlem. Then the gas had run out, and they were in no shape to seek out a filling station.

Charybdis had another option; one that she guessed would be safer anyway. The tunnels.

Sean was skeptical, but he knew it made the most sense. He could pass unnoticed among the crowds. Both she and the still-bleeding Maggie could not.

Once they had walked for about an hour, Maggie stumbled. Sean tried to pick her up, to carry her the rest of the way. They saw that she needed rest more than anything else.

Sean set her down at a junction where two old IRT lines had once met. The darkness of the underground swallowed them, so deep within the bowels of the city that the stench of rot and grime enveloped them fully. The reek no longer bothered them. They didn't even notice it anymore.

They were safe, for a time.

The pause left a gaping silence that seemed to magnify every drop of sewer water and every skittering shuffle of a rat in the darkness. Sean finally broke the pall.

"Now you've seen me. Now you know what I am," he said, exasperated.

"I know who you are, I think. But what? I haven't a clue, Sean," Maggie replied, wheezing from the pain, more animated by her anger than anything else.

He nodded, and let himself ease backward, out of the filmy light. In the wet shadows, she could barely see him.

"The other day, at Vince's, you asked me about where I went, what I did after I left. I never really answered you. Now I suppose I can," he said.

"I'm waiting," she answered.

There was a second long pause, so long in fact that Maggie thought he was not going to make good on his word. But then he spoke, and she found herself quickly in awe.

"Obviously I am not like you. I guess I've always been this way, but I never knew for sure until the first time I saw another one of my own kind. That, I remember, was a freakish thing," he began.

"Your own kind?" she asked.

"In a manner of speaking. Most of us are not like me. In fact, I'm really quite the oddity, even among a bunch of the oddest folk walking the good Earth. I don't molt, at least not unless I want to, which is why I never really knew what I was back here all those years ago. Oh, I had my suspicions, but I never really *knew*, not until France."

Though she couldn't have been sure, with the darkness hiding most of his face, Maggie thought he took on a different expression then. If she was right, then Sean was sad, and she wasn't entirely sure why.

"I met Howie on the trench-line. He wasn't an original member of the Fighting 69th like me, but he got placed with us like a lot of newbies after things got rough and we starting losing our New York boys. I'd describe him to you, how tall he was, how his blond hair was cut or the way he smoked a Camel, but it really wouldn't be worth the effort, since, as I eventually found out, none of that was really him anyway.

"Men tend to make friends pretty quick when bullets are whizzing by their heads, and that was how it was with me and Howie. Being the way that I was, why I'd left New York in the first place, I didn't have many friends in the regiment. I kept to myself mostly, even when the fighting got heavy.

"Howie ended up with us after his own boys were wiped while he'd been laid up with what the docs first thought was the flu. It turned out to be just a head cold, so the brass wasn't about to send him home short of his commitment.

"Anyway, he didn't know anyone else, and we happened to be bunked next to each other, so we ended up talking. Small talk at first, mindless conversation. What I noticed right away, though, was that it wasn't the same shit everyone else talked about. In a trench, in the mud and the trenches, when you know that every day might be your last, all anyone wants to tell you about is his sweetheart back in East-wherever-the-fuck. Or maybe the smell of the prairie grass in South Dakota or something. With all the new guys coming in from regiments outside New York, I'd heard it all by that time.

"Not from Howie, though. He talked about all the places he'd seen, all the things he'd done. And he'd been everywhere, and done almost everything. At least it sounded that way to me, a little punk from Hell's Kitchen who had never left the city, much less the country, until Uncle Sam came calling.

"When I couldn't sleep one night because of the noise from the Kraut shelling, he told me I'd get used to it, just like he had in Cuba during the Spanish-American War and in South Africa during the Boer War. I didn't know a damn thing about either one at the time, so I just acted like I knew what he was talking about.

"I remember once a bunch of guys in the unit got real severe gangrene, since we never had dry socks and it rained all the time. Howie said it was like Korea, all the mud, that is, only it was a lot colder there.

"Then, and even I knew this one was a little weird, we started taking heavy casualties trying to take a German machinegun nest over a hill. He said it reminded him of *Fredericksburg*. Said he could still see the horror of Irish volunteers just like us charging toward him behind a stone wall. Cut down in the grisliest piece of human carnage he'd ever laid eyes on. Human blood mixed with pieces of men and scraps of blue uniforms on a great big, cold field. That's what he said, anyway.

"I really didn't want to hear any more about that under the circumstances.

"When I finally did ask him how many places he'd been

to, though, he just laughed and rattled off a list of cities I'd mostly never heard of. Milan, Istanbul, Jerusalem, Cairo, Baghdad, Moscow, Tokyo. You name it. He'd seen it.

"Seems he had no family to speak of, no wife, no special someone waiting at home, not even a home to go back to. As far as I could tell, he'd spent most of his life just wandering around from place to place, staying a while and then moving on.

"I thought that sounded terrific. But almost anything sounds terrific compared to stale rations, French mud, and German bullets. He didn't seem to think so, though. That was what struck me about him. He'd been all over the world, over a time span I later figured out would've made him something like eighty years old by the time we shared a tiny corner of hell in the summer of 1918—even though he didn't look a day over twenty-five. But all it left him with was a bunch of stories. That, and the saddest set of eyes you'd ever want to see.

"Looking back, I think I know why he latched on to me the way he did."

"He knew you were both of the same sort?" Charybdis asked, not quite following Sean's logic, if that's what it was.

"No, not yet. At least I don't think he did. He was just alone, and he wanted someone to talk to. It was only the dumbest of luck that we ended up having so much more in common than either of us suspected."

"So how did you find out about his . . . secret?" Maggie questioned.

"It was July 1918. We were fighting at a place called

Champagne, if you can believe that. We were starting to pick up steam. Our guys were pushing the Hun back day after day. There were a lot more ground assaults then. We spent more time running around from trench to trench than sitting and waiting.

"Things didn't go our way forever. One night our squad was doing a reconnaissance sweep over some cottages. We were hit by a German ambush. The crossfire downed most of us right off the bat. Only a few, including me and Howie, managed to find cover.

"We ducked into a hole, just barely. Howie was hit bad by the time we settled in. The previous residents were still there, two German gunners, but they weren't much more than rotting corpses. As it turned out, we ended up stuck there for a while, because the Germans who'd hit us were the leading edge of a counterattack. Their fire kept us pinned down for two days.

"It ended up being Howie's last two days.

"I knew he was dying, as soon as I set him down in a puddle of blood and muck, tracers constantly buzzing overhead. There wasn't much I could do for him, but that was just about the least of my concerns, because by the end of the first day things had already gotten so weird that I was scared out of my mind.

"First he got all pale, which is not so strange when you're shot. But then other things started happening, things I never could have imagined."

Maggie stopped fiddling with her hair. She fell still as Sean's voice got lower, and quieter.

"His eyes got all white, like a snake, and he quivered. The bullets had shred his coat and his shirt underneath had fallen away from his body when I set him down. I tried to move him, not that I thought it would help, but I didn't have any idea what else to do. That was when I first saw it.

"It looked like his skin was petrified, like those trees in Nevada or Arizona, all purple and hard like he was turning to stone. I thought the blood might have congealed and dried on his back, and that he must've been wounded worse that I'd thought. But there was no blood. Not a drop. With all the smoke there wasn't much light, and it was hard to make out what was going on, but the closer I looked the weirder it got.

"He was cocooning, preparing to die," Charybdis stated.

"Right, but I had never seen that before," Sean agreed. "After a while his whole body got like that, his chest, his arms and his legs, even his face froze up and hardened like a statue.

"At this point I was ready to ditch the foxhole and take my chances with the Germans. Howie was a good guy, but the shit that was happening to him scared the hell out of me.

"I stayed, though. I watched him lay there, entombed in his own skin, or whatever it was, for a whole day. By the next morning, something had happened. The shell cracked. Just a little at first, but by the evening it was breaking, and I could see something pushing from inside, trying to get out.

"I don't know what kept me there. What I was watching was the most disgusting thing I'd ever seen. For some reason, I didn't mind looking at it. As he lay there, hatching like a big, ugly slug, I knew that we were more connected than two lost soldiers. I knew I had to stay.

"Once the shell had broken away, I could see what was left of him. Howie, the Howie I knew, anyway, was just a memory.

"Instead of skin, he had this grayish, gelatinous covering. I was afraid to touch it for a while. When I finally did I kind of shuddered. It had the consistency of something soft, almost unformed, the way you'd imagine the skin underneath your fingernails to feel if you peeled them away.

"*It's okay to touch*, he managed to say. *I won't bite. No teeth anymore.*

"I think he started laughing then, but it wasn't like a regular laugh, and that's something I don't think anyone could describe.

"In a few minutes his entire cocoon had broken off him. What lay there in front of me was truly a sight. They say that nothing can really prepare you for the horrors you encounter in war. Well, this was way beyond any of that. He didn't even look human anymore, more like a slug drowning in its own slime.

"He didn't seem to have much time left, and he motioned with what used to be his left arm—it was by then more like a flipper or a tentacle—I knew he wanted me to lift up his head.

"That mop of blond hair had almost all fallen out, but

some of it lingered, suspended in the slimy film that covered what had once been his cranium. His eyes weren't white, but they weren't even really eyes anymore. More like dark holes where eyes had been. The mottled yellow-gray skin of his head was writhing, moving around like there was some dirty liquid sloshing underneath, pushing the surface up in one place and sagging down in another.

"I could see he was fading. I'm not sure if that was why I did it, or if it was something else. Empathy for a friend? I still don't know, but that's when it happened."

"When *what* happened?" Maggie asked.

"I let myself change."

"I don't understand," she said.

"Maybe it was a macabre camaraderie, a bizarre attempt to comfort a dying fellow, I don't really know. I tore off my own coat and shirt so that the skin of my torso was visible, and I concentrated. I hadn't let it happen over my entire body before, only little pieces and only for short times, but I think I probably expected to die right there too, so that sort of apprehension didn't hold the same weight as it once had.

"Soon enough, as my dying friend watched, my own skin hardened, turned purple and then cracked and fell away. Just like his had, only much, much faster. When it did, what was left underneath was the same grayish-yellow ooze and vague features that he had.

"*Dionysus* is what I think he muttered through his sagging mouth. *I don't know how I missed it. You're one of them. I've heard stories, but I've never seen one before.*

"*One what?* I asked him. In the moment the irony of *him* being shocked by *me* was lost to the circumstances. *A trickster. You are one, aren't you? You change whenever you wish, not like the rest of us poor, sad souls.*

"*I don't know what you mean. What rest of you?* I asked him.

"*Rest of us,* he corrected me.

"I think I just stared at him, and I let my human form retake my body.

"*Oh . . . you don't know yet, do you?* he said, almost laughing. It was one of the last things he said to me.

"Howie died a short while later. He managed to tell me one last thing, which I didn't really understand at the time."

"What was that?" Maggie asked.

"That I should go to Russia. That I should follow the call, and find the Keeper."

"Russia? Why?"

"He didn't have time to say. But somehow, and I can't really say why, I knew I had to go. I felt something pulling me there.

"So I deserted the Army. I spent the next several months trying to get across Eastern Europe, not an easy task in those days, maybe even harder than it is now. Several times I thought about giving up, but I knew I couldn't. If not for Howie, then for something else. He'd sent me on the path, but somehow I think I would have found it on my own eventually. The pull was too strong. I had no choice."

"None of us did, none of us ever do. Her power is too strong," Charybdis echoed.

"St. Petersburg was where I ended up, it's Leningrad

now, but it was still *Sankt Petersborg* in 1918. The city in those days was a magnificent place, but it was dangerous too."

"Indeed," Charybdis said. "Many years later, I heard a man much more eloquent than I compare Peter's city in those times to a rare gem seized inside a workman's vice. Though its facade gleamed with a sparkle hardly rivaled anywhere else under the sky, he said, the cracks within the jewel were growing, and the pressure was not soon to relent."

"Very true," Sean agreed. "To anyone who looked long enough, the signs of collapse were clear enough. But nobody was looking in those days. Not the deposed Romanovs or their foppish retainers, not the seething generals and their dying charges, and certainly not the peasants and their Bolshevik rousers. That, I think, may have been why we were all drawn there, and why the Morrigan chose that place for the most surreal episode of what has surely never been the world's most grounded affair."

"Morrigan. There's that name again. Who, or *what*, is that?" Maggie demanded.

Charybdis was about to reply, but Sean stopped her with a wave. She wasn't ready for that, not yet.

"In time," he counseled. "First I need to explain why we were all gathered there. It was for the high festival of our people."

"Ah, the St. Petersburg feast," Charybdis mused. "Now that was a time. Days and nights of feasting and ritual. The time truest to the roots of our tradition in centuries."

"I can't really comment on that, since it was the only one of those grand events that I've yet been privy to, but

I do know this. For all our depravity and excess, and all of our, *peculiar* affectations, from what I can tell, the locals didn't even notice us," Sean continued. "What an initiation, I can tell you. I still recall the sounds of the city, the chaos. Cannons from the Peter and Paul Fortress booming across the Neva. Gunfire echoing through the Hermitage pavilion, and the cries of starving men and women clamoring for help in the cold. Help that would never come.

"I was drawn to a palace south of Nevsky Prospekt, along a canal that ran near St. Isaac's. Whose abode it was I do not know, but it was fantastic, and it was ours."

"A noble of Tatar descent, or so I was told," Charybdis answered. "The Morrigan inhabited his form. She used his position to provide safety for us all, to seclude us from the revolution outside within his giant palace."

"The actual festivities were held beneath the palace, and that's what I remember most," Sean said. "When I entered, it was dark, and poorly lit. Steam was rushing from old, broken pipes. There were hundreds of figures, gathering in rows upon a wide floor. Some wore shrouds that covered most of their forms, leaving only grotesque faces of every shape and sort imaginable; as well as some not even dreamt of in the nightmares of the mad.

"Those who were not cloaked paraded about naked, although it was an uncommon nudity, for though most walked on two legs, few bore any more resemblance to ordinary folk than that. Some were formless, their skin no more than a shifting sea of pus and ooze. Others had very distinct features, some bestial, the bastard offspring of reptilian and mammalian parents.

"Then there were others, who stood out boldly among the deviant throng, though no one paid them any more mind than the scores of stranger celebrants. These were the few who looked entirely and completely human. They were, almost without exception, both young and beautiful.

"Then someone stepped to the fore, it looked like a man at first, but I know now how silly that seems. A weirdly glittering robe was all about her, and very little of her actual body was visible beneath it.

"I think I stared at the shroud for the longest time before I even noticed anything else. The colors of it had a way of mesmerizing you when you watched it, because it seemed like it moved on its own, as though it was alive too. I remember that especially, since there was no wind at all in the place, damp and dank like a sewer or a subway tunnel during a rainstorm. And every time a fold or a flap lifted or bent, the shade of the cloth shifted. Pale blue became jade green, and then black and then red.

"Who knows how long I stood there just watching the colors change? But I know that I finally looked up, and I know that because I have never been as frightened in all my life as I was at that very moment. Never before, and never since."

"What was it?" Maggie asked.

Another long silence followed that simplest of queries, but it didn't appear that Sean was thinking as he sat quietly there, or even that he was preparing any response at all. He merely sat still, as though he couldn't speak any more.

Eventually, though, he cleared his throat, and he began talking again, not quite where he had left off some moments before.

"*A reading from the Book of Nestor,*" the . . . *person's* voice said from the dais.

"I had no idea what that meant, but I couldn't take my eyes off of her, and the words weren't really all that important to me anyway. I do recall them, oddly enough, all these years later. I suppose that might have something to do with it being my first time. You always remember your first time, even if it really wasn't that memorable when it happened.

"*Column seven of the Nineteenth Scroll.*"

As Sean recited the passage from memory, Charybdis joined in with him. She knew every word by heart as well.

"*Long had he dwelt there, among the ice and the clouds atop the citadel Asgard, when there came to the place of the Changeling King Loki a pilgrim of the lower race. It was in the form of a hawk that he met the visitor, a man with one eye who entered the great hall under a promise of brotherhood.*"

"All of those gathered around me then began chanting, and I think I joined them, somewhat, even though I didn't really know what they were saying," Sean continued. "Truth is, even if I'd known the words, most of what was being said would still have been incomprehensible. Even among our own kind, the true voice of many of us only barely resembles anything human. That's how it was that night. Mostly it sounded like a herd of livestock with their throats being slit all at once. That, or a thousand starving children screaming for a morsel of food."

"Actually, I'd say it was something like a cross between those two things. Really very hard to put your finger on, to be perfectly honest, and I've never tried to describe it to someone who hadn't experienced it personally before," Charybdis explained.

Maggie was aghast now, unsure if their macabre words were true, only certain from Sean's demeanor that he at least believed them. That may have been chilling enough.

"Is that what frightened you so? What you spoke of a few minutes ago?"

"No."

"Well then, what was it? What was so terrible, so much more horrible than what you've just told me? Was it a voice? A face?" Maggie questioned.

"She didn't have a face. Not one like you or . . . or other people have."

"The man, or woman, on the podium?"

"Was it a man? I couldn't have said at that moment. Now I know that such a distinction is fairly meaningless among my kind, but then I had no clue."

"A woman, then?"

"Well, this is what I'm saying. Neither one. Or maybe both. It depends on which way you'd prefer to look at it. I mean, if you're asking if it was a man as in *hu*-man then the answer is really quite a bit simpler.

"Not even close."

"Then what?" she asked.

"It was the Keeper. It was the Morrigan."

The words left a chill in the air. It lingered for a long moment. Then Maggie spoke again, trying to absorb it all.

"I don't understand. What was all of it for? All the pomp and circumstance?"

"The Molting," Sean replied, almost in jest by his tone.

"What?"

Here Charybdis took up the lion's share of the explanation. She could see that Sean was reluctant to speak further.

"It means different things to different people, I guess. To the Morrigan it is a celebration of her own greatness. To my master Argus, I suppose it is an observance of our long history. But it was not always so. Once it was a glorious affair, a paradise of pleasure, a respite for the hunted."

"The hunted?" Maggie interrupted.

"Yes. The one moment in time when the persecuted and the damned could revel free of their oppressors, free of the fear that followed them through every other day of their lives. Free, for a short while, anyway," Charybdis answered.

"The damned?" Maggie asked, still not quite following.

"Indeed. Despite what the current appearance may suggest, before you stand two changelings. And near this place there are gathered hundreds more of us, revealed this night in all our glory as we could never be to the outside world."

"Where do they, *you* come from?" she asked.

Sean shrugged. It was a question he himself had never much cared about. Charybdis nodded, however. She knew.

"Everywhere. We are born, as you were, of human parents. But we are not human, not by any ordinary measure, anyway. For thousands of years, as long as there have been people, so have we been."

"I've never heard of such a thing," Maggie protested.

"And yet here we stand," came the simple, dismissive answer from Sean.

"But how could . . . ?"

"How could no one know of us?" Charybdis said, anticipating her next query.

"Right."

"The humans knew us, once. That memory lives on in their stories, their folklore. Have you ever read the tale of Daphne, the woodland girl who was pursued by Apollo and transformed into a laurel tree? Or perhaps Medusa, the beauty who offended Poseidon and grew snakes from her crown? The tales are many, and not just from the Greeks and the Romans. Tales of our kind come down from every people: the Native folk of America, the varied tribes of Africa, the Norse, the Chinese, and the Celts."

"So what happened? Obviously, you're still here. How did you, how did all of this . . . ?"

"Become folklore?" Charybdis said.

Maggie nodded.

Charybdis sighed, suddenly a little sadder as she spoke. "Times changed. People changed. One superstition died and another rose up to take its place. In the dying days of the Roman Empire, the Christians saw us as devils. They massacred our covens, killed our leader and called us servants of Satan. Later, they demonized us as witches and werewolves and vampires. Where we had once been honored, we became hunted. In the Islamic world it was much the same, we were seen as abominations, and driven underground, forced to hide our true selves in order to survive.

"And survive we have, and we shall continue. That is why we have festivals such as we have here described.

"Every year in this season, we begin the change from our human-looking outer selves, back to the true beings that lurk within us. It is a dangerous time for us, a vulnerable time, and for safety's sake many of us band together. In seclusion from the outside world, often at safe houses called Havens, we cocoon, and undergo the molting. It is then that our true forms emerge.

"Once together, we recite tales of the old ones, so that we may never forget. We induct all newfound shifters into our fold, as well. They shed their human name and take on a name from the rolls of the ancients. That is how I became known as Charybdis."

"Then?" Maggie asked.

"As I told you, we celebrate," Sean broke in.

"But what exactly are you celebrating?"

"Life," Charybdis said.

"Life?" she asked.

"For us it is often difficult, and fragile. Every time we change, we know that our new form may be frail, or worse," Charybdis answered. "After we emerge, we remain in our true form for a period of days, even weeks. Then we grow tired, and we are forced to cocoon again. When we emerge the second time, we have grown into a new body. Usually different than what we have been before. For most of us, in fact, the change is totally random. We mutate into a wholly new shape, and remain that way until the next molting season.

"Some of us emerge from the cocoon in aged bodies, some as little children, some as animals. We have no control over it, so we celebrate living while we can. Every year there are those who are not strong enough to survive on their own until the next season."

"So that's how it goes. We read, we have a party and we change," Sean said.

"We molt, yes. We cocoon and regenerate, and after several days, we are born anew. It is the most dangerous time for us, for if we are discovered in that vulnerable state, we are defenseless," Charybdis followed-up. "But I must tell you, the feasts are truly inspiring, for that reason alone. Debauchery. Hedonism. Whatever you'd like to call it. Drinking, sex, opium, hashish, and other drugs. We indulge in everything that can provide pleasure. Because every changeling knows that it could be her last night alive."

Sean finally elected to offer something other than sarcasm.

"Once every seven years," he began, "there is a gathering of all the changelings the world over. At that time, we are all drawn to the Keeper, and we join her in one great, bacchanalian festival. A renewal for the community, just as for the person. That is what brought me to St. Petersburg in 1918. And that is what has drawn Charybdis and the rest of our kind here to New York now."

"Drawn to this Morrigan?" Maggie said.

"Yes. The Keeper. The guardian of the scrolls and

the protector of the lore. She is our queen, and one of the most ancient of us, besides. She took the mantle in the year 1587."

"She's four hundred years old?"

"Unlike humans, we completely regenerate our bodies every year. If kept free from harm, sickness or violence, we can live almost forever."

"Who's the oldest of you?"

"That would be Argus. He is the only one left who saw that bygone age when we were honored, rather than cursed. Some say he seeks to restore it. But the Morrigan will not do as he wishes."

"But why do you need a queen?" Maggie asked.

"We don't. That's what I've been trying to tell them for thirty years," Sean said.

Charybdis ignored him.

"The Keeper is not truly a queen, or a king. The Keeper is a very special being. A changeling of rare ability—what we call a trickster—from the stories of the ancients."

"I've heard that word before, in your story, Sean," Maggie said, turning toward him.

He paid her comment no attention, but Charybdis kept talking.

"Among us it refers to a changeling who is liberated from the bonds of ordinary molting cycles. One who can mutate spontaneously, change form at will, into whatever he or she wishes. One who does not require the cocoon to regenerate.

"Since ancient times, the Keeper has always been a trickster. Not only the watcher of our lore, the Keeper is our protector. The Keeper stands guard while the lot of us are in hibernation to insure that our race will live on."

"Wait, Sean?" Maggie stammered, suddenly understanding, though she wasn't yet certain if she'd really gotten it all. "Sean is a trickster?"

"He is," Charybdis said, looking over at the dejected sight of him.

"And the Morrigan is too," Maggie said.

"The Morrigan believes that Sean is a threat to her. She believes that Sean is the one we call Lucifer, the trickster spoken of in the prophecies of Nestor. In ancient times he was our greatest king, the greatest of all changelings. The heirs of Constantine slew him, smearing his name with the taint of deceiver for all time.

"But it was written that Lucifer will return one day. He will come out of the west. He will seize power, and he will lead our kind back to their rightful place of honor among mankind. He will return us to the light."

"Sean?" Maggie said, turning to him, still sitting quietly, almost morose by his expression. He did not answer.

"He refuses to accept that he is Lucifer," Charybdis explained, somewhat pedantically. "My master Argus first told him of the prophecy in Prague, many years ago. He attempted to tutor him, to instruct him in how to become a leader. But Sean rejected the idea. And despite our best efforts, he rejects it still."

"So why don't you just get rid of this Morrigan? Why

can't someone else kill her?"

"Someone else could, if they caught her at just the right moment, but such moments are rare. A trickster can mutate his flesh at a moment's notice. One who knows you're coming can avoid almost anything. Swords, even bullets. *The trick*, so to speak, is to catch one when they don't expect it. Then they're just as vulnerable as you or me."

"As happened to me a few days back, when you first saw me," Sean said. "The Morrigan's agents surprised me. I was shot before I had the chance to change. Once I was wounded, my talents, so to speak, were rather compromised. I could barely manage to change form once before almost losing all my strength entirely."

"But those moments are rare," Charybdis said. "And as Sean has now proven, it is exceedingly difficult to kill a trickster, even if you do get them when they don't expect it. But another trickster, well that's a different story altogether."

She turned back to Sean. He still seemed completely uninterested.

"Why don't you do something Sean? Why would you not want to help your own people?" she asked.

Sean stood up then, and he stepped very slowly over toward Maggie. He ignored Charybdis. After a long, pregnant moment, he was back in the half-light, his face very near to Maggie's.

"I am not Lucifer," he said, out of breath as though he had repeated the same thing a thousand times before.

"But how do you know, if everything else fits and . . . ?" she began, but he did not allow her to finish.

"Do you want to know how I know? I'll tell you. Because I'm no one. I'm not the Sean that you once knew. I'm not the Vince that I pretended to be. I'm not anyone."

Maggie stared back. She had nothing to say. His gaze was so weary, so empty.

"When you change so much, so often, for so long, you lose sight of what you were before. I've been a thousand different things, people, animals, even. And I can't figure out anymore if there's a little bit of all of them in me, or if there really is no me at all."

"What are you talking about? With the power you have? I've seen it myself. You can be anything. You can be anyone to anybody," she replied, astonished at his reticence.

"No. I can *pretend* to be anything," Sean said, stepping back into the shadows. "But none of it is ever real. I'm not even me anymore, and if I'm not real, then what's left?"

She just stared blankly.

"Nothing. That's the answer," he replied. "Nothing."

BOOK IV

"Prophecies and Other Vagaries"

THIRTY-NINE

THEY WALKED ON IN NEAR SILENCE FOR SEVERAL MORE hours. It was likely drawing close to midnight, though none of them had a watch. Charybdis seemed to know the abandoned tunnels at least as well as Arachne. Her path was determined and as heedless of the squealing rodents they disturbed at one turn and the warmed-over stink of rotting, besotted sewage they slogged through at the next.

Finally, with Maggie fading in and out of consciousness, they came to a place the trickster recognized. It was the tunnel Arachne had led him to several days before. Abandoned subway construction interrupted by a new corridor, torn out of the dirt and stone by hand.

"You've led us right back to Argus. To his lair," Sean said.

Charybdis stopped and turned. There wasn't much light, but Sean could see her eyes.

"She wished to see after your friend Vince, did she not?" the changeling said.

Sean looked down at Maggie, held fast against his chest as he walked. He knew that was what she wanted.

"In any case, where else could we have gone? We need a safe place to rest, and to contemplate our next move," Charybdis continued.

Through the newly carved tunnel there was, strangely, no light. The distance wasn't far. Charybdis was able to feel around in the darkness for the rope ladder that she knew would be suspended from the cathedral's subterranean entrance.

She climbed up first, and opened the grate. When she turned to help her companions up the rope, however, she found that Sean did not need her aid. Only a moment after she had made her way out onto the church floor, Maggie arose through the open hole. A triad of leather-winged bats deposited her gently beside Charybdis, the three acting in perfect unison. Once she had settled herself against the edge of a pew, the bats released their grip. They flittered softly upward into the dark rafters.

Then, after a pause that seemed like several minutes under the brooding still, the animals fell from the ceiling. One after another, they tumbled to the floor as though suddenly dead. Defying chance and gravity alike, all three landed in the same place, upon an open spot on the church floor behind both Maggie and Charybdis.

At first seeming to topple into a mere pile of dead creatures, Charybdis quickly realized that the stricken animals did not fall haphazardly. They came together purposefully, like the pieces of a gruesome puzzle. Joining and interlocking into place, assembled by unseen hands, the bats molded themselves into human form even as

Charybdis looked on, astonished despite her many years among the Children of Nestor.

Her initial surprise yielded to horror an instant later, though, but not from anything that Sean did. It was when she looked around to see what had become of the cathedral.

The church was smoldering, and dark. No torches burned. The braziers that had rested along the pews were toppled, their coals spilled. Flat moonbeams poked like swords through the ceiling, revealing a mess of ash and blood spread across a morose tableau. At least a dozen gutted corpses punctuated the deathly mosaic.

The bodies were not human.

"Safety?" Sean said.

His bloody human shape was still fighting to emerge from the twisted conglomeration of wings and fur and pus.

"I don't understand. When I left . . ." Charybdis began, shaken by the devastation.

It was silent and still for a moment longer. Soot filled their lungs with the stench of death. A scavenging fly buzzed. It was ignored.

Then came a whisper. Faint words filtered out from the shadows.

"Come forward, my children. You have nothing to fear."

It was Argus. His accent was unmistakable; the unique cadence of a being whose native tongue had been dead for more than a thousand years.

"Master?" Charybdis questioned.

"It is I, barely," came the hoarse response.

The wounded voice was centered on the other side of

the church. It staggered out from somewhere in the dark recesses, where the confessional booths had been appropriated by the nesting cocoon-makers.

Sean lifted Maggie up on the ledge of a pew, laying her down across the hard oak. He almost kissed her cheek, but decided it against it. Instead he ran a gentle stroke along her shoulder. She barely acknowledged the gesture. He turned back to the skinny albino.

Their eyes fighting to discriminate shadow from illusion in the dim, both he and Charybdis navigated their way through the debris. They could hear Argus breathing, wheezing really, huddled someplace in the clutter.

He was cowering beneath a pile of burned wood and broken stone. A gold-rimmed dispensary leaked a tip-tap trickle of holy water into a sanctified puddle beside him.

He was almost lost underneath the broken timber, the left side of his peculiar face a pincushion of splinters in red-seared flesh. Only one badly sliced arm was free. He waved for them when they got near enough to see it moving against the rear wall. It took a while for the pair to clear off the refuse, careful not to injure the old being any more in their attempt to free him.

"What happened here?" Charybdis asked, once they had him pried loose.

"The Morrigan exacted her final vengeance," Argus answered. Slowly, they walked him over to where Maggie rested. His legs dangled, but he was able to shuffle along.

"I don't understand," Sean said.

Charybdis was clearly stunned. "Someone must have

betrayed our location."

"I'm afraid your lover Scylla was not as loyal to you as we had thought," Argus replied.

Charybdis did not take the suggestion lightly.

"Scylla did not betray us. She gave me her word that she had joined with us. She never would have broken that bond!"

The injured, crimson-haired being did not waver, despite his obvious weakness.

"I wish it were not true. But that is the only explanation," Argus answered. "The Morrigan's agents told you she had died, but the Morrigan, like her namesake, has always been a master of deception. She must have killed Arachne in that hotel room, and then given our location away to the Keeper."

"I can't accept it," Charybdis said.

"How exactly did this happen?" Sean questioned.

Argus was already nodding before he finished his question. He answered as though he had expected the query, or had been preparing an answer long in advance.

"Servants of the Keeper surprised us. They massacred those few who remained with me. I was wounded as well, and left for dead. The Morrigan knew of my treachery, you see, and I posed a threat to her that she could no longer tolerate," the old being said, more like a recitation than a reply.

"I never should have left," Charybdis said.

Argus did not give her a chance to continue.

"There was nothing you could have done. The Morrigan planned to be rid of me from the start. I realize now that she did not call the Festival here merely to settle affairs with Lucifer. She did it to free herself from the leaders of all the other Havens."

"She planned to be rid of you all along?" Charybdis asked.

"Indeed. The inhabitants of the Chaligny/Bastille Haven in Paris were mostly killed in the War, as were mine in Prague. So it was with those of our kind from Leningrad, Hong Kong, and most every other city in which we have made permanent homes. The Morrigan brought us all here to consolidate her power, to form a single community in New York, under her direct control."

"And now she has done it," Sean said.

"Not quite yet," Argus answered. "You yet draw breath, and so the prophecy remains. There is still a battle to be fought."

Sean sighed.

"I've told you. I want no part of it. Fight your war without me," he said.

"Argus is right," Charybdis continued. "This is more than just your ordeal now Sean. All of our futures are at stake. If you aid us, we all may yet succeed this night. We all may finally get what we wish."

"What do you mean?" Sean asked.

Charybdis gritted her teeth, almost growling as her fists clenched under her robe.

"We have only one course left to us. We must destroy the Morrigan once and for all," she said. "Perhaps Lucifer is right, and we no longer require a Keeper. Certainly not

one as cruel as the Morrigan. She may have turned Scylla
against us, but I will not serve her again. Tonight we will
be free, and the rest of our kind with us. Or we will die in
the effort."

Sean yet seemed unmoved, stirring though the pale
woman's speech had been.

"If the Morrigan has been here, then she has your
friend Vince as well," Charybdis said, directing her words
to both Maggie and Sean.

Maggie glared back at him. He knew what that look
meant. The years had not dulled it at all. After a long,
quiet moment, he finally melted under the glare of her dag-
ger-blue eyes.

"We'll need to find our way into the festival," Sean said.

"I can lead us there, through the underground tunnels," Argus said.

"Once inside, I'll locate Scylla, to see after this report
of her treachery," Charybdis added, thinking out loud.

"And if she has indeed betrayed you?" Argus asked.

"Then I will kill her myself," she replied, her voice
practically devoid of emotion. "You blend in with the
revelers Sean, get close to the Morrigan. We'll cause a
commotion and . . ."

". . . and you can kill her," Argus said, as though it
were a proposition far easier than they all knew it to be.

"It's no longer just about you, Sean . . . Lucifer. A few
days ago you addressed our people on this very altar. You
talked about freedom. If you meant what you said, then
you'll do it. Damn the prophecy if you wish, you need not

replace the Morrigan. But help the rest of us be free," Charybdis said. "Do at least that much for us, and we will ask no more of you."

Maggie motioned for him to sit near her. He didn't, but she spoke anyway.

"If you ever felt anything for me, then you'll do this," she said. "And for Vince. Don't forget about him. You got us both into this. You owe us at least that."

Sean was quiet again, for another lengthy stretch. It seemed that everyone in the church was looking at him, waiting for his answer.

"Okay," was all he could offer.

FORTY

ONCE THEY PASSED BEYOND THE NEWLY CARVED TUN-
nels directly beneath the cathedral, it became dark and
cold. The air was damp with waste-polluted water. Everything was black, but for occasional hints of moonlight that
slipped in from sewer grates and manholes above.

Argus was at the lead. His gleaming red eyes reflected what little light there was in a weird crimson glow; off
and on, off and on as they walked, like a scarlet lighthouse
shrouded in the mist.

"The Morrigan has purchased a waterfront property
for the festival. It's accessible from these tunnels. My followers who have preceded us left markers for those who
might come later," Argus finally said, after they'd been
walking for nearly an hour.

With his slinky, bluish-white fingers, he pointed out
just such a milestone. A dress had been draped over a rusty
outgrowth of pipes and wires. One arm of the outfit had
been hoisted up at a right angle to the floor. In the murk,
with only the reflected light from Argus's scarlet eyes for
illumination, it looked as though a headless ghost pointed

the way.

"Fine silk, such a waste. Likely discarded by a change-ling who no longer required clothing," Argus commented.

Sean held Maggie in his arms now, carrying her through the slime. Her breathing had grown irregular. She was coughing up phlegm. She was shaking.

"Vince never smoked Parliaments," she whispered.

It was too faint for anyone but Sean to hear.

"What?"

"Cigarettes. He hated Parliaments. Only smoked Lucky Strike, and sometimes Marlboro, or maybe Pall Mall," she continued.

"I don't understand," he whispered back.

"At my apartment, Paddie offered Vince . . . you . . . a Parliament, and you smoked it. Vince never would have done that."

Now he knew what she meant.

"I was hoping you wouldn't really notice," he said.

"Well I did, but I didn't care. I wanted Vince to be back so badly. I just didn't care. Seeing him . . . seeing you looking like him . . . it was easy to believe."

"What can I tell you? I never quite get it exactly right."

"What do you mean?" her reply was made almost out of reflex. She wasn't even sure she cared anymore.

Sean answered regardless. "Getting close to the appearance of someone is actually pretty easy. I can mimic the outside without a problem, but not everything else."

"So you've done this often? Impersonated other people?" she quipped.

"Most of my life, actually," he answered, without even a hint of humor. "I've been hundreds of different people. I read Shakespeare at Oxford as a Scottish war vet. I took classes in Bologna as a girl I met in Florence. I studied impressionism in Marseille as a beggar I encountered in Toulouse. I even learned how to dance the waltz in Munich in a program given for retired folks. But no matter how often I do it, there are usually a few details that I miss."

"Nobody's perfect, huh?"

"Perfect? No, not unless you want to absorb someone."

"Absorb?"

The thought left her momentarily aghast.

"You've seen it, that day with Paulie Tonsils outside of Vince's place."

"I only caught a glimpse, but it really shook up Vince. For a moment, I thought I saw two Paulies, but just for a second. Then he died."

"Yeah, that's the drawback, as you might guess. A long time ago I discovered that if I actually touch someone, come in contact with their skin, I can become them. Everything that makes them who they are. Thoughts, feelings, even the rhythm of their heart. I can absorb the whole lot; draw it out of them and into me."

"Is that how you got better so quickly after that morning?" she asked.

"In a manner of speaking," he answered. "I took everything Paulie had, every breath of life in him. That's what restored me. Now I have it all in me. Every memory. Every little quirk. I can tell you everything about him."

"Like what?" she asked.

Sean didn't even need a second to think. The words rattled off his tongue.

"He hated spaghetti but not elbow macaroni. Never drank white wine. When he was twelve he killed a neighbor's cat with a kitchen knife and buried the body in his mother's garden on the roof of their building. Best tomatoes they ever grew that season. And he had a thing for women's feet that I'd rather not get into."

She was silenced. Sean laughed.

"He even convinced himself that his comb-over actually fooled people," he joked. "I could actually become him now, if I wished. Even his wife wouldn't know the difference."

Maggie had no idea how to answer something so surreal. So Sean kept talking.

"The problem is, as you saw, taking all of that away from someone usually kills them. In Paulie's case that wasn't much of a loss."

Suddenly the thought struck Maggie. Her head turned sharply.

"What about Vince?" she demanded.

Sean realized what she must have been thinking. He put his hand on her cheek, just for a second.

"Don't worry, he's fine," he assured her. "At least he was the last time I saw him. As much as I resented him for what happened with the two of you, as much as I wanted you for myself, wanted to be rid of him, I couldn't bring myself to do that. He was the only real friend I ever had."

"Touching, I guess," she replied. "So you faked it with him."

"I faked *being him*, yeah. But I haven't really known the guy for the last thirty years, so obviously I missed a few details. Animals or objects are easy, but people are complicated. It's easy to get things wrong. Especially when you do it quickly. Truth is, as long as you get the major aspects right, most people will overlook the little things, even if they've known someone . . ."

Sean paused then, as though the words had jarred something in him.

"Sean?" she prodded.

He stopped walking, leaving both he and Maggie a few paces back from the others. For a moment, there was just the silence of the tunnel, and the constant, *synchronized* red flashes from the eyes of their leader.

"What's wrong?" she whispered.

". . . even if they've known someone for a long, long time," he continued.

"What's the matter?" she said.

Her teeth were chattering.

Sean didn't answer. He remained transfixed in the dark, his gaze stuck on the rhythmic red flashes.

The next voice she heard came from a few yards away, from ahead.

"The exit is just up here," said Charybdis, her stark white features brightened by light from above. "Argus has found the doorway to the Morrigan's domain."

✤ ✤ ✤

The doors closed behind them, silent and still. Nothing penetrated the shadows. Not the rusty clang of the docks or the evening lilt of the Hudson.

It was dark, lightless aside from a single pink sparkle that seemed to flicker far, far in the distance; like a flower lost amid a starless night. Quickly the lone sparkle became two, and then four and then a full blaze of rose-colored light. Within the aura was a frame, and two behind. Silhouettes of women and men with thin, curved bodies. The figures seemed to illuminate themselves, with a reddish glow that came from nowhere but around them.

The one at the lead was cloaked, although her shroud might merely have been a trick of the shadows. Her beautiful canine face was lit only by the blush of scarlet lips. Her feral-eyes were blank, and dark as opal stones. Her crown was half hidden, either bald or lost beneath a hood of darkness that rested heavily upon it.

"The Daughters of Cerberus," Charybdis said. "The Guardians of the Molting."

"Will they let us pass?" Maggie asked. Her voice was hushed to a near whisper.

"They will do nothing to impede us. They are only gatekeepers, not guards. Anyone, human or changeling, is permitted to cross into the festival," Argus said.

"But how do you keep such a thing secret?" she asked as Sean set her down beside Charybdis.

"I said that anyone may enter. If you tried to leave,

then you'd see," Sean answered, slowly edging backward from both Maggie and the others.

"Welcome to the Molting," Argus said.

The doors beyond the Daughters of Cerberus opened, flooding the antechamber with light and smoke and noise. It was warm. The humid draft carried a sting, weighted down with the sharp odor of musk and incense.

Maggie choked when the scent assaulted her.

"Forward, quickly, if we're to enter without attracting much attention," Charybdis urged.

She noticed that Sean had drifted a few paces back, beside the gatekeepers. But she paid little mind to it.

"That won't be a problem, Charybdis," Argus said.

His tone was strange, almost hostile, but Charybdis did not have long to wonder after it. A second, very familiar voice continued the ancient one's thought.

"You already have my attention."

It was mellifluous, more like music than simple words. When Charybdis turned, she knew why.

"What's going on?" Maggie asked.

She was suddenly very conscious that Sean was gone from her side.

"We've been tricked," Sean said.

"Very true, very true," Argus said, stepping to the fore. A cadre of white-robed Maenads streamed into the chamber, circling the weary travelers with a ring of pointed steel. "You have been fooled, and now the game is over."

As he spoke, Argus sucked a huge breath into his lungs, inflating his chest in an absurdly distended fashion. When he exhaled, his entire body twisted in a way that no normal person's could ever do, like a band of tightly woven rope uncoiling.

His skirt fell away with the torque. There was no hideous mutant nudity beneath. His lower limbs were somehow merged into one icy-white stalagmite. A delicate shimmer glazed his skin.

As they watched, horrified, his smile dissolved and his eyes fell shut. Then his head melted into the thick of his shoulders.

They would have continued staring, revolted and drawn in at the same time. But the glow of his flesh coalesced, spinning away from his chest in a sudden flare. Those who did not immediately turn away winced and shielded their eyes with their hands.

The burst of heat and flame lasted only a moment. The shadows of the entranceway quickly fell back down over them, except for one place. And that was where they all looked.

Argus was gone. Something far more beautiful, and far more terrible, stood in his place.

"Who?" Maggie said.

"Morrigan," Sean said.

His voice was now eerily disembodied. It echoed as though spoken from a distance.

When the others turned to see why, they found not three Daughters of Cerberus lingering in the shadows, but four. Their black hoods stood out darkly against the gleaming white cloaks of the encircled Maenads.

"It is over Lucifer. I will spare no one now to end it forever," the Morrigan said, her hands raised toward the quartet of gatekeepers, three genuine and one an imposter.

A second flare sparked from within her open palms, illuminating the dark again. The light struck the Maenad guards, igniting red flames on the edges of their blades. Without hesitation, they hacked down all four of the canine sentinels.

The savage murders took barely thirty seconds.

Maggie gasped as the four obedient women dutifully fell, none offering up so much as a yelp. Their cloaks covered over their remains when they landed, and the guards wasted no time in spearing the mantles. The Morrigan seemed to float toward them, her fingers glittering with captive lightning.

One cloak came away to reveal a bloodied, pale cadaver. A second revealed the same. Two remained. One, they all knew, was not a Daughter of Cerberus.

The Morrigan waved off her attendants. She would have the final honor for herself.

With one motion, she yanked the bloodied cloaks from both fallen watchers, and found two more corpses.

"My queen!" one of the attendants shouted.

It was a moment too late.

From behind, the first of the fallen ladies rose. Her corpse was corrupted, torn by a dozen gashes and fouled by violent, red-drooling cavities. But even as she stepped toward the Morrigan, the wounds were mending themselves in a mess of bone and blood and jagged flesh.

She was smiling through a toothless, oozing mouth.

The Morrigan nodded. She recognized a fellow trickster and opened her arms. Twin blades were growing out of the pliable shapes of her fingers. She slashed each sword in turn, but the steel passed through the risen corpse like liquid. A Maenad beside her made a third strike, a thrust. Sean's cadaverous torso opened to accommodate the weapon, wide so that the blade cut only air.

The Morrigan recoiled, though the rest of her guards were already in motion. They charged Sean, but his body, whose features had now begun to regain their original form, was too quick.

Sean took hold of, and withdrew the Maenad's blade from his chest. It exited as harmlessly as it had entered. The skin closed up where it had opened to allow the sword entry. With a swift hand, he slashed across a pair of the guardians. Two deformed heads tumbled to the floor, and as the rest watched helplessly, Sean vanished into the haze and the noise of the Molting.

FORTY-ONE

SWORDS AGAINST THEIR BACKS MARCHED THEM AHEAD, motivated by the Morrigan's angry command. Behind, the doors that had once been guarded by the Daughters of Cerberus slammed shut. They were sealed off from the outside.

"Enjoy your peek into our world. Brief though it will be," the Morrigan sneered.

As Maggie looked on, disbelieving yet, the war goddess fell backward into her own shadow. Then, just as she had cast off the physiognomy of Argus like others might discard a coat, the Morrigan shed her human aspect. A glowering black raven grew up from the midst of her remains.

It eyed Maggie with a knowing glare before vanishing into the hidden reaches above.

Their leader gone, the silent Maenads forced the two through a shifting glow of candles, torches, and electrical lamps. Charybdis had taken Maggie up in her arms. She was now too weak to walk.

From her vantage, Maggie couldn't see much. The veil of smoke from braziers and opium pipes stung her

eyes. Tears and shadow-soaked clouds obscured her view.
There were people everywhere. Or maybe not people. In
the haze it was hard to be sure.

They negotiated a living maze. Charybdis carried her
through a sea of tangled flesh broken by occasional vacant
eddies. Glimpses and glances hinted at horrors half-drowned
in the haze. Screeches and squeals suggested worse. She
saw depravity, raw and shameless. She shuddered.

At one turn, a woman was bent over a wooden saw-
horse, her wrists and her ankles chained to the base. Red
sores and blisters befouled her exposed ass. Two beastly,
hunched creatures hovered over her predicament, scandal-
ous delight spread across their faces.

Whips dangled from their hairy fists. They took turns
flailing them against her despoiled buttocks. She shrieked
with every hard crack of the leather, but Maggie wasn't at
all sure if they were screams of agony, or of pleasure. They
might have been one in the same.

Just a few yards away, sheltered behind a ragged curtain, four figures sat around a table clothed with purple
velvet. Each one was unique, and none of them paid even
the faintest attention to the continuous screams stirred up
from the whipping post.

Two had heads that were triangular in shape, with a
snout-like mouth and nose. Their torsos were elongated
and tubular. Both had drooping arms that seemed to lack
joints. Each was hairless. Their skin glistened the color of
slate, but one had clearly defined female breasts while the
other did not.

Something sat between them with a face that resembled an African ritual mask; wide, long, and flat with tufts of straw-hair jutting up from the crown. Thick, gnarled fur hid its body. Across the table from it was a woman, human in all respects. She was naked and perfectly shaped, but covered in a coat of fine, blond hair.

There was a pint glass in front of her, the mouth covered by a large silver spoon marked with diagonal slits. She placed a series of sugar cubes on the utensil, reciting an adage as she did so.

The slate-skinned one beside her handed up a large black bottle, the glass tarnished, old, and opaque. Only a fragment of a paper label still clung to the face.

She raised and uncorked the bottle, pouring a pale green liquid over the spoon. All four of them breathed in deeply as they watched the sugar cubes dissolve, and the mixture drain through the slits.

Once it was done, the absinthe glowed jade-green. She removed the spoon and set it down. The four joined hands, those with something less than traditional appendages offering what they could to their neighbors. A solemn moment of prayer passed, a phrase repeated by each one in turn.

Then the leader took hold of the glass, sipped it lovingly and passed it to her left. Each one did the same.

"Hmm. That's something I haven't seen in ages, I thought no one was doing it anymore. Even for our kind, the wormwood can be deadly," Charybdis remarked.

Maggie would have said something, but the next group

snared her attention instead. Her expression said it all. Her eyes were opened as wide as they could go. Her jaw hung down quite un-self-consciously.

"I realize some of this is shocking to you, but it is all perfectly normal for us," Charybdis attempted to assure her.

"Normal? *That* is normal?" she said.

She pointed to the seven or eight naked males stroking each other's genitals. They were gathered in a wide circle around a bald, blue-skinned woman who moaned deeply as she was penetrated by the organ of a rearing canine.

"Sex with animals is normal?"

"Those animals you see will look like ordinary people in a few days, and some of those ordinary looking people will look like animals."

"But . . . still, sex?" she muttered.

"Certainly. Intercourse doesn't have the same meaning for us as it does for you," Charybdis said, not at all disturbed by the debauchery. "For our kind it's merely one more form of gratification. Because of our constant molting, most of us cannot reproduce."

She hardly seemed convinced.

Underscoring the squeals and the sighs, and the occasional scream, a rhythmic chant kept constant pace throughout the hold. It was incomprehensible, an endless stream of words. Each one blended so seamlessly into the next as to resonate in a ubiquitous hum. It seemed to have no single source. Somehow, it grew stronger when they stopped at the foot of the towering throne dais, like an invisible, euphonious tide.

"What are those sounds?" Maggie questioned.

She was beyond fear now. The pain in her side had made her weak. All she had left was her horror, and her anger.

"They're called the Odes of Dionysus," Charybdis answered. "Songs that were ancient when Rome was a village, hypnotic tunes that once heralded festivals in dark, haunted forests. Some say they're meant to drive the revelers into ecstasy. And to drive outsiders into madness."

"They're not in English. What do they mean?"

"I'm afraid I don't really know," Charybdis answered.

"Aren't these *your* people?" she asked.

"They are, but in all my years I never learned this language. It's Greek. I know that. A very old form called *Koine*," the pale changeling replied.

"Why Greek?"

"Tradition," a familiar voice interrupted. "So I'm told, anyway. This particular custom predates even me."

It was Argus, *the real Argus*. He was chained like a beast, his neck constrained by an iron collar. The links kept him fettered to the floor of a pit at the base of the Keeper's throne. His limbs were shackled in like fashion.

He smiled, peculiarly, as Charybdis and Maggie were forced to rest upon the damp concrete next to him. The white-robed Maenads clamped manacles on their wrists, locking them all into place in the shadow of the Morrigan's great seat.

"The Havens, where changelings gather in secret today, are the continuations of ancient pagan temples. It was there that our words and our history were born, in the lost days of Mycenaean Greece. Later, they were written down during the waning years of the Roman Republic. At that time, Koine and Latin were like English and French today," Argus continued, lecturing like a sage despite his confinement. "We were honored in those times. The pagans saw our molting as a reflection of the endless cycles of nature. Continuous change. Continuous renewal. As the winter becomes the spring, as the seed becomes the flower, and even as the caterpillar becomes the butterfly, so do we change.

"The ancients gave us sanctuary. For many thousands of years they used us in their rituals, and spoke of us in their stories. Now their descendants fear us."

"Enough of the tales, Argus. For all your distrust of the outsiders, it is by the hand of our own kind that we face death today," Charybdis gibed.

Argus was about to respond, to admonish his aide, when the Maenads returned. They brought another prisoner. It was Vince. He was shirtless, haggard, and pale. Regardless, he immediately interrupted.

"Maggie? Goddamn Sean! He said he was going to keep you out of this. Son of a bitch!" he exclaimed as he too was forced to his knees and shackled beside the others.

"He tried, I think. No thanks to your friends," Maggie answered, not nearly as happy to see him as he might have expected.

"My friends? What the hell are you talking about? Jesus Maggie, I don't know what anybody told you, but I'm not . . ."

"We were sold out! By your ex-partner," Maggie said,

cutting him off with a sharp tone. "He set us up, told us he was going to help. But he led us right to them."

Vince shook his head. He banged his hand against the stone blocks.

"Pat Flanagan? No way. Not Paddie. He's the most honest cop I've ever known."

"Yeah well, all I can tell you is he took us way out of the city, and that's where they got us. They knew right where to find us, too."

"We did have advanced knowledge. That is true," Charybdis spoke up.

"I can't believe it, not Paddie," Vince continued.

A dark and sonorous voice answered him.

"You needn't, Mr. Sicario. Your friend was quite loyal. To the end, I imagine. Little pity, his death, he was an annoying sort," the Morrigan said.

No longer a raven, she stepped up to survey them from the edge of her dais. The comment was more of a mention. It carried no hint of emotion.

"Loyal, but not at all tight-lipped. And those around him, those within his precinct, owed their favors to Salvatore Calabrese. They were more than happy to keep me abreast of his comings and goings. Truly invaluable in obtaining all of you," the Phantom Queen continued, floating away into the teeming masses, leaving only the oversized shadow of her opulent seat, just beyond their sight.

FORTY-TWO

SEAN MOVED WITH EYES SHIFTING IN EVERY DIRECTION, through shadows and varieties of light. He glided anonymously between the grotesque and the beautiful, seeing for the first time in three decades the celebrations of his estranged brethren.

His every step was registered with utmost caution. The Morrigan could be lurking behind any one of the faces that passed by in the revelry. The Keeper, like him, could change shape at will, and could stalk him without his ever realizing it. For that reason, Sean submerged his human form, the face of his never-faded youth. With every dark corner he slipped into, and every cloud of narcotic smoke that wafted over him, he shifted his appearance.

To the three reptilian women wagering sexual favors over hands of five-card draw, he was a hunch-backed giant, clambering by like some Grimm Brothers ogre.

Two squid-headed men, one cooking his heroin on a spoon over a flame, the other tying off his flipper in preparation for the needle, saw him as a lovely young Asian girl, naked and prancing.

But neither was really looking.

In the girl's form, he skipped his way into a circle of dancers, cavorting and twirling to the throbbing beat of kettledrums. Spun about, his breasts fondled and his ass slapped, he just as quickly slipped away from the coterie.

Then he passed beneath a mesh tarp, slung from the low-hanging ventilation pipes in the rear corner of the warehouse. It was a bit quieter there, sheltered from the debauchery. Several figures were reclined on cushions, one on an antique couch. When he came to the only person sitting upright, a thing with shimmering silver skin and a head with two faces, he had sprouted pointy ears and shifted into an elf-like form.

The twin-countenanced man smiled with both mouths. He offered a pipe, and an empty set of cushions lay upon the floor. Sean nodded, placed his lips on the pipe and sucked in some of the warm opiate smoke. He pretended to inhale, then lazily reclined.

When he did, and he set his feminine head down, he noticed a figure walking by just outside of the tarp's shadow. There was nothing peculiar about him, plainly humanlike and non-threatening, but it was the way he walked that caught Sean's eye. He stepped slowly, turning his head in every direction as he did. He seemed to be looking for something, or someone.

Was it the Morrigan? Or merely one of the Maenads, uncloaked for the hunt?

Whoever it was, they were seeking him. Even he would not be able to hide forever.

✣   ✣   ✣

Scylla, as yet unaware of her lover's capture, or the presence of Lucifer besides, rested where she had been for the past day. The wounded warrior was tended to in a sheltered chamber near the Keeper's dais, by some of the least unusual changelings, nearly human looking attendants who betrayed their true race only through slight physical anomalies.

Under their expert care she had recovered some, but was still weak, and required more rest before she would be able to molt again. When the Morrigan stepped into her abode, at the lead of six faceless Maenads, she sensed something was amiss.

The six-armed woman arose at the Keeper's entry. While the renowned slayer did not look to be entirely herself, limping as she stood and wearing a bandage over the wound in her midsection, she yet made a fearsome stand. She was naked, but for the bandage and a black leather belt around her waist. Twin scabbards hung from each side of her waist. Her skin was golden and gleaming, her eyes fierce and black as night.

"Master?" she said, twitching her fingers to reach for her swords, as yet uncertain if that would prove necessary.

"Scylla, my foolish child," the Morrigan scolded. "I had hoped you were near to rejoining my side, with the sacrifice of Lycaon."

As she spoke, the Maenads drew forth their curved scythes. Now there could be no question.

"Sacrifice?" Scylla asked.

Though heedless of the blades suddenly pointed at her, her heart sank at the realization that her plot had somehow been uncovered.

"Yes. My wolf-child is gone. Fallen in the pursuit of Lucifer, but thanks to you and your lover, his sacrifice was not in vain. In fact it was exactly what I had wished for. The prophecy has now come to affect us all, hasn't it?" her silky, melodious voice said.

"You sent Lycaon after Lucifer, knowing he could never subdue a trickster."

"Of course, he was loyal to a fault, much as I once thought you to be. His absence will be lamented, but it was necessary. For the sake of our kind, I must endure, above all.

"You see, as bold as your plot against me was, your own actions doomed it to failure. When Lycaon rescued you, he did far more than save you. He captured your friend Arachne as well. She was reluctant to give up any information at first. I allowed her to molt, however, and after I had three or four of her legs removed and barbequed for my hungry servants, she became quite forthcoming.

"Once I knew where Argus was hiding, I let Lycaon rampage. He slaughtered those few who had remained loyal to the old one. He also, quite by accident, discovered that Mr. Vince Sicario rested within the cathedral. With the word from our contacts in the New York City Police Department, I suspected Lucifer had sought to deceive me by taking on his old friend's form. So I elected to answer deception with deception."

Scylla snarled. It was the only gesture she could make without risking a blade in the back.

"And now Lucifer himself has been drawn into my realm, soon to join Charybdis as my prisoner. Tonight I have been given a rare opportunity. I will settle these affairs once and for all, and finally, mercifully, prove the Book of Nestor wrong.

"Perhaps you would like to watch?"

✣ ✣ ✣

Scylla was marched out to the foot of the throne dais. Charybdis saw her and cursed. She echoed her lover's sentiment, even as the white-robed servants chained her up, shackling all six of her arms. The pit was now crowded full.

"How far we have fallen," Scylla said, looking up at the platform with the seat of the Morrigan atop it.

"Fitting, though, that we shall meet our end where we had our beginning," Charybdis replied, making a bitter, somewhat strange introduction between Maggie and Scylla.

"What will happen here?" Maggie asked.

"The Morrigan will solidify her power. She will exact her final judgment on the two of us," Charybdis said.

"For aiding Sean?"

"No, our transgression dates much further back than this latest travail. Our history with the Morrigan far predates Lucifer's," Scylla answered.

She left it at that, perhaps unwilling to tell more, perhaps not. Argus, however, broke the momentary still when it became clear that neither Scylla nor Charybdis intended to continue.

"Why don't you tell this human your tale? It might help to reconcile you with the end, unburden your soul, one final time," the ancient one suggested.

Ever the counselor, even while awaiting his own execution.

Charybdis shook her head. She looked over at Scylla, frowning. Each regarded the other for a long while, and finally, both smiled. Then they relented.

"1918 was the year of our disgrace. The last year in which we laid eyes upon one another, until these current days," Scylla began.

"What happened?"

"Lucifer," Charybdis replied.

"Sean? So he is responsible?"

Scylla looked certain, but Charybdis wavered, and it was she who continued.

"He was the impetus, but he is no more responsible for what happened than we were."

"How, then?"

"He simply appeared," the pale woman said. "Do you recall what he told you in the tunnels beneath the cathedral? About how he was drawn to St. Petersburg, to the underbelly of that deserted Tsarist palace?"

She nodded.

"Scylla and I were there as well, standing by the side of the Morrigan, as we had for three hundred years. We were once her most trusted aides, you see, her guardians against harm. Deadly to all comers, and loyal to the death."

"We were feared. Feared perhaps as greatly as the Morrigan herself," Scylla boasted. "It was our most glorious time."

"But as with all glory, it was not to last forever," Argus added.

"True enough. When Lucifer entered the hall, he was unaware of who we were, or of who he was. The only reason he knew as much as he did was his experience on the battlefields of France. It left him, I'm afraid, with a somewhat *mistaken* impression."

"One which cost us our place of honor, and nearly our sanity besides," Scylla added.

"I still don't understand," Maggie said.

"After several days spent observing us, silently, it came time for the initiation rite. All the new changelings were urged to come forward to shed their human identity and take on a name from the rolls of Nestor. Many did so, and Lucifer joined them."

"But he didn't know our customs, and our prejudices. He expected that we were all like him," Scylla said.

"It was a moment that I will never forget," Argus said. "When he stepped up to the foot of the Keeper's chair, before all of us gathered, he greeted the Morrigan."

"Greeted her by changing his form to mirror the Keeper," Charybdis interrupted.

"I don't think anyone in the hall was spared a startle in that instant, the Morrigan first among us," Argus said.

"She flew into a rage, accused us of betraying her and

immediately struck a blow to slay the youngster," Charybdis stated.

"But why?"

"Because the Morrigan believed that a rival trickster had come to claim her throne, and that we had been complicit in the attempt," Scylla answered.

"Lucifer was too quick, however. He escaped both the Morrigan and the palace itself. No one saw him again for several years, until I found him, wandering lost in Prague," Argus said.

"Ultimately, the Morrigan realized what had happened. We were absolved of any suspicion, but her anger did not abate. She still blamed us for not protecting her," Scylla noted.

"As our punishment, we were stripped of our status, banished from her side and sent away. Each of us was forbidden to have any contact with the other, until Lucifer was slain," Charybdis said.

"Until our failure was rectified," Scylla concluded, finishing her lover's thought.

"That is how Charybdis came into my service, in fact," Argus said. "For I have long sought to cultivate relations with those who are disgruntled with the Morrigan's reign. It was as my aide that Charybdis came to know Lucifer, and to befriend him."

"All in an effort to kill him, at first," the pale woman considered, nodding. "But I waited, bided my time. Tricksters are resilient creatures, you see, very difficult to kill. In truth, they're almost invincible if they know you're coming. I needed to find just the right combination of circumstances."

"But she went soft on him instead," Scylla joked.

"Under Argus's tutelage I grew to know him, and I grew to like him," Charybdis smiled. "He was a wounded soul, very much like I was then. He too loved another that he could not be with. But he did not stay long, and even as I came to understand him, and his desire to be free from all of this, he left our Haven. And vanished for over twenty years."

"When he came to our attention again, with the killings in Venice, and the trail he left that led back here, I knew that our chance had come. Together I had hoped that we might end the rule of the Morrigan, and free all of our kind," Argus said.

"But we have now failed in that endeavor as well. And soon we will pay the final price," Scylla said.

FORTY-THREE

THE WAREHOUSE WAS COMPLETELY SEALED OFF FROM the outside world. They had been chained up for hours, long enough for their weariness to overwhelm their fear.

A bath of crimson light washed over them like the hand of death, but only for an instant. Each of the five prisoners looked up to see the lovely, horrible sight of the Morrigan.

"The time for feasting has arrived," the Keeper said.

A small horde had gathered before the face of the throne platform. They were clambering, alternating between shouting and humming in some peculiar pattern. Bodies pressed tightly against one another, strange flesh meeting scales, and fur, and naked skin.

They cheered when the Maenads led Vince and Maggie to the side of the throne, and they howled when Argus was led there from the pit. But the crush of revelers cried the loudest when Scylla and Charybdis emerged from the shelter, and marched up to the top of the platform inches ahead of pointed Maenad blades.

Their cries then became something other than fervor or cheer. In sight of the two who had once been the Morrigan's aides, their voices fell into a rumble that was utterly different in its tone.

It almost sounded like hunger.

"And the last, the one who has made this night's wonderful harvest possible," the Morrigan shouted. "Bring her forth, that the blood of the traitors may slake the thirst of the loyal."

From someplace below the throne, though it wasn't exactly clear where, two more white-hooded, faceless Maenads ascended. Between them, braced limply in their arms, there rested the strangest creature of all. Long, spindly limbs branched off from a hairy, rounded torso, four or five of them, at least.

It didn't look like much of anything in fact, until the Maenads set it down before the Keeper, and its proper shape became clear. It was a giant spider, with a body that lay parallel to the floor, though clearly missing several of its eight legs. A human head looked up from the front of it.

It was Arachne. Though her blond hair was gone, and her skull was half-merged with her stunted neck, the features of her face had hardly changed. But she was now bloodied and cut, her eyes swollen and her mouth dripping red.

"Argus, I believe you are acquainted with tonight's first guest," the Morrigan said, waving her followers forward again.

The two who had brought Arachne up pulled down on a series of rusted chains suspended from the rafters, holdovers from the previous life of the warehouse. There were clamps attached to the ends of three out of the four links, and they duly fettered them to three of Arachne's remaining legs.

"This one has been very helpful. She did require some coercion, of course," the Morrigan began. "But once I had severed a few limbs and, I think, had an eye plucked out, she really became quite talkative."

Argus sneered, though his androgynous features were rendered somewhat comical when expressing anger.

"You are to be credited, old friend, now that I remember to mention it. She is very strong, an excellent choice for a bodyguard. If only she had come under my supervision earlier, she might have served me. Instead, she chose to follow you. Now she suffers the price of disobedience."

The Maenads stepped back, and took up a place at the edge of the platform. The other ends of the chains were secured there, slung like pulleys over the pipes and rafters. Slowly, they unfastened them from their locks, and they increased the slack.

The Morrigan, now behind Arachne, pushed her like a child on a swing. Dangling, she swung helplessly over the waiting crowd. Claws and hands and other things reached up to touch her, to grab her, but her momentum carried her back over the throne dais unscathed.

As a Maenad handed the Morrigan a great book, the text of ancient lore that she alone was master of, she cued her musical players. Quickly, the tunes of the orchestra drove the revelers into frenzy. Many shed what little clothing they still wore, revealing their forms, both hideous and magnificent. Churned like a storm tide, roused by the ancient song of Dionysus, they formed a mob of fury.

Again the Morrigan pushed her captive charge, harder this time. When Arachne flew out over the howling masses, the Maenads increased the slack once more. She dropped ever farther, twisted by the uneven length of the chains, dangling within reach of some of the largest of the weird revelers.

She screamed. The chains dug into her flesh and tore her limbs from their sockets.

The crowd loved it.

Her return swing only brought her to the edge of the platform, sobbing and squealing for mercy. The Morrigan, the very old leather-bound volume in her hands, merely kicked her off the dais, and for a third time, the chains carried her careening out over the assembled.

This time, the Maenads ended their torture, and released the chains fully. The clatter of the clanking metal was quickly drowned out by the rush of screams when Arachne's body fell into the sea of adherents.

She vanished beneath the living waves.

Their ardor reached a fever pitch. A geyser spray of blood and flesh-shards sprang forth.

The Morrigan smiled.

"She revealed it all, Argus. Your plotting. Your scheming. She betrayed you," the Keeper declared.

The great tome in her grasp was now opened, exposing dusty, crinkled parchment. Upon the pages, complex script was scrawled in the classical Greek alphabet.

The Morrigan read. Her melodious voice rang out over every other noise; the screams, the music and the sounds of tearing flesh. The words were incomprehensible to most, only Argus of all those gathered on the dais understood. He recognized them as the writings of Nestor, preserved in their original tongue. The Morrigan was reading the full text of the prophecy.

"He does not wish to replace you, Morrigan," Argus shouted. "He doesn't even believe in the prophecy."

The dark goddess seemed to hear the ancient changeling. She turned from the sight of the blood-feast to address Argus.

"Then we have at least that much in common, don't we?" he answered. "I'd like to say the same for myself. But as you advised me wise one, the best way to ensure that the prophecy is false is to prove that Nestor was mistaken. And to do that, I must prove that Sean Mulcahy is not Lucifer."

"But Sean wants no part of us, of this. I assure you, he poses no threat to your reign," Argus continued.

The screaming faded, and the gathered slowly stilled. Many turned their faces upward, blood-soaked and crazed. They sought the next words from the Keeper.

"Mulcahy! I know you can hear me. I know you're among us still. I know you're listening," the Morrigan proclaimed.

"What if he's already gone, Morrigan? All that Sean has ever wanted was to be free from our world. Now that he has that chance, I see no reason why he wouldn't take it."

"No reason? I can think of at least one," the Morrigan replied, her gaze shifted from the ancient one to Vince and Maggie. "I can think of two, in fact."

FORTY-FOUR

THE GROTESQUE ORCHESTRA CONTINUED TO PLAY. Slowly, the Maenads drew the chains back up from the crowd. Blood lubricated the rust, dripping from the iron. Jagged fragments of skin and bone clung to the wet links.

All other traces of Arachne were gone.

The Morrigan had her servants bring the fetter-ended chains over to where she stood. Then she called forth the next victims for her cannibalistic feast.

"My two disgraced servants, together before me once more," the Morrigan said, turning to Scylla and Charybdis. "I had hoped you both bent upon repentance here. But I know that your actions were little more than a ruse."

"Somehow, I suspect you wanted to believe it," Scylla replied.

The suggestion elicited a slight smile from the Keeper. She nodded with grim satisfaction as she considered the thought.

"Wanted to believe? Yes, perhaps so. Perhaps that is why I feel so very disappointed in you both now," the Morrigan answered.

"All that I will say is that I love Charybdis. Everything that I have done was to that end," Scylla said, her teeth clenched and her lips held fast.

"And I love Scylla. What was done here was for no less of a cause. However our betrayal has made you feel, you can rest assured that we have suffered more in these past decades than you can ever understand."

The Morrigan sighed, again seeming to ponder the sentiments for a long moment. But when she raised her gleaming red eyes to bear a moment later, there was not a hint of congeniality in her gaze. Only malice resided in her stare.

"Suffer? My children, I have not yet even begun to make you suffer."

She winced as the Keeper lifted her hand so that her cloak fell away. Instead of fingers, a single, translucent hook pointed toward her.

The Maenads swept in from behind her, leaving Scylla chained to the stone blocks at her feet. Charybdis twisted her head as she was hauled forward. One last time she mouthed the three simple words she had been kept from saying for thirty years.

Scylla nodded, a tear on her golden cheek.

"I love you too," she said.

Charybdis kept her expression harsh. She stared into the glittering, burning eyes of the Morrigan. The Keeper frowned. She looked genuinely regretful, right up to the moment when she impaled the changeling who had once been her most loyal.

The Morrigan dug into her flesh with her self-made hooks. Once in each shoulder she drove her poniard-hand deep through skin and muscle, ripping joints and slicing flesh like carrion.

Charybdis did not even whimper.

The Maenads carried forth the orange-brown links again. Instead of the clamps that had held Arachne's limbs, ice tongs were now fastened to their ends.

Scylla gasped, held at her distance by the blades of the white-cloaks and the chains on her six wrists. She strained against the metal, tearing red swatches into her skin. And though Charybdis remained stoic, the agony of her ordeal played out across her lover's face as though it were her own.

With uncommon gentleness, the Morrigan herself set the pincers in place, buried deep in the torn muscle and sinew of Charybdis's torso. Still, she kept her gaze fixed directly on her. She would not permit the Morrigan the pleasure of a single cry.

The Morrigan stepped back, and she waved for the Maenads to take hold. They pulled on the chains at their base. Soon Charybdis was hauled into the air above the dais, a living effigy for the maddened, blood-starving crowd.

The Morrigan turned her attention to the carnivorous masses, moaning in anticipation of the salty-rich flavor of not-quite-human meat. They could smell her as she dangled just beyond reach. Her pheromones and her dripping innards drove them into ecstasy.

"The price of defiance," the war queen said.

The crowd roared.

With a shove, she thrust the hanging body of Charybdis away from the throne platform. This time, however, the throng did not have to wait for their feast. When her gibbeted form swung out fully across the gathered, the Morrigan waved to her Maenads.

They released the chains.

Charybdis tumbled into the crowd. She was promptly swallowed up by their rush of savage longing.

Strange music echoed through the chamber, screams of pain and cries of hunger mixed with sounds of pure, inhuman delight. The center of the masses, where Charybdis had fallen, surged upward like a wolf pack in the madness of a feeding. Blood sprayed in every direction, pieces of arms, legs, and other, less-identifiable chunks of flesh went flying.

But again, the horror did not last long. Soon the horde quieted once more. The deed was done. Their prey was torn limb from limb. Their peculiar taste was quenched.

The Morrigan nodded. She turned for the next offering to the bacchanalian death-rite.

But there were gasps. Screams followed by shouts from within the throng. The horde sprang to life again. Carnage erupted once more as though set in motion from the start. A second time the supplicants to the throne of shadows swelled in a rage of cannibal lust. Another round of shrieking followed, another flurry of raw meat and savagery set to delicate orchestral tunes.

And a second time, the deed was done. The horde

settled again.

The Morrigan gave it no more thought. She looked away from her flock one more time. But her attention was drawn back only a moment later. Once again, a disturbance rippled through the mob. Its source remained unseen, though clearly situated within the crowd. Something was still brimming beneath.

The adherents pounced for a third brutal course, continuing their Dionysian savagery. But this time, some of the wild masses backed away, shaking their heads in disbelief; horrified, if anyone so soiled with blood could still know such a feeling.

Intrigued, the Morrigan stepped to the edge of the dais. She was about to inquire after her subjects. It quickly became unnecessary.

All the revelers stepped away. A barren circle opened in their midst. Pieces of a human, barely recognizable for the thrashing pile of remnants, sat in a heap on the floor.

But the fouled corpse was alive yet.

The remains continued to move, despite their ruined state. A chill slipped over the otherwise crazed changelings. The blood on the floor congealed. Shredded flesh slithered in a wet mess, a pile of red worms swimming in a puddle of crimson filth.

Everything fell silent. Even the Morrigan was brought to a pause.

Animated by some will, by some power whose source was unseen, shattered bones mended. Torn muscles healed. Tattered skin re-formed. The pieces joined, and built themselves into a figure. A blood-dripping silhouette at first, but then with features that emerged from the repaired anatomy.

Some of the throng chanted his name, even before his face had fully reshaped itself.

"Lucifer."

The Morrigan had no time to quiet them. The curdle of a death scream, followed by the gurgle of a severed throat, turned her to the left.

Beside Scylla there stood a Maenad guard, its face lost beneath the shadow of a great hood. The pristine of its white robes became quickly savaged as the Phantom Queen watched, stained a deep scarlet from within. Its sword dropped harmlessly from its grasp. It collapsed.

There was a woman standing behind.

"Charybdis," the Keeper muttered.

Alive, though wounded by her own hand, the pale changeling stood defiant atop the dais. Warm red splatter stained her breasts, spilled out both from her own gashes and from the Maenad she had just killed.

The Morrigan did not even need to look to know that she had already loosed the chains binding Scylla. Below, the chanting surged. The clatter and the rumble of Lucifer shook the rafters.

But the trickster was already gone.

On the dais, Scylla picked up the fallen Maenad's blade. Charybdis was already armed. Then the two who had once sworn to guard the Morrigan circled her.

There was nothing but hatred left in their eyes.

FORTY-FIVE

ARGUS TURNED WITH A START WHEN A HAND GRIPPED his shoulder. His head twisted to his left. He found Sean staring down at him. The trickster's face was still emerging from a bloody chaos of veins and muscles. Under other circumstances, the ancient one might have been repulsed by such a hideous sight, or at least have shuddered.

Instead he extended a greeting.

"I thought we might not see you again, but I am pleased to be proven wrong," Argus began. "A penchant for memorable entrances, undiminished by the years. But I must confess that your appearance this time perplexes even me."

Though the exigency of their circumstances did not lend themselves much to conversation, Sean obliged the old being with a reply.

"No mystery. I saw what happened to Arachne. I made my way into the crowd. When Charybdis was lowered, I set her loose and took her place. Not so hard among that mob. In their frenzy most can barely see straight," Sean answered.

"I understand. Then you must have realized by now that you are indeed Lucifer, as I have always said. Will you bring an end to this foolishness? Take your place among us, once and for all?"

This time Sean did not answer. Instead, he turned the use of his unnatural hands to work. He snapped the chains that bound Argus to the dais floor with little effort. Then he moved to Vince and Maggie.

Vince did not hold his tongue. "Sean, what the hell are you . . . ?"

Sean did not let him finish.

"Forget it Vince. Do what I say and this will all be over for you soon."

He broke the chains around Maggie's wrists; delicately, though. She was ashen pale, and sweating. The wound inflicted by Anubis had gone untreated for almost eight hours. She had nearly bled out.

Once she was free, Vince pushed past his old friend to kneel beside her. He lifted her head and tried to wake her. She hardly responded. A groggy nod was her only reply.

"Goddamn you, Sean, what the hell did you do?" he shouted, bracing to make a run at the trickster. Argus placed a stringy white arm in his path before he could move, however. He offered the angry man a succinct admonition.

"I wouldn't," the very old changeling counseled.

✠ ✠ ✠

Across the dais, Scylla and Charybdis whirled their sabers

with the poise of practiced masters. As swordsmen, they had no equal, for the two former guardians wielded the blades with the acumen of centuries.

But their foe was a measure beyond the need for such skills, and the Morrigan parried their every thrust. The Keeper turned back blow after careful blow, her own hands mutated into scythes every bit as deadly as the Maenad steel of her adversaries.

Several of the torches and ritual braziers had already toppled from the fight. The embers had set fire to the cloaks of the dead Maenads. Their corpses now burned atop the platform, almost-human bonfires to light the battle of three very inhuman combatants.

The flames spread as the trio continued their artful, murderous fencing. Down from the dais, the tapestries and cloaks of the crowded floor caught fire. Black smoke flooded the narcotic-tinged air.

✠ ✠ ✠

"Look, Scylla and Charybdis battle the Keeper, but they will not hold against her for long, you know that. Only one of the Morrigan's own kind can truly put an end to her," Argus urged. "Fulfill the prophecy, Sean. It is time for Lucifer to be reborn."

Sean did not look up to the fight on the dais. His eyes were dead set on Argus. His face betrayed nothing but contempt.

"It was you in Venice, wasn't it?" he said.

"What are you talking about?" Argus answered, taken aback. He had not expected such a question, especially not given their predicament.

"You shouldn't have known about that, about the girl I lost there that night. I killed all of the men sent to capture me, and I didn't tell anyone of the details until I got to New York. But you knew. Were you there, watching me butcher your servants, too cowardly to step into the light yourself?"

Argus attempted a denial. Sean silenced him before he could finish.

"Enough lies. When I first came to you in the cathedral, you spoke of it. I had assumed the Morrigan to be responsible, but that was what you wanted me to believe. You wanted me to blame her, to hate her as much as you do. You needed me to. After all, you couldn't very well expect me to join your crusade knowing that your people nearly killed the only other woman I've ever loved."

Argus waved his arms, nervously, but with an air of urgency. "This isn't the time for recriminations, Lucifer. We can deal with these issues later, but now you must act. You must strike at the Morrigan."

Sean remained unmoved.

"Why? For your benefit? So you can rule the loyal flock through me?"

Argus feigned an indignant glare.

"I never said I wanted that."

"But that's what you were after. We both know that."

"I only wanted what was best for us all, you included."

Finally, the trickster looked over at the ongoing fight.

The Morrigan was winning. Scylla and Charybdis would not last much longer. He raised his own hands, fists clenched.

"Save it. There's no need."

"So now you'll have your vengeance, I expect," Argus said, resigned to his fate.

"What's done is done. By whatever way we have come here, this is where it will end," Sean answered.

He turned to Vince, still knelt over Maggie, who was barely conscious on the ground. The fire on the floor had spread to the tapestries and nets slung all about the rafters. The hungry crackle of flame joined the cries of the revelers. It was almost too loud to think.

"Vince, you have to go," he said.

The ex-cop didn't even look up.

"Not without her," he said.

Sean lowered himself to eye level with his old friend. He placed a hand on Vince's shoulder. Despite the noise, and all that had gone on between them, his voice was some-how calm—and eerily reassuring.

"Her ribs are cracked. Her lung has probably been punctured. She's lost too much blood. There's no way she can stand up, let alone walk. If we move her in this condi-tion, she'll die. You have to leave her."

"Not a chance. Not again. If she dies here, I'll die with her." He meant what he said. There was a tear on his cheek. He had no intention of leaving his wife.

But Sean did not waver.

"Vince, look at me. She's not gonna die. You two are

both gonna make it, but you have to let me do what needs to be done here. Trust me one last time buddy. I promise. Do as I say and we'll all . . ." His voice faded in the noise.

"What?" Vince demanded.

Sean stared back at him for a long while, almost too long considering the situation. Finally he smiled in a way that Vince hadn't seen from Sean since their childhood.

"And we'll all get what we want."

Somehow, that answer seemed like enough. Vince stood up, grabbed Sean by the arm and stared him down. He didn't say a word. The expression on his face told Sean he would agree.

Then the trickster turned to Argus.

"See that he gets away safely, and you'll leave here free of the Morrigan forever."

"You're going to do it then?" Argus asked.

Sean shook his head. "No. You don't need me. You'll have what you came for, Argus. After all these years. Lead those who wish to follow, and leave everyone else free to find their own way."

"What will you do?" Argus asked.

"It would appear that my road will end here. Right where it began, of all places."

FORTY-SIX

CHARYBDIS WAS HOLDING TWO SWORDS. ONE SHORT. One long. She twirled them like deadly batons, her eyes locked on the Keeper. Scylla fell, knocked across the dais by a strike from the Morrigan's hand. She struggled to get back to her feet.

The Keeper was outlasting them. Blood streamed from the shoulder wounds where Charybdis had been hung. The stress of combat had opened the slash across Scylla's gut. It surged red from under the bandages.

The Morrigan showed no sign of harm. No sign of slowing. Her ephemeral form shifted like the clouds of smoke churning through the roof beams. Even the two most skilled of her flock could not strike her.

Scylla charged, her blade held like a lance. The Morrigan's hand met the blow in the shape of a scythe. At the moment of impact her flesh melted into a hand, grasping the saber and heaving its owner into the air.

Charybdis leapt toward her as her back turned. But the Keeper spun around. She swatted down the white-lady, her other arm having taken on the form of grizzly's paw.

Scylla, undaunted, rose up and made her charge a second time. The Morrigan neither turned, nor moved to avoid it. But when Scylla made contact, her steel met only an empty cloak. The body of the queen had liquefied, leaving only the shroud behind.

Though she tried to regain her bearings, the Morrigan was faster. Her shape reconstituted itself from under her very feet. The force of it lifted her and tossed her aside like a doll.

Though it seemed futile, Charybdis rushed again. The thrust of her broadsword cut the heated air. Her blade met only the clang of another deft parry. Wheeling without pause, she shifted her weight and swung the heavy weapon anew. Again it was stopped in mid stroke, and again there came a counterblow that threw her back.

Graceful, despite her still-healing gash, Scylla slipped behind the dark goddess. She planted her legs for a body blow.

But the Morrigan could not be struck easily. Her body shifted like a wind-blown sapling just as Scylla launched herself. The bronze-skinned warrior-woman tumbled to the edge of the platform, falling into the frenzied crowd beneath.

Her shape re-formed a moment later, but Charybdis jumped off from the dais before she could reach her. On the floor of the warehouse, she found Scylla under attack by three Maenads. One's cloak was burning as she wore it. Charybdis came to her lover's aid, slashing the three servants dead. Then both looked up and saw the approach of their former ruler.

The Changeling Queen stalked her foes. She floated down from the dais as a malevolent raven, coming to rest with the softness of a feather. All in her way parted to allow her to land. The twin guardians were huddled together, their backs pressed against the wall of the platform.

The fire raged. Cinders and embers sweltered across the warehouse floor. The Morrigan ignored it all. She approached the two with her hands open.

Crazed revelers scampered everywhere. Among the smoke and flames their fury was fueled more by fear and confusion than by the bacchanalian frenzy that had set them into motion. Even in their stupor, each gave the Morrigan a wide berth.

That was why she never saw the figure that crept up in her shadow. Someone whispered a hint, but it was too faint. By the time the Morrigan realized that someone near her had said Lucifer, she tried to turn. She only sensed Sean's presence when the trickster's hands made contact with her throat.

By then it was too late.

"You've come for me, finally. I knew you would," the Keeper said.

Her hands reached up to seize Sean's wrists.

"I don't give a shit about you," Sean answered. "But there's no other way."

"You can't defeat me. You're not strong enough. I will absorb you."

Sean smiled.

"I know," he said.

His hands had lost their human appearance. His pliable flesh was beginning to merge with the Morrigan's. The Keeper answered with a grin. She mutated her own hands. Her fingers melted into Sean's arms.

Two were becoming one.

The Morrigan's laugh blended with Sean's. Sean's wail fused with the screams of the Morrigan. As the warehouse burned around them, and the astonished revelers looked on, Lucifer and the Morrigan came together. They joined into a single, terrible creature.

The union was not peaceful.

As their flesh congealed, two changelings merged into one, a fury raged under boiling skin. The grotesqueries of a dozen different creatures, some real and some only imagined, sprang out of the joining. Limbs and tails and other things twisted and whirled. Cries and howls in myriad voices rang out.

The beast battled itself.

Within, all that had been Sean Mulcahy, his thoughts, his memories, and his desires, flooded the mind of what had been the Morrigan. In return, all of the Keeper's five centuries flowed out of her.

Back and forth. Hatred and fear. Longing and lust. Loneliness and anger. It churned from one consciousness to the other, and then back again. A constant, maddening loop as both beings absorbed each other.

Those few who had braved the heat and the fire fell still, even as the walls fell around them.

Then, something altogether different happened.

While the hybrid monster writhed, arms and legs flailing in every tortured direction, one segment slowed. It was near the core, close to the heart of the gurgling, bubbling thing. The shimmering flesh drew still. A familiar human face fought to emerge from within.

Charybdis recognized him immediately. It was a vestige of Sean, reaching out from the middle of the beast. Drawn apart for a moment, clearly pained beyond measure, the face of the ageless wanderer fixed his gaze at the two warrior-lovers.

He could only manage a few words.

"Raise your swords! For your freedom! For our people! Kill me!"

Scylla winced. Charybdis fought back a tear. But they both understood. They did not waste a moment hefting their swords. In a single motion, as though possessed of one mind, the two lunged hard upon the beast. With terrible force they buried their blades to the hilt in the mutant's deformed chest.

The thing that had been the Morrigan and Lucifer staggered. A half-dozen mouths howled through pointed teeth. It threw back both Scylla and Charybdis, but it did not pursue them. Cries in two voices peeled from its many throats while something like blood streamed out of its middle.

Then it collapsed. Its movements slowed. Its shape devolved into a strange, shapeless mass.

And it died.

A surreal quiet fell over those who had remained to watch the death struggle, despite the crackle of flames, the choking carbon-black fumes and the heat.

"Perhaps he was not Lucifer," Scylla said, after a long moment regarding the combined mess that had been both their friend and their enemy.

"Perhaps not. And perhaps the prophecy was never more than words," Charybdis answered, the shock beginning to overcome the changelings as the fires burned around them. "Very old words to which we paid too much attention. But Sean was real. Of that there can be no question."

"Now he's gone too," Scylla said.

"Yes. We have finally done what we swore to do. We are finally free."

A ventilation tube, the metal heated to an orange glow, broke free from the ceiling a moment later. It came crashing down in the center of the floor, scattering ash and debris. Scylla took hold of Charybdis and yanked her out of the way.

Then the two vanished into the black smoke, seeking a way out into the world beyond.

FORTY-SEVEN

ALL THAT REMAINED WITHIN THE WAREHOUSE WAS THE fire and the chaos. Those few who had braved the flames long enough to see the death of the Keeper now sought escape. In every direction they scattered, unable to see in front for more than a foot or two.

Many found death before freedom.

Abandoned by the faithful, the slobbering, blood-soaked husk of the Morrigan and Lucifer remained where it had fallen. The strange flesh bubbled and singed as the flames crept near. Smoke swept over it like a death shroud.

But within, some hint of life remained.

A shadow of a person, a mockery of human form, melted away from the broiling trickster corpse. It was Sean, or what remained of him. He crawled through the dense blanket of super-heated smoke, hardly able to see or to breathe. He moved like a serpent, his legs not fully formed behind him. He clawed himself forward, upward, and over to where he knew she was waiting.

Half the roof collapsed, too far away to see, but he could hear it. Pipes and girders and concrete crashing down upon itself, sucked into a torrent of flame. The cries of his people echoed, those dying few who had not made it out, and would now meet their terrible end.

Finally, he managed to pull himself up the dais. Maggie was there. Like him, she rested very near death.

Sean took hold of her. He cradled her in his arms and brought her close to him. She was barely breathing. Her skin was pale and wet with perspiration. She hardly had the strength to shiver. Somehow, she managed to speak, though the words were soft, and hoarse.

"Are we going to die, Sean?"

Strangely, he smiled. "No, in fact you're going to be fine."

"And you?" she replied.

"There is no me, remember?"

She coughed. Blood spilled out on to her chin.

"Still joking, even as we . . ." She wasn't able to bring the last breath to her lips. He answered anyway.

"In a way, I'll always be with you. Now don't speak, this might hurt a little. But in a few minutes, you won't feel a thing. I promise."

With a touch as delicate as a child's, he settled his hands on her bare skin. "You know I always loved you," Sean said, placing his hand on her cheek as if to kiss her.

But he didn't.

He gently moved his other hand across her bare chest, just over her heart. The beats came slowly, with a stunted, irregular rhythm. Her breathing was labored, strained by the noxious smoke and the wound in her side. Sean closed his eyes. He let the touch of his bare hands rest softly against her.

He inhaled, just a little at a time, while she did. When he exhaled, he felt what she felt. He knew her pain as though it were his own. His heartbeat slowed as well. Within moments the rhythm of it matched Maggie's in perfect sync.

She opened her eyes again. And she smiled too.

Sean laughed, despite the pain. At last, he had found what he came back for; the only thing he had ever really wanted.

FORTY-EIGHT

WHAT REMAINED OF THE ROOF OF THE LARGEST WARE-house on the Pier 33 lot caved in just as the first truck from Engine Company Number 17 arrived. The flames were reaching up high above the waterfront by then, unleashed from within the center of the inferno. The black sky over the Hudson glowed a violent color, despite the hour.

Across the vacant lot, Vince huddled on an overturned dinghy. Argus had vanished from sight moments after they'd escaped. Now the strange figure was nowhere to be found. Vince was shivering as he watched the flames tear apart the old storehouse. He was shaking not just from the cold, but from anger too. Tears clouded his sight, rolling down his soot-stained face.

Sirens blared, from behind, from the side, from nearly every direction. A ladder truck raced on to the scene. Fire-fighters scrambled from the back, hauling hoses and axes. There were still people, if you could describe them that way, streaming out from the smoke. Some were scamper-ing for cover. Some were leaping into the river.

But he didn't care about any of it. Sean had lied to him

one last time. Things weren't going to be alright. Maggie was still inside. Without her, things would never be right again.

He was about to scream. To let loose his sadness and his rage. But when he wiped his eyes, he saw something that stopped his heart cold.

A woman was walking toward him. Not fast. Not slow. She was just walking, as though there were no fire, and no sirens. It was as though there were only the two of them.

At first she was just a silhouette, a black figure against the sea of fire. When she neared, though, there was no doubt in Vince's mind.

It was Maggie.

He dropped the blanket from his shoulders. He ran toward her and threw his arms around her. Though her hair stank of smoke and her clothes were covered in black dirt, she was unblemished. There was no hint of the wound that had put her so close to death only minutes before.

After everything he'd seen, it hardly took a moment to suspend whatever disbelief still lingered in his mind.

They held each other for a long time before Vince finally asked a one-word question.

"Sean?"

"He's gone," she answered.

"Gone? How? He said we'd . . ."

"We'd all get what we want," she interrupted.

Vince looked dumbfounded. That was always how he looked when he got emotional.

"I don't understand," he said.

"Don't you see? This is what we both wanted. What

we all wanted," she answered, moving into his arms again, and laying her dry lips against his.

It wasn't the most passionate kiss. But it said as much as either one needed to say.

EPILOGUE

FREEDOM HAD COME TO THE CHILDREN OF NESTOR, for better or for worse. Leaderless, those who survived the tumult dispersed from that place in New York, and ventured out into the world that they had feared for so many years. They remained among us, wandering, watching, seeking to live as Lucifer had told them.

But still they waited. Waited for that day when they could finally emerge from their secrecy. The day when humanity would come to know them again.

AUTHOR'S NOTE

THIS WAS TO BE A BOOK ABOUT IDENTITIES. WE ALL have several. There are the ones we show to the world and the ones we hide. The ones we take on out of necessity, and the ones we allow only a few people to see.

Which one is our "real" self, or are they all just guises?

What if you had no identity, if you could be anyone in the world that you wanted to be? Would it be a blessing, or a curse?

Maybe there are no answers to these questions.

What Sean always wanted was an identity. He doesn't have one of his own. He spends most of the book stealing other people's, and in the end he just wants to belong somewhere. He wants a home, he wants to love and be loved.

Does Sean become one with Maggie? I think so. But is that really what he always wanted?

Only time will tell. When I know the answer to that, I'll have another story to tell.

RICHARD D'AGOSTINO
RITE OF PASSAGE

CHAPTER 1

Watch your step, Jack. Those ancient builders set
traps all over the place."

"Frank, what do you think we'll really find?"

"I'm not sure."

"Sure you are. What does it say? Tell me what the
crystal says."

"If you must know, it says treasure, treasure of Thoth."

"What does it mean?"

"You idiot! What do you think it means? Gold, lots of
gold, mummies, statues, like that."

Sand crunched beneath their feet as they inched along
a passage so black it ate the light, oblivious to the small
mounds nesting here and there. Sweat beaded. Hearts

pounded. It seemed the air was thin. Their flashlights lighted, in bouncing rings, a featureless corridor hammered out of stone thousands of years ago. A dank musty odor reached into their nostrils, signaling the absence of life for a very long time.

"Oh, Jesus, Frank!" Jack stumbled, dropping his light.

"God damn it, Jack, watch it."

Jack picked up his light and shined it. "What the hell is that?"

"A figure carved in the wall. Let's go."

"Well, shit. It scared the piss out of me. What is it for?"

"You wouldn't understand."

"You don't have to talk to me like that, Frank. I can understand if you give me a chance."

"I don't know why I brought you along."

"I know. Because you need me, Frank. You need me to help you, that's why." Jack's feelings were hurt. He was a slow person and knew little about archeology, but he would do anything for Frank, even when he talked bad to him.

"Jack, what is that?"

"What?"

"That!" Frank shot his light at chunks of broken pottery on the floor. "You broke it. Damn you, Jack, you broke it."

"I didn't. I stumbled right here. I didn't touch that."

"Who did?"

"I don't know, I . . ."

"There's just you and me in here, Jack."

"Yeah, but I thought I saw . . ."

"Don't give me any shit, Jack. I told you this place was booby trapped."

"Yeah, you told me. But, I didn't do it, honest."

"There! Shine your light over there."

"Frank, it's just some sand trickling . . ."

"SHUT UP, damn it! Do you hear that?"

"Yeah, I hear it. It's the dirt under your boots."

"I'm not moving, Jack."

"Frank? What is it?"

Stone ground against stone. The earth shook. Walls trembled. In a gush, sand poured from slots in the wall. Dust swallowed the air.

"I can't breathe." Jack fumbled his light. He clutched his nose, his mouth.

"Let's get the fuck out-a-here!" Frank screamed.

"What about the treasure?"

"We can always come back for the treasure. Now go, damn it!"

"I can't see, Frank!"

"God damn it, this way!"

Jack's arms flung in the darkness. He grabbed Frank's shirt.

"Let go! Follow the goddamn wall!"

"I don't wanna die, Frank. I can't see."

"Use your fuckin' light."

"It's dead, Frank. I dropped it."

In the thick dust-soup, Frank's light was less than a

glow. Gasping, lurching forward, their fingers were torn ragged as they grasped and pawed the wall. With the next several steps, the quickened, tumultuous rasping of stone on stone drowned Frank's reply. Jack did not hear Frank say, "We've got to make the corner," as a huge granite plug smashed him to the wall.

Just making the elbow of the tunnel, Frank could not see what happened to Jack, but he smelled hot blood and felt the splatter of body fluids drench his head, his back.

In the sudden silence he whispered, "Jack?" He shouted, "Jack!" His voice slammed back, repeating in the dust filled passage.

Again, he heard the hiss of pouring sand and scrambled for the mouth of the opening as another monolith rumbled somewhere, shaking him to his knees.

Frantically, he crawled toward the mouth, trying to stand, sucking air, and reaching out in pitch darkness. His brain said twenty feet more, just twenty feet more. A breeze . . . Another thunderous clap.

Once more . . . absolute silence.

ISBN#1932815546
ISBN#9781932815542
Gold Imprint
US $6.99 / CDN $9.99
March 2006
www.rdagostinobooks.com

For more information

about other great titles from

Medallion Press, visit

www.medallionpress.com